First published 2012 by Solaris
an imprint of Rebellion Publishing Ltd,
Riverside House, Osney Mead,
Oxford, OX2 0ES, UK

www.solarisbooks.com

ISBN: 978 1 78108 050 4

10 9 8 7 6 5 4 3 2 1

A CIP catalogue record for this book is available from the
British Library.

Designed & typeset by Rebellion Publishing

REBELLiON

Printed in the US

JAMES LOVEGROVE
REDLAW

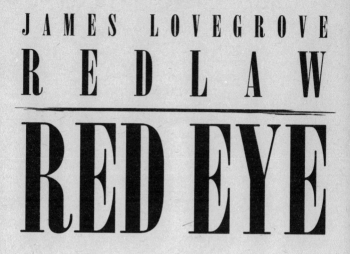

RED EYE

SOLARIS

NEW YORK IN *winter*.

The city is white, white, whiter than white. Snow has fallen freshly today, and more is forecast to fall later tonight. The city is featherbedded in thick drifts of the stuff. Manhattan, all twenty-two square miles of it, is no longer its usual muscular, hard-edged self. The skyscrapers and wharves instead look soft and strangely fragile. This urban island has become like some massive, impossibly intricate snowflake, lying quiet beneath a grim grey sky.

Down in the canyon streets, the valley avenues, traffic moves, but sluggishly. Yellow cabs make up most of it, crawling in long lines between the heaps of banked-up slush at the roadside. People are out and about but not in great numbers, and although in a hurry, because New Yorkers are always in a hurry, they walk with care. The ground is icy. Even boots with the ruggedest soles are no proof against slipping.

It's January, Christmas nothing more than a bauble memory, New Year a forgotten hangover. The whole of the eastern seaboard of the United States is in the grip of the freezing weather, and no one is finding it at all festive. The band of snow extends as far inland as Chicago and as far south as Florida, where frostbitten oranges are dying on the bough and retirees who thought they'd escaped the cold forever have begun to succumb to hypothermia and pneumonia.

Here in New York, the Hudson is locked solid, a single rumpled floe. You could probably cross it on foot, if you were crazy enough to try. Icicles twice as long as a man is tall hang from the Statue of Liberty's torch and crown. The wind that shoots in off the river lives up to the bird of prey it's nicknamed after, the hawk. If it catches you, it sinks talons into you which seem to carve clean through your flesh to the bone.

So let's try and find some warmth, shall we? I know of a place. You might not like it, but at least there's no snow there and the wind can't penetrate.

It's underground. Deep down. Come with me.

We glide below the city into the subway. We go from the lighted areas, platforms where evening commuters grumble and stamp, into the tunnels. We travel through the transit system, following labyrinthine twists and turns of track, shunning the roar and clatter of trains, heading for darker, deeper, silent parts.

Now—yes—we're where few dare venture, where maybe even angels fear to tread. We've come to a region of the subway that's found only on old outdated maps. Its existence is a matter of debate even to the Metropolitan Transportation Authority itself. The assumption is that this and all the other disused sections have been walled up, fenced off, made safe and inviolable. They were taken off the grid long ago, and no one has really thought about them since.

In recent years, people have inhabited these manmade caverns. The homeless. The destitute. Human moles. They've built little shanty villages, furnished them with scavenged scraps, and made themselves as comfortable as they could. They've established their own neighbourhoods, their own rules and laws, and gone about their business more or less free from interference from above.

Lately, they've moved out. They've had to.

Another kind of dweller has taken up residence.

Down here, where it's pitch black.

Where it's sunless.

Where it's always night.

CHAPTER ONE

THE NEST NUMBERED twenty in all. Sometimes the total might be a couple more than that, or a couple fewer, as newcomers arrived or existing members departed, but by and large it stabilised at twenty. Twenty seemed optimal. Sustainable.

Food was the one regulating factor. There wasn't much of it to go round. Rats were the main source of nourishment, followed by stray cats and dogs, the odd pigeon or bat. Enough prey could be found to keep twenty bellies full, twenty thirsts slaked, but only just.

Humans?

Not advisable.

Tempting.

But off the menu.

To abduct and kill a human would be to risk drawing attention to the nest's existence. The nest members were trying to be as unobtrusive as possible. They didn't want to advertise their presence. That way, they might just survive.

There were, after all, dangers.

Vampires were not welcome in this country.

No one wanted them.

More than that: no one had any sympathy for them.

Feelings ran deep in America. There were powerful social currents at work. Certain hostile forces at play.

Dangers.

MLADEN WAS NOMINALLY in charge. A vampire community really needed a shtriga if it was to be orderly and at peace with itself, but in the absence of a shtriga an ordinary vampire would do. In this instance, Mladen was the smartest among them, or—which amounted to the same thing—the most cautious. So the others listened when he spoke and, unless they strenuously objected to something he said, they complied with his wishes.

Mladen hailed from the former Yugoslavia. He had grown up watching his nation tear itself apart during the civil war, neighbour turning against neighbour, friend against friend, like fighting dogs let off the leash. He had seen his hometown, Sarajevo, bombed to rubble, with certain streets becoming shooting galleries for snipers bearing cheap Russian rifles and ancient ancestral grudges. By the age of seventeen he had witnessed more death than any youngster should.

His memories of that time were perhaps hazier than they would have been if he were still just a man. Mladen's old life, before he was turned, often seemed little more than a dream, a succession of loosely linked events that may well have happened to someone else.

The memories were still sharp, however. They filled him with the belief that what mattered, above all else, was cohesion. Societies could fall apart in an instant, with little prompting, unless their leaders remained vigilant. Someone had to watch out for everyone else and take care of them.

That was why Mladen was on sentry duty, carrying out a self-imposed routine of patrolling all the tunnels near the nest. Now and then he would assign the job to one of the other vampires, but nobody performed it as thoroughly and diligently as he did. And nobody treated it with the same level of seriousness. The vampires felt cosy where they were, safe from intrusion and harm. They were pleased with this little haven of theirs.

Mladen could never be that complacent himself.

Alert as always, he picked his way along the old rusted rails, pausing every so often to listen out and sniff the air. He was alive to the minutest of stimuli: the scurry of mouse paws, the drip of distant water, the invisible patterns of draughts and breezes. He had established a detailed picture of his environment in his mind. He knew every inch, every nuance of his subterranean home. He knew when things were as they should be...

...and when they were not.

Mladen caught a stray scent. Something shadowy and pheromonal. Hard to identify. Anomalous.

Halting, he lifted his nose, drawing in a deep breath.

A part of his brain recognised the scent and understood it to be familiar and no threat.

Another part said the opposite.

It was a hybrid smell. A composite of known and unknown.

Mladen's hackles rose. Unconsciously, he bared his fangs.

People were coming. Vampires? Not-vampires? Mladen was confused as to what they were, and his confusion was in itself alarming.

Instinct urged him to flee, find refuge, save his own skin.

But Mladen was responsible for the others in the nest. He was their alpha male, their protector.

So he turned and ran back to his fellow vampires.

And by doing that, doomed them all.

"Sir? Got a hit. Motion, dead ahead. You got it?"

"Loud and clear. This is Red Eye One to all units. We have probable V-contact. Converge on me and prepare to engage. I repeat, converge on me and prepare to engage."

"Roger that. Red Eyes Four and Five on their way.

"Reading you, Red Eye One. Six and Seven also en route."

"Hee hee hee! Here we come. Who you gonna call? Nestbusters!"

"Seven, kindly stow that shit. We are not a bunch of beer-chugging hillbillies out on a duck hunt. These are military-grade operations, and if you do not treat them as such I will personally put a nine-millimetre round in your goddamn skull. Do I make myself clear, soldier?"

"Sir, yes, sir."

"Sir?"

"Two?"

"Sonar suggests a cluster of at least a dozen V's. Maybe more. Half a klick due north. And, uh, nasal-input data confirms it."

"Yeah, I smell 'em too. Gentlemen, lady, let's go do what they're paying us to do, and make some undead properly dead."

MLADEN DIDN'T NEED to shout out a warning. The nest members sensed his panic from a distance. They detected the sharp, fearful odour radiating off him as he approached, long before they could see or even hear him. It had a distinctive sour tang, like milk gone bad.

Some of the vampires had been asleep; now all at once they were not. They sprang from their beds— the creaking cots and stained mattresses left behind by previous occupants of the tunnel—shedding their threadbare blankets and quilts.

Others, already awake, set aside whatever they were doing and rose to their feet. Two of them, a husband and wife, laid down the half-drained carcass of a black cat they had been sharing. They wiped their mouths and peered in the direction Mladen's scent was coming from. A pair of teenaged girls—they looked like teenaged girls—abandoned the game of chess they had been playing in the dark.

The air was filled with expressions of uncertainty. Hisses. Growls. The vampires looked at one another, hunching into defensive postures.

Mladen appeared at the furthermost visible point of the tunnel, where it curved out of sight. He was running full tilt, helping propel himself along by digging fingernails into the brickwork of the wall.

"Quick!" he yelled. "We must go! They are coming."

"Who?" enquired one of the others. "Who is coming?"

"I don't know. It doesn't matter. They are enemy, I can tell. We go or we die."

Now the other vampires could smell what Mladen had smelled, that inexplicable mix of human and something else, something essentially vampiric. It threw them into consternation.

"Don't just stand there!" Mladen cried. He had covered most of the distance between him and the nest, some two hundred metres, in a little under ten seconds. "Do as I say. Go that way, further into the tunnel network. Split up. If they catch us, they will—"

And then Mladen was no more. He exploded in a spray of particulate matter that scattered along the tracks with the momentum of his running. The *boom* of a gun report rumbled like thunder.

The vampires gaped.

Seven armour-clad figures were spread out across the width of the tunnel. They were sprinting as fast as Mladen had been, if without the same feral urgency. They had rifles in their hands. Their bodies were festooned with other weaponry: pistols, knives, grenades. Their heads were helmeted and their faces entirely masked save for their eyes, which gleamed crimson.

Boom!

One of the pair of teenaged girls recoiled, flying backwards. She was dust before she hit the ground.

Boom!

The husband of the married couple disintegrated before his wife's eyes.

Overcoming their shock, the vampires counterattacked. As a pack, united in fear and rage, they hurtled at their assailants. Several of them took to the walls, scurrying horizontally along on all fours so as to be able to leap off and hit their opponents from above. The rest charged, a loping nightmare of talon and fang.

"ALL OF YOU, stand firm. Make every shot count. The man who writes our cheques likes us to put on a good show. Let's give him his money's worth."

"Affirmative, Red Eye One."

"Heard, understood, acknowledged."

"Hell, yeah!"

THE VAMPIRES LAUNCHED themselves into a withering salvo of gunfire. It wasn't a fair fight. Really, it wasn't a fight at all.

Most of the nest members were annihilated in the first few seconds. Those that survived managed to get within striking distance of their foes, secure in the belief that their superior strength and speed would win the day. One on one, at close quarters, no human was a match for a vampire.

But *these* humans, or whatever they were, had astonishing reflexes. Knives were drawn. A single flickering sideways slash, and a vampire head was lopped clean off at the neck. Hardwood blades plunged into hearts and were pulled out again almost instantly, the action so swift that the victim had time to look down and actually see his own ribcage crumbling in on itself, his own torso hollowing into a cascade of ashes.

Even hand-to-hand, with no weapons at all, the combat was asymmetrical. The vampires were startled to encounter a level of muscle power that was at least equal if not superior to their own. Their talons raked uselessly on armour-sheathed chests and limbs. Crushing fists squeezed their necks and splintered their upper vertebrae.

Perhaps a minute passed between Mladen's demise and the elimination of the last member of the nest. It was certainly no longer than that.

Seven armoured figures stood surrounded by the ashy remnants of almost three times as many vampires.

No one was even breathing hard.

THE TEAM COMMANDER, designated Red Eye One, unclipped the mask covering his mouth and nose. It was a contoured bulge of black polycarbonate, miked-up and soundproof. Useful in the theatre of conflict, but also stifling.

"And that, people," said the stern-jawed man, "is how you exterminate a nest of vamps."

There were nods and grunts of assent all round. A couple of the other Red Eyes unclipped their masks too.

"Hope you got all that back home." Red Eye One tapped the infrared microcamera affixed to his helmet. He cocked his head as a reply from base was transmitted to him via an in-ear feed. "Clear as day? Good. I was a mite concerned. All this brickwork and bedrock above us. Nice to know there was no signal interference."

Red Eye Seven lurched into the camera's scope, grinning. "We came, we saw, we dusted their asses!" he crowed, both thumbs aloft.

Red Eye Three, the sole woman on the squad, rolled her eyes.

Red Eye Five, a hulking African-American the size of a bedroom wardrobe, dragged his toecap contemplatively through one of the piles of dust littering the ground. "Guess they ain't so tough after all."

"Fuck, no, they're not tough," said Seven. "And you know why? 'Cause we're tougher. We're Team motherfucking Red Eye! Baddest of the bad. Ain't that right, Six?"

Seven and Six hooted and high-fived.

Three shot One a look that said, *Children*; One just shook his head at her in return. High spirits at the end of the successful mission were permissible. Men would be men, and indeed boys would be boys.

He secured his mask back into place. "Let's evac. Job's done, and if God is in His heaven there'll be hot coffee and turkey sandwiches waiting for us at the debrief."

"I'd settle for a pint of haemoglobin," said Four.

"Man, me too," agreed Seven, his eyes lighting up.

And in the eyes of all of them, even One's, there was a similar sudden glint of greed.

They all knew what their metabolisms should have: meat and drink.

They also all knew what they really wanted: something that was both meat *and* drink.

They craved it, in fact.

PERHAPS IT WAS the prospect of fresh human blood. Perhaps it was the exhilaration that came with completing a potentially hazardous task.

Either way, Team Red Eye weren't on high alert as they marched back through the system of abandoned tunnels towards their exit point, a defunct station somewhere below 9th Avenue. They had lowered their guard and weren't paying full attention to their surroundings.

Otherwise one of them would surely have spotted the bright scarlet LED status indicator light glowing in a trackside alcove once used by subway workers to avoid oncoming trains.

And the hi-def digital camcorder to which the status indicator light belonged.

And the young woman who was holding the camcorder and who crouched in the alcove, eye to the viewfinder, hand trembling, scarcely daring to breathe as the seven heavily armed and armoured paramilitaries filed past.

CHAPTER TWO

JOHN REDLAW WAS in an alleyway, on his knees.

He did not like being on his knees. Not unless he was praying, which at this moment he most assuredly was not.

His knees were old knees, clicky and stiff from fifty-plus years of running, fighting, beat-pounding and general wear and tear.

They often ached. Chronic progressive cruciate ligament and meniscus damage in both of them. A doctor had once suggested the possibility of titanium replacements. Redlaw had not visited that doctor again, preferring to think that the knees God gave him at birth ought to see him out the rest of his life.

They ached particularly badly at this moment because they were buried in snow some ten inches deep. The cold and damp were making them throb.

But worse than that, the reason why Redlaw was truly not enjoying being on his knees, was the gun which was pressed against his head.

Not just any old gun, either.

A Cindermaker.

Now, there was irony.

Or, perhaps, poetic justice.

"So I'M THINKING," said the young man holding the Cindermaker, "all that cash you just flashed, that nice thick stack of Benjamins, you should hand it over to me. 'Cause why should an old geezer like you have so much of it, you knowum sayin'? 'Cause you're, like, eighty, and I'm just turned eighteen. My whole life ahead of me. Got bills to pay, ho's to lay, you get me?"

He was a white kid who dressed and spoke like a hip-hop star and went by the name of D-Funkt, which was doubtless not what his parents had christened him. He wore a huge thick quilted jacket and had a do-rag tied round his head, and a fur-trapper hat on top of that with the earflaps fastened under his chin. A silver lip ring lent him a perpetual sneer. A fuzz of beard clung to the underside of his jaw like moss.

"Whereas you, mister"—and D-Funkt ground the barrel of the Cindermaker harder still into Redlaw's temple—"don't got more'n a few years left. Way less than that, you don't do like I say *right now*."

"I don't want any trouble," Redlaw said, as calmly as he could.

"'I don't want any trouble.'" D-Funkt mimicked Redlaw's accent badly, sounding more Australian than British. "Izzat so? Then how come you're on the Lower East Side after dark, buying a motherfucking gun?"

"That's all I want. The gun. I've paid you the amount you asked for. We have a deal."

"Yeah, and you know what I have to say to that? 'Fuck you, nigga' is what I have to say to that. I don't want to give you the goddamn gun no more. I want you to give! Me! All! Your! Money!" He accompanied the last five words with several harsh jabs of the Cindermaker that bent Redlaw's head further and further to the side.

"All right, all right." Redlaw reached inside his overcoat and produced his wallet. He held it out to the kid between index and middle fingers. It was, he had to admit, rather ostentatiously stuffed with dollar bills. In hindsight, he should have been more careful.

"Now that's what I'm talking about, old man." D-Funkt plucked the wallet from his hand. "See? Wasn't so difficult, was it? And now I don't haveta put a cap in yo' wrinkly white ass. Everyone's a winner, baby."

He proceeded to tuck the wallet away in a pocket. For that moment, barely even a second, his attention was divided, not fully on the gun and Redlaw.

That was when Redlaw struck.

He grabbed the wrist of the hand holding the Cindermaker and twisted the gun away from his head. At the same time, he drove the elbow of his other arm into D-Funkt's knee, hard as he could. He felt a satisfying *pop* as the patella dislocated. More satisfying was D-Funkt's sharp, startled howl of agony.

Keeping a grip on the kid's wrist, controlling the gun, Redlaw rose to his feet. He turned to see a once-jubilant face now crumpled in distress.

"Jesus, man!" D-Funkt blubbered. "My motherfucking knee! Oww! Jesus fucking Christ..."

Redlaw punched him in the face.

"Don't."

He punched him again.

"Take."

And a third time.

"Our Saviour's name in vain."

D-Funkt sagged to the snow, nose broken and gushing blood. Redlaw wrenched the Cindermaker out of his numb grasp.

"Ohhh, man," D-Funkt groaned. "Oh, God. Don't hurt me. Don't hurt me no more. I'm begging you."

"I said I didn't want any trouble," Redlaw said. "I gave you every chance."

"I'm sorry, I'm sorry, I'm sorry."

"Wasn't it enough that you're charging me a thousand dollars for this gun? How much money do you really need?"

D-Funkt mumbled something about rare imported items, backstreet deals, a guy had to do what he could to get by in this economy.

Redlaw sniffed in disdain. He reached down and groped in the kid's pocket for his wallet. "I'll have that back, thank you," he said as he restored it to its rightful place in his own pocket. "And you owe me a box of Fraxinus rounds too. I believe that was included in the price."

"There." D-Funkt nodded to indicate the other side of his jacket. Redlaw delved into that pocket and found the box. Fifty 9mm ash-wood rounds, all present and correct.

"You want your grand back? Take it. It's in my jeans," D-Funkt snivelled. "Please. Just leave me alone. I ain't gonna give you no more problems. Take it and go."

"No. We had a deal," Redlaw said. "And I, at least, am a man of my word. The money's yours. You could probably do with it anyway. I've heard the healthcare system in this country is extortionately expensive, and you don't look to me like the type to take out insurance."

LATER, IN HIS hotel room, Redlaw sat at the dressing table and field-stripped and cleaned the Cindermaker. As he did so, he reflected on the fact that he ought to have foreseen D-Funkt's attempt to mug him. Really, what had he expected? It was a furtive, illegal exchange taking place in a blind alleyway in one of New York's roughest districts. The surprise would have been if the kid *hadn't* tried to rip him off.

Maybe I'm getting old.

But there was no maybe about it. He *was* getting old. Every day, one step further away from the acuteness and resilience of youth. Every day, one step closer to the grave.

With deft, practised movements, Redlaw reduced the gun to its components. The guide rod and recoil spring were a little rusty, but he'd bought some oil and a lint-free cloth. He'd also bought a bore brush and some solvent to clean out the dirt and carbon build-up in the barrel. A bit of a scrub, some lubrication for the moving parts—the hammer, the trigger assembly—and he'd have the Cindermaker working as good as new.

A television bantered in the next room, a late-night chat show, the volume up too loud as if to hide something bad going on. Directly below, a man and a woman were arguing, voices escalating as their tempers rose. The heating vent in the floor wheezed, pumping out air that was lukewarm at best. The hotel, occupying a slender brownstone just south of Gramercy Park, was hardly the Ritz Carlton. But then Redlaw was on a tight budget. The Cindermaker was a hideous but necessary expense. Aside from that, he was having to make every penny count. He had plundered his savings in order to make this trip. A few thousand quid, all he had in the bank. Not much to show for thirty years' loyal service in both Her Majesty's constabulary and the Night Brigade, but it would have to do, because he had no income now. As far as SHADE was concerned, John Redlaw was persona non grata. If he showed his face around headquarters, he would be arrested on sight. He was on wanted lists, technically a fugitive from justice.

He had nothing.

Nothing except a promise made to a woman he'd barely known but greatly admired. A woman he might go so far as to say he had loved.

That promise and his faith were the only two things keeping him going.

And he wasn't so sure about his faith any more.

Reassembling a gun was, Redlaw always found, a therapeutic act. Barrel into slide, slide into frame. Slotting the interlocking pieces together, like solving a jigsaw, or a crime.

When it was done, he racked the slide on the Cindermaker, checking that the action was smooth. Then he loaded the clip with Fraxinus rounds and slapped it into the magazine well.

The Cindermaker rested nice and heavy in his hand, intimately familiar, lethally fit for purpose.

Unable to take a Cindermaker of his own through customs on the transatlantic flight, Redlaw had made it his first priority on arrival to find one. Enquiries at a firearms dealership in Little Italy had met with shaken heads and puzzled frowns. British-manufactured pistol?

Ash-wood bullets? Not in this country, buddy. No call for that sort of thing in the US of A, no sir. Leastways, not yet.

But a customer in the shop had overheard, and had drawn Redlaw aside and told him in a low voice that he knew a guy who could get him what he was after. It would take some greasing of the wheels, but...

A hundred-dollar arrangement fee had set up the meeting with D-Funkt in the Lower East Side alleyway.

Now Redlaw was armed. He had protection, just in case.

It was time to go looking for vampires.

CHAPTER THREE

REDLAW HAD NO contacts in New York. He had never been to the Big Apple before, never even travelled to the States. In his entire life he'd left British shores on only two occasions. Once was a brief jaunt to Spain to walk the last section of the Way of St James, the pilgrim trail leading to the cathedral of Santiago de Compostela in Galicia. The other time was a SHADE-sponsored cultural exchange trip to Paris to compare notes and swap tips with the Sûreté, whose zero-tolerance policy toward the Sunless had been proving unusually effective in dealing with the issue of vampire immigration. Neither excursion was exactly what you'd call a holiday and, anyway, Redlaw was not the holidaying type.

He was certainly not in America to see the sights and do a spot of shopping.

He had come to chase down a rumour and divine the truth of it, or otherwise.

He had nothing to go on other than stories. Vague reports, mostly second-hand. Starting with something a vampire had told him back in London...

"...KILLING US," THE vampire said.

He was originally from Turkmenistan, Uzbekistan, one of the Caucasus -stans at any rate. And Redlaw had just saved him from a staking.

Two Stokers lay sprawled on the slimy floor of a vacant lockup beneath some railway arches in Leytonstone. They were unconscious and surrounded by their homemade anti-Sunless paraphernalia: several rather blunt-looking stakes, a plastic Coca-Cola bottle containing what they were evidently convinced was holy water, and a makeshift flamethrower constructed from a pesticide spray gun with a cigarette lighter duct-taped to the nozzle.

Sometimes these vigilantes were such idiots, it was a wonder they could tie their own shoelaces.

"I hear it from friend," said the vampire. "Good friend. Human. We keep in touch, even after I become vampire. My family, they turn their backs on me, chase me away." He mimed spitting, to illustrate his relatives' contempt for him, or perhaps his own for them. "I am monster, they say. No longer can be talked to. But my friend Nurzhan, he not so bad. We know each other since school. I sometimes phone him. He is in America, studying health sciences. Temple University in Philadelphia. He is to be doctor. We talk. Nurzhan, he tells me recently there have been bad things happening to my kind in that country. Because he knows what I am, he is interested in vampires. He goes on internet, reads things. I think he hopes to find cure for me, if there is one. He doesn't find cure yet, but he does find rumours."

"That someone's slaughtering vampires over there."

"Yes. Yes." The vampire nodded animatedly. "As I tell you, killing us. Like these men try to." He gestured to indicate the Stokers. Redlaw had spotted the two men behaving suspiciously outside a pub in West Ham that was a known Stoker haunt, and had followed them to the lockup. Morons they might be, but they had possessed enough basic cunning to choose to attack the vampire during the daytime, when there was every chance he'd be asleep.

"But America has hardly any Sunless."

"And it is busy destroying the ones it has already got."

"What I mean is, there isn't really an anti-vampire movement there. Not a well mobilised one like here, with cells and meetings and ringleaders."

"According to Nurzhan, there is. Or there is *something*. Two, three nests have been wiped out. So the internet says."

"The internet says a lot of things," said Redlaw.

"I know. But I tell you because I think you should know. You are John Redlaw. Once we feared you. Now you are vampires' friend. This is what everyone says, and today I see for myself."

"I don't know about 'friend', but I do have a new set of priorities." Redlaw rubbed his fist. His knuckles still throbbed from cold-cocking the Stokers. "A burden of care."

"And I thank you for caring for me," said the vampire sincerely.

"You'd be better off, you know, in a Sunless Residential Area. Safer. Then you wouldn't be vulnerable to attack."

"Safer? In SRA?" The vampire gave a gruff, scoffing laugh. "I think not. We do not trust SRA now. We do not trust government. We take our chances out in the city, the countryside. You yourself know what happened when we did trust government. Can you blame us for not wanting to again?"

Redlaw looked at him. "In all honesty, I can't."

LATER, AT AN internet café called the Java Crypt, Redlaw surfed and searched. The content of various US-based forums and chat rooms backed up the vampire's assertion. People were posting comments suggesting there was some kind of clandestine backlash taking place in the States. The oldest of these dated back to three weeks ago and purportedly came from an actual vampire. Since there were so many wannabes and fantasists out there, it wasn't difficult for Redlaw to discount the authenticity of *that* claim. Had the poster chosen a more original username than Dracul12345, he might have stood more of a chance of being taken seriously.

What he wrote, however, had a distinct ring of plausibility:

> There were three of them near my place in Trenton, NJ, nosferatu like me, holed up in this old timber mill down by the river. I've been watching them come and go at night. This one night, I swear, there was shooting. Saw gun flashes and everything inside the mill. After that, no more nosferatu.

Another poster corroborated his testimony, to some extent:

> I'm from New Jersey too, Hopewell, just north of Trenton. I don't know about any timber mill, but I go hiking in the woods round Kuser Mountain County Park and lately I've been coming across dead raccoons, woodchucks, this one time even a deer. And when I say dead, I mean no blood in them. Just laying there *empty*, if you know what I mean. Like deflated balloons. I make sure I don't go in those woods any time near sundown, you can bet on that, not now. But even so, I've noticed there've not been any dead animals for a week. Seems to have stopped.

A third poster said:

> Don't know about you guys, but if it *was* vampires, could some local gun nuts have gotten them? Like a posse or something, gone in there blazing away with wooden bullets? Or else maybe the cops?

To which someone calling himself StarzNStripes retorted:

> Good to know somebodys doing SOMETHING coz our a-hole of a President sure as fuck isn't, and neither's any of those loudmouth cocksuckers in Congress tho their sure as hell making plenty noise about it. ;-)

There were other similar accounts of anti-vampire activity, centring on Trenton and two further New Jersey locations: Newark and Atlantic City. The more Redlaw read, the more he sensed there was substance beneath the surface. The seemingly discrete incidents had a clear common link, even if it was only that groups of Americans could no longer tolerate the presence of vampires in their midst, or stomach their government's continued refusal to treat the matter as urgent, and had elected to deal with it themselves, by force.

It was interesting, but no real concern of his. He had enough on his plate in London without having to worry about events three thousand miles away.

REDLAW SHELVED ALL thoughts of the American attacks at the back of his mind, and he had every reason to believe that that was where they would stay.

His view changed after two close brushes with the authorities that very same evening.

The first occurred as he was leaving the internet café. A police car trundled past him in the street, the two officers inside apparently just cruising the area, keeping an eye out, nothing more. Nevertheless, Redlaw shrank into the shadows of a shop doorway, sinking his head into the pulled-up lapels of his overcoat like a tortoise withdrawing into its shell. The police car drove onward... then halted. The reversing lights winked on. Redlaw spun out of the doorway and walked at a fast lick in the opposite direction, back past the Java Crypt. He wanted to run, but didn't, for fear of making himself look more suspicious. He rounded a corner and dived into the front garden of the nearest house. Peering over the privet hedge he saw the police car reverse past the end of the street, then turn in. He ducked out of sight. The police car crawled by his hiding place more slowly than he thought any automobile could. And just when he believed it had gone and he could emerge, back it came the other way. The officers certainly now seemed to be hunting for someone. Was it him, specifically? Had one of them ID'ed him from the warrant that was doing the rounds? Had they recognised the man the tabloid press had dubbed "Redlaw the Outlaw" and "the Shady Dealer"?

He stayed hunkered in that front garden until well after nightfall. By then, the coast seemed clear and he finally dared to venture out and head homeward.

Home wasn't his flat in Ealing, to which he couldn't return for the time being and maybe not ever, not as long as a SHADE patrol car remained parked outside twenty-four seven. Home was a squat above an abandoned curry house on the fringes of the Stoke Newington SRA. The roof leaked; pigeons played havoc in the loft. But at least whoever owned the premises hadn't got round to having the water cut off, so the toilet and the cold taps worked.

Redlaw was dog-tired and looking forward to burrowing down inside his sleeping bag and getting some kip.

An uninvited guest, however, had other ideas.

REDLAW FAILED TO draw his Cindermaker in time. The figure standing in the living room of the squat, silhouetted against the curtainless window, had a Cindermaker too, and was aiming it at Redlaw's head.

"Drop it, Redlaw. Nice and slow. On the floor. That's it."

Redlaw laid his gun down, wishing he'd been feeling a little less weary, a little more awake. Wishing, too, that he didn't know the owner of the voice and the gun.

"Sergeant Khalid," he said. "You found me."

"*Captain* Khalid," replied Redlaw's one-time nemesis at SHADE. "But then, you've obviously not been keeping up with the promotions situation at HQ. There've been a lot of changes since you went rogue on us, Redlaw. Positions vacant, new blood replacing old. It goes all the way to the top, and for that we have you to thank, seeing as how you're the one who cleared the space."

"So happy to help with your ascent up the ladder. Last I saw of you, Khalid, you'd just been beaten up by rioters. How are you feeling now? Bruises all healed?"

The other man's grin was mirthless. "I'm fine. Qureshi's fine too, although he carries a nasty scar on his forehead. We call him Harry Potter. He hates that. As for poor old Heffernan..."

Redlaw felt a twinge of guilt.

"Wheelchair-bound," Khalid went on. "Surgeons couldn't reconnect his spinal cord. He's started a desk job with us, using voice recognition software to run his computer, but it's quite a comedown for someone as physical as him. You should see the look on his face whenever your name's mentioned—which happens quite often. This awful combination of loathing and frustration. The things Heffernan would do to you, if only he could."

"It wasn't me. I didn't hurt him."

"No, it was the shtriga. But she was with you. She snapped his neck protecting you. If it wasn't for your association with that bitch, Heffernan would still be playing rugby every Sunday afternoon."

"Don't call her that."

"A bitch is a bitch." Khalid cocked his head. "Aren't you at all curious to know how I tracked you down?"

Redlaw shrugged.

"It wasn't hard," Khalid said. "Interrogate enough 'Lesses, you soon get the answers you're looking for. Truth is, they can't stop going on about you. They hear your name and it's hard to shut them up. The ones you've saved from Stokers sing the praises of the mighty John Redlaw, and the rest just love the idea of this ex-shady becoming the vampires' champion. How come you've turned, Redlaw? Why are you their new hero?"

"You wouldn't understand and I can't be bothered to explain."

"And did you know that vampire-on-human incidents have been on the up since you switched sides? Some of the figures put the increase as high as eighteen per cent, in just a few months."

"That's nothing to do with me. Blame the government. After the whole Solarville episode, the Sunless don't trust anyone any more, least of all SHADE, and they certainly don't want to have anything to do with Residential Areas if they can avoid it. Once bitten, et cetera."

"Well, anyway," said Khalid. "Thanks to your newfound pals showing you so much love, all we then had to do was collate the data, triangulate, and reconnoitre. I had an entire unit dedicated to just one goal: locating the murderer of Giles Slocock,

MP, Nathaniel Lambourne, businessman, and Gail Macarthur, SHADE commodore. They worked round the clock for me, with the full cooperation of the Met, and they'd be in this room with me right now, only..."

"Only you wanted to hog all the glory for yourself," said Redlaw. "And the credit. No doubt you've an eye on the commodore's chair."

Khalid tried to look affronted.

"You know that I didn't kill Lambourne? I'm innocent of that one. It was Macarthur."

Khalid puffed out his lips. "What does it matter?"

"And with Slocock and Macarthur, it was self-defence, not murder."

"Frankly, I couldn't give a toss. Those are matters for a judge and jury to establish. Me, I just want to be the one who drags you back to HQ by your ear. Don't worry, we'll look after you once you're there, you can count on it. There's any number of officers who'd like to drop in on you in the interview room, pay a nice social call, and I'll make sure Heffernan gets a ringside seat for the whole event."

"I won't come quietly. You must realise that."

"I'm really hoping you won't. Injured, intact, it doesn't make any difference to me. This way, I get to see you squirm in pain before anyone else does. A win-win. I believe a leg shot ought to do the trick. I'll try my best to miss the femoral artery."

Khalid re-sighted his aim at Redlaw's thigh.

Redlaw leapt.

The bullet splintered the floorboard just beneath his feet.

At the same time, Redlaw struck Khalid horizontally like a battering ram.

The force of the collision drove them straight into the window... and through.

They plummeted onto the pavement outside, Khalid underneath, Redlaw on top. It was a drop of some twelve feet, and Khalid took the brunt of the impact on his back. He and Redlaw lay together amid shards of glass and splinters of frame, both stunned, but only one of them was capable of getting to his feet. Khalid moaned as Redlaw pushed himself up off him. Redlaw suspected the SHADE captain was hurt pretty badly, but that was the least of his concerns. Khalid might have been in the squat alone, but he wouldn't have come without backup. There would be other shadies somewhere around, lurking out of sight, and the sound of the gunshot and the window smashing would surely—

"Hey!"

A voice from across the street. Someone emerging from the door of another empty house. Footfalls, rapid, running.

Redlaw snatched up Khalid's Cindermaker and fired it wildly in the direction of the voice. His intention was to deter, not hit, and he succeeded. He glimpsed the SHADE officer scurrying for cover behind a lamppost. He fired again, to convince the man to stay put, then sprinted off along the road.

Return fire came his way, but belatedly, not before he was more or less out of range.

Round the next corner, Redlaw came face to face with a SHADE patrol car rolling towards him. Without hesitating, he loosed off two bullets at it. One pierced the radiator grille, the other the bonnet. Whether he had fatally damaged the engine, or just startled the driver, the car skidded to a halt. Two shadies sprang out and started shooting.

Redlaw doubled back, racing past the end of the curry house road. Fraxinus rounds pinged and ricocheted around him. Out of the corner of his eye he saw a couple of SHADE officers standing over the supine Khalid, concerned. Several others were haring up the road and quickly joined in the chase with the pair from the car. Redlaw ran, and ran, and kept on running, London a blur around him, until his body couldn't bear to run any longer. When he finally stopped, staggering to rest against a wheelie bin, his lungs felt as though they had been stripped inside out, his legs burned, and his heart was hammering so fast and hard that he seriously thought it was going to give out or else seize up like an over-wound alarm clock. He bent over and heaved his stomach contents onto the paving stones. For a time, everything went hazy. He may even have blacked out, while somehow still managing to remain upright.

Only as his head cleared did he realise that he had given his pursuers the slip. Up until that moment, he had been beyond caring. He dimly recalled zigging and zagging through the city, darting down side streets and up back alleys and across patches of park, using his knowledge of the lay of the land to throw his pursuers off. He sagged against the bin in relief.

For the rest of the night he wandered the wintry city, twitchy as a trodden-on cat. Every unexpected sound, every wail of an emergency vehicle siren, was a sharp reminder that he was a hunted man. By dawn he had come to a decision. It wasn't so much a choice as an acceptance of the only course of action available to him. The Hand of God seemed to be pushing him in a definite direction. The usual divine strategy of closing all other doors and leaving just a single exit. Free will? Well, you didn't *have* to take the exit...

Redlaw found a branch of his bank, and the minute it opened he cleaned out his savings account.

Luckily, he had his passport on him already. Even more luckily, no one had considered that John Redlaw might be an international flight risk and taken steps to warn the Border Agency.

From Heathrow to JFK, and a bridge as wide as the Atlantic lay in smouldering ruins behind him.

IF THERE WAS one thing Redlaw knew how to do, it was locate vampires. He was in a strange, alien city, and the weather was diabolical. But wherever you were and whatever the conditions, certain aspects of vampires' behaviour were constants. They took refuge in shabby, tucked-away places, mostly through necessity but also by preference. They tried to draw as little attention to themselves as possible. And they always left traces, signs that the eye could be trained to detect.

It might be a litter of dead vermin, rats especially, heaped in a basement lightwell. It might be a pile of faeces, unusually red, spattery and pungent. It might be the urine with which, doglike, they left their scent and alerted other vampires to their presence. Vampires were not the cleanest or most foresighted of creatures. They were as much animal as human, and didn't think to tidy up their own mess or consider that others could track them by their detritus.

Redlaw, with Cindermaker lodged in trouser waistband, steered clear of the well-lit avenues with their shops and restaurants. He ranged southward, down to where the city's grid pattern broke up and intersections were no longer invariably right-angled crossways. The rigid geometry of upper Manhattan and midtown gave way to something he found more recognisable: unplanned urbanisation, a street layout that seemed to have occurred naturally rather than been imposed by ruler and set square.

Here, between the ruins of the World Trade Center and the vaulting arrogance of the financial district, was the sort of warren of cramped old buildings he could see vampire immigrants favouring. He assumed that, like the City of London, this part of New York tended to be busy by day but unfrequented at night, which also suited the Sunless.

Patiently, doggedly, Redlaw trudged through the snow. He bent to check doorsteps for the telltale, acrid-smelling stains that betokened territorial marking. He scanned the upper-storey windows of the more dilapidated tenement blocks, looking for crude methods of blotting out daylight, such as newspaper pages and scraps of cardboard box taped inside the panes. He was a big game hunter searching for spoor, but to passers-by—of which there were few—he looked like nothing so much as a madman, one of those quietly tormented schizophrenics of which New York seemed to have more than its fair share, performing arcane public rituals to stave off some private apocalypse.

Midnight deepened into the small hours, and Redlaw had nothing to show for his efforts except sodden shoes, damp feet, and an uncontrollable shiver that came and went but was more violent each time it returned. He had never, ever been so cold. *Tomorrow—note to self— buy warmer clothing*.

To add to his woes, around 2AM fresh show started falling. The flakes were huge and silent, floating down like autumn leaves. They clumped on his eyebrows and built up in white epaulettes on his shoulders. His unprotected head was soon snowcapped, which made his scalp ache, especially at the crown where the covering of hair was thinner.

He forged on because that was the sort of man he was. A bit of snow—no, a *lot* of snow—wasn't going to deter John Redlaw. He could almost hear Róisín Leary telling him he was an idiot and he should get his arse indoors now or he'd catch his death. His former SHADE partner had not been one to mince her words.

Similarly, he could almost hear the voice of Illyria Strakosha, the shtriga he had allied himself with not so long ago, saying much the same as Leary. Putting it less bluntly, perhaps, but with an equal amount of eye-rolling exasperation. *Really, Redlaw, stop this bally nonsense. You're only human, old bean*.

Ghosts of the dead. The sounds of his conscience. Redlaw knew they were just memories, disembodied echoes haunting the hollows of his mind, but sometimes he thought of them as angels.

And then, at last, success. A result. Persistence rewarded.

He had passed the deconsecrated church twice already, and only on the third time did something about it strike him as anomalous. A small round window high in its façade appeared to have been neatly removed. Not vandalised, as some of the others were, with starred holes in their stained-glass panes where stones had been hurled at them. This one window was simply not there any more, leaving a circular aperture that was just large enough to permit a human-sized body to squeeze through.

Looking closer, Redlaw discovered scratches in the stonework below the empty window. A column of little runic scuff marks led up the wall, the kind that might be left by unnaturally sharp, powerful talons. For a vampire, climbing up the sheer face of a building was a far from impossible feat.

The church was tall and sandwiched between two former warehouses that had been converted into blocks of fashionable boho loft apartments. In its day, it would have been quite something. No doubt a property developer was eyeing it up with a view to making it quite something again in the near future. For now, though, it was very much nothing. A useless, hollow excrescence. A place of worship that was no longer needed, especially in a part of the city where money was God and the general opinion of religion was that it was a madness that made people fly jumbo jets into skyscrapers. The world had moved on and left this church behind like a large, steepled gravestone.

The handles on the double doors were secured by a padlocked chain. A laminated notice warned that, by civic ordinance, trespassing on this property was an offence punishable by a steep fine and a possible jail sentence.

Redlaw glanced both ways along the street. Nobody around as far as the eye could see. Nobody but him. The snow tumbled in thick flurries, encrusting streetlamps and burying parked cars. His gaze fell on the railings that fronted the church. Vandals had been busy there too. Several of the railings had been worked loose from their settings; a couple lay discarded, poking up out of the snow. Redlaw fetched one. The sturdy iron rod promised to make a decent crowbar. He inserted it inside the loop of chain. Several minutes of wrenching and twisting him did him no good. The chain held fast. He tried another tack. He stuck the railing inside the shackle of the padlock. Bracing the tip of it against one of the doors, he leaned back like a signalman pulling a lever. The padlock resisted. Redlaw strained, putting his back into it, all his strength. He grimaced. Breath steamed through clenched teeth.

There was a loud metallic *snap* and the shackle sprang open. The sudden release caught Redlaw by surprise and he collapsed backwards.

The chain rattled loosely to the ground. Redlaw picked himself up and grasped one of the handles. He dragged the door open, heaving it against the knee-deep snowdrift that had accumulated in front, until he'd made a gap just wide enough to slip through. Drawing his Cindermaker and chambering a round, he went inside.

THE MOMENTS IT took his eyes to adjust to the gloom were the most dangerous. Anything could happen while he was temporarily blind.

At SHADE, image-intensification goggles were standard issue equipment. Now that he was "freelance," Redlaw was having to learn to do without the things he had once taken for granted.

Dimly, the church interior took shape. Pews stood in haphazard rows, some overturned. The font had been removed—presumably a nice piece of marble masonry, worth reselling—leaving just a bare plinth. The pulpit was intact, and so was the life-size crucifix that stood in the apse behind the altar. On it hung a Christ depicted in that pose that so many ecclesiastical sculptors seemed to think appropriate: the Son of God wasn't exhibiting any apparent pain. There was only profound sorrow written across His face, His anguish spiritual rather than physical.

The presence of the crucifix gave Redlaw pause. Perhaps he'd made a mistake. He had assumed the church would be bare inside, stripped of its holy regalia. How could there be vampires here with this large sacred symbol still dominating the place? To them it was as toxic as radioactive waste.

Then he caught the distinctive, meaty whiff of vampire scat. It smelled fresh.

And, above his head, he detected faint, furtive movement.

The rafters.

Vampires were up there. Watching him. He could sense pairs of crimson eyes staring down.

He walked further into the church, along an aisle over whose flagstones countless congregations must have passed, and many a bride; many a funeral procession, too. He tried to exude an air of calm and peaceability. He didn't want to alarm anyone. The Cindermaker hung by his side, concealed discreetly in the folds of his overcoat.

As he reached the end of the nave, he sensed vampires descending behind him. It was instinctual as much as anything, a prickling of his nape hairs. They were putting themselves between him and the doorway, guarding his exit route. Some were coming down the church's pillars as well, with near-perfect stealth, shadows shifting amid shadows. They weren't going to challenge him openly. Not yet, and maybe not at all. They were waiting to see what he did. If he turned round and left, they would most likely let him, sinking back into the darkness as if they had never been there.

The vampires had nothing to gain by being aggressive, and nothing to lose by adopting a cautious stance.

Redlaw halted at the altar, a bare block of stone not unlike a raised tomb. Experience was telling him he was in the company of at least two dozen Sunless, perhaps as many as thirty. He could read the acoustics in the church much as a bat could map its environment by sonar. The tiny scraping clicks of talon on stone, which to most ears would have seemed just random background noise, to him spoke volumes.

His right shoulder gave a sudden involuntary spasm, reminding him of the last time he had been in a large building full of vampires. An industrial unit on the Isle of Dogs. A trap laid for him by one of the few people in the world in whom he had had complete, implicit trust.

The episode had left him with extensive scarring and an arm that was stiff every morning.

His faith in his fellow man had suffered greatly, too.

"I am here," he said in a loud, clear voice, "only to talk. I mean you no harm whatsoever."

His words were met with absolute hush. He pictured the vampires hanging from the walls and pillars, stock still, ears cocked, listening.

"You're probably aware that I'm carrying a gun," he went on. "You can smell the cordite and the ash-wood bullets. I promise it is only for self-defence. I have no intention of using it unless necessary, by which I mean unless I am provoked and in fear of my life. As a show of earnest, I'm putting it down here on the altar and stepping away."

He did so, taking three paces backward.

"Now it's out of easy reach. You have the advantage over me. Like I told you, I'm not out to harm. I really only want to talk."

Whispers crisscrossed the gulfs of the church. Nervous chatter. He caught the gist of it. Who was this? Could he be believed?

"I can give you my name, though it may not count for much here. John Redlaw. Formerly my job was to police your kind. I've since assumed a more pastoral role."

It occurred to him that many if not most of these Sunless were not native English speakers. He should simplify his language.

"You might call me a human shtriga."

That set tongues wagging. The word *shtriga* carried weight. Non-vampires weren't even supposed to know it.

"How interesting," said someone to Redlaw's left.

He spun.

A man appeared from the transept on that side, sauntering round the base of the pulpit. He was dressed like a priest, from dog collar to ankle-length black cassock, yet he didn't move like one. His gait was delicate, feline, full of grace and sinew. He had a pronounced widow's peak and a lean face that tapered to a very pointed chin.

He was no 'Less. His eyes were normal-looking, not bright vampiric crimson.

But he wasn't just a man, either.

"You do yourself a disservice," he continued. The accent was American, but bore a trace of east European. Russian, perhaps. The way the "r"s rolled and the intonation rose and fell. "You're too modest by far. The reputation of John Redlaw has spread beyond the borders of the United Kingdom. I wouldn't go so far as to say it's global, but it's undoubtedly international. Within a certain stratum of society, that is."

"And you are...?"

The priest, if he was a priest, smiled. And all at once he was no longer standing in front of Redlaw, he was behind him, crouched on the altar with the Cindermaker in his hand.

"Faster than you," he said, levelling the gun at Redlaw. "And ready to blow your head off if you make the slightest false move."

CHAPTER FOUR

SHTRIGA, THOUGHT REDLAW. *Not a pretender like me. The real thing.*

"Come, my children," said the shtriga priest, beckoning to the unseen vampires all around. "It's quite safe now. I have this under control. There's nothing to be afraid of. Captain Redlaw knows full well that his fate rests in my hands. He could no more disarm, defeat or outrun me than he could fly to the moon. So come closer and see. See this man who has turned so many of your brothers and sisters to dust, and who now dares to invade our private sanctuary, carrying a weapon whose sole purpose is to make dust out of you, too."

The vampires crawled down from their perches, dropping silently to the floor. They gathered round Redlaw in a shuffling, tightening circle. Red eyes blinked. Fangs parted to reveal wormy, purple-black tongues. The creatures were all sizes, representing a wide range of ages and ethnicities. What they had in common was an indifference about appearance—they were strangers to laundering and the use of a comb—and a hunched, stooping posture, partway between that of a lion and a hyena.

Redlaw had been surrounded by vampires before, but every time he'd had a small arsenal of dedicated weaponry on him—stakes, garlic smoke bombs, *aqua sancta* grenades and the like. This time he was completely unarmed, and didn't even have the consolation of knowing there was a team of shadies nearby to provide reinforcements.

"Two points," he said to the shtriga, as coolly as he could. "One, it's not 'captain' any more. It's Mr Redlaw, or simply Redlaw. Two, I was telling the truth when I said I'm here to talk. If you know anything about me at all, you'll know that I'm no liar. I mean what I say and I say what I mean."

"And you claim to be shtriga?" The priest dipped down and grabbed Redlaw's jaw, none too gently. "Show me your teeth."

Redlaw peeled back his lips.

"Human teeth," said the priest. "And yet..." He subjected Redlaw to a lengthy appraisal with his nose, sniffing up and down his face, neck and shoulders. "There is shtriga scent on you. Minute traces. I can only just smell it, but it's there. You've met one of us, not so long ago. Known him well. No, not him. Her. Yes. Her. She has left her mark on you. This was not some casual encounter. The two of you became close. Were you maybe even sexual partners?"

"That's my business," Redlaw said stiffly.

"Oh, I think you'll find it's my business, too. While I have this"—the priest brandished the Cindermaker—"everything about you is my business."

"Yes, about that." It was the third time in as many days that Redlaw had been held at gunpoint. With a Cindermaker, moreover. He was heartily sick of it. "Either get that thing out of my face or use it. One or the other. Just stop waving it around like it actually means something to you. You don't need it. You can kill me with your bare hands, and we all know it. I wouldn't stand a chance against you. The gun's just a prop, so you can show these 'children' of yours how you've turned the tables on me, how completely at your mercy I am, the irony of threatening me with my own weapon. I'm sorry, but I find that sort of cheap melodrama a total waste of time."

The priest studied him, and for a moment Redlaw wondered if he hadn't just bravado'ed himself into an early grave.

Then another smile appeared on that gaunt face, and the priest flipped the Cindermaker round so that he was holding it by the barrel, the grip extended towards Redlaw.

"Go on. Take it," he said. "You're right. I have no need of it. Although, should you attempt to use it, I assure you it will be the last thing you do."

"We seem to understand one another," said Redlaw, uncocking the gun and pushing it down the back of his trousers. "Now then. I'm here for answers."

"You are, are you? And you expect me to give them to you?"

"I'm hoping so."

"Well... I suppose it all depends on the questions," said the priest.

"There's really only one question," said Redlaw. "Who's killing vampires?"

*　*　*

THE PRIEST HAD a name. It was Rudi Tchaikovsky. Yes, Tchaikovsky. Like the composer. They had been distant relatives, or so he had been led to believe. The famous Tchaikovsky had been a cousin of a cousin, something like that, with perhaps a "once removed" thrown in. Although that may just have been a tall tale, a desperate grasp at the coattails of fame by his family.

Where that other Tchaikovsky's vocation had been music, this Tchaikovsky had been destined for just one calling since birth, namely the church—Russian Orthodox, of course. His father had been a priest, as had his father's father, so young Rudi was never likely to do anything but follow in their footsteps.

Nor had he ever wanted to be anything else but a priest. During his boyhood, the mysteries of God had been as exciting to him as any book or toy. Growing up in a rural township outside Kostroma, some two hundred miles north-east of Moscow, he had discerned God's influence everywhere around him, in every tree and blade of grass, in the sparkle of sunlight on snow and the lonely howl of the wolf on the taiga. God's love interpenetrated Rudi's world at an intimate, almost cellular level, and he could imagine nothing nobler than sharing that passion, that joy, that sense of divine omnipresence, with local churchgoers.

All of this Tchaikovsky told Redlaw as they descended a narrow spiral staircase down to the crypt. Half of Tchaikovsky's vampire "flock" followed at a respectful distance, with the other half remaining behind in the nave of the church to keep watch. All night, vampires stood sentinel in the rafters, and all day too, at pains to avoid stray sunbeams. Vigilance was crucial, according to Tchaikovsky.

There were more Sunless in the crypt. The place was packed with them. They occupied the shelf-like alcoves where coffins had once lain. They stretched out on three-tier metal bunk beds, with scarcely any room between the top mattress and the low vaulted ceiling. Some slumbered. Others peered at Redlaw with wary wakeful eyes. So many unwashed undead in such close, airless confines generated an overwhelmingly repugnant stench. Redlaw thought he was pretty inured to such things, but even he had to shield his mouth and nose.

"You get used to it," said Tchaikovsky, seeing his discomfort. "I myself hardly notice any more, and they of course aren't troubled by it. To them, this musk is community, a cementing in scent."

"You were a priest," said Redlaw, staring sidelong at Tchaikovsky, "and now you're a shtriga. How does that work?"

"Better than you'd think."

"But aren't the two mutually exclusive?"

"Who says so, Mr Redlaw? God? I believe in God's plan. Nothing happens that He does not allow. It was His will that I became what I am, a century ago. It is His will that I now use the abilities I have been granted to help those who need help, to embrace the less fortunate and elevate them, to be a good shepherd. I did that as a priest back in Kostroma Oblast, before the Bolshevik Revolution came along and the persecution of the religious began, and I do that as a shtriga here, in modern-day New York, New York."

"In a deconsecrated church."

Tchaikovsky grinned, revealing for the first time his fangs, which were tidier, more discreet, and nowhere near as snaggled as the average vampire's. "It has a nice... I was going to say *irony*, but you've shown yourself to be no fan of that, so let's call it symmetry instead."

"But with holy symbols everywhere. The windows. That crucifix."

"Me they don't affect in the least, and as for this lot..." He gestured at the huddled vampires. "They build up a tolerance. Repeated exposure seems to inoculate them. But also, bereft of meaning, of significance, what are those saints and angels in the windows? That Jesus on the Cross? Coloured glass and painted wood, that's all. They derive their potency from the beholder, and there haven't been beholders in this church for years, not of the devout kind. Faith infuses inanimate objects with power, charges them up like a battery pack. The objects in themselves are meaningless. You have something round your neck, yes? I see a chain. A crucifix, would be my guess."

Redlaw nodded.

"Just a few ounces of moulded metal," said Tchaikovsky. "The small piece of ore it originally was could have ended up as part of a car, or a piece of scaffolding, or the leg of a desk chair. It just happens to have been forged into an item of neck attire, an icon of a particular shape. What makes it in any way special is the person wearing it. When John Redlaw holds up that crucifix to ward off a vampire, it isn't the crucifix itself that repels, it's the faith of the man whose hand it sits in. You empower it, or the Lord through you. And that," he concluded with a slight apologetic bow, "is my rather longwinded explanation for how a nest of vampires can survive in what was once holy ground but is now simply vacant urban real estate. Forgive me, the habit of sermonising is hard to break. You haven't come to learn about any of that."

"No."

"We're down in the crypt for demonstration purposes," said Tchaikovsky. "Today, as you can see, you can't swing a cat in here. A month ago you could have. Several cats. I had to buy these bunk beds—military surplus—and I'm cramming people in as tightly as possible, but we're at capacity. I've even had to institute a rota system, like they did with the crew's quarters in galleons of old, sailors sharing berths, sleeping in shifts, so that everyone gets somewhere to rest. And the reason for that is—"

"New arrivals. Fresh intake."

"Precisely."

"They're coming in from elsewhere."

"From all over New York state, New Jersey, even up in New England. Fleeing to the city. Drawing together. Seeking safety in numbers."

"Because they're scared. Because someone *is* busy killing vampires."

"Just so."

"I heard reports."

"This is the proof of it, Mr Redlaw," said Tchaikovsky. "Right here. More and more of them turn up each night. They follow scent trails and word of mouth and find their way to my door, and I take them in, as is my rightful duty, and give them succour and shelter. Someone has begun targeting vampires in this country, systematically unearthing nests and eradicating them."

"Who?"

"This we don't know. It could be civilian vigilantes, like your Stokers."

"They're not 'my' Stokers," Redlaw snapped.

"Figure of speech. But I must say it seems better organised than that. There's a distinct pattern and consistency to the attacks. They began in New Jersey and have been progressing steadily northwards through that state, heading this way. That doesn't seem like the actions of a civilian lynch mob. That, to me, smacks of planning and direction. It even, I daresay, looks a bit like herding."

"Driving the vampires into a heavily populated area," said Redlaw. "In which case, besides the 'who', there's also the 'why'. This isn't just some spontaneous upsurge of anti-Sunless sentiment. There's an ulterior motive."

Tchaikovsky regarded him with something like respect. "You're genuinely concerned, Mr Redlaw."

"You sound surprised."

"Precious few humans care for, let alone about, vampires. In fact, hardly any. Fear is the commonest response, with revulsion a close second. Both understandable in their way, if not pardonable. However, it's almost unheard of to come across a man who actually, sincerely puts a premium on vampire welfare. And an ex-SHADE officer, no less. What could have brought about this Damascene conversion, I wonder?"

"Not so much Saul to St Paul as poacher turned gamekeeper. No, make that gamekeeper turned conservationist."

"And this change of heart was prompted by...?"

"Events. Circumstances. *Force majeure*."

"You don't reveal much about yourself, do you? The Redlaw cards are played very close to the vest."

"That way I'm more likely to win the game, aren't I?" said Redlaw. "Now, if you don't mind, I'd like to go back upstairs." The smell in the crypt wasn't getting any more bearable. On the contrary, Redlaw was beginning to feel nauseous. Even the shallowest of breaths was drawing more of that noxious miasma into his body than he would have liked.

"Of course, of course," said Tchaikovsky. "Forgive me. I just felt a visual illustration of the situation would be more effective than any words of mine. We can leave. Children? Make room."

The crowd of vampires who had followed Tchaikovsky and Redlaw down now parted to let them through.

Near the entrance to the staircase, a hand shot out from one of the alcoves and seized Tchaikovsky's sleeve.

"Father," said an imploring voice. "Please. I'm so hungry. I can't remember when I last ate. I feel empty. I'm begging you, feed us. Feed us again."

Redlaw's hand crept under his coat, making for the Cindermaker. He was all too conscious of being a living creature, the only one in a building full of Sunless. Prey among predators. A meal on the hoof. The pumping of blood in his veins beating as loud as a dinner gong.

For all his pretensions to wanting what was best for vampires, Redlaw could never forget that they didn't necessarily reciprocate the feeling.

"It's been so long," the vampire continued. He was of Latino extraction, his ochre skin now a sallow, sickly yellow. "I'm so weak. I hurt inside."

"I know, Miguel, I know," said Tchaikovsky soothingly. "There will be food soon, I promise. When have I ever let you down? Please just be patient."

Miguel sank back into his alcove with a disconsolate sigh. Here and there, other vampires echoed his plea with yelps and soft mewling cries.

"What *do* you feed them on?" Redlaw enquired as he and Tchaikovsky climbed the spiral stairs.

"The usual. Any vermin that can be scrounged up from the street. What else?"

"Must be difficult. So many mouths."

"Hard as hell, but we get by. Jesus fed five thousand with next to nothing. I'm not Him, but I do my best."

"You're not tempted to...?"

"Get thee behind me, Satan," Tchaikovsky said over his shoulder, with some asperity. "You know as well as I do how unwise that would be, to say the least. There've been vampires in America for longer than you think, Mr Redlaw. Not many, but their presence here predates the recent diaspora out of eastern Europe by several decades. And how have they managed to survive? By staying well below the radar. By refraining from doing the one thing that would be guaranteed to bring swift, brutal retaliation down on their heads."

"Surely there's been the odd human victim."

"I don't doubt it, vampire nature being what it is. Nevertheless, they've been careful. And with numbers on the rise, it's more vital than ever that that caution continues. We can't have the sort of public backlash here that there's been in France and Spain, or even your own fair country. America shouldn't be like that. This is the land of opportunity, after all. Famously welcoming to all those who fetch up on its shores. A nation forged and bolstered by immigration. I'm certain that, in time, vampires will become as accepted a part of American life as any of its other diverse component factions— but only if we abide by the rules and don't rock the proverbial boat."

"You're an idealist," said Redlaw.

"Merely someone attempting to put into practice the teachings of our Lord. Even if the world we find ourselves in nowadays is one that Jesus Himself would scarcely recognise..."

TCHAIKOVSKY SHOWED REDLAW to the door of the church much as though he were a minister seeing the last parishioner off the premises after a service.

"I feel it was destined that you and I should meet, Mr Redlaw," he said at the threshold. "Don't you? Do you not feel that you were guided here?"

Redlaw looked noncommittal. Destiny, the hand of God, a foreordained universal plan—these were things whose reality he was having trouble acknowledging at present. If the Lord truly was steering him through hardship and humiliation towards some ultimate goal, then that goal was a mysterious one indeed. Right now, divine purpose could easily be confused with vindictive spite, God bullying one of His staunchest supporters simply because He felt like it and He could.

"I'll be in touch," was all he said by way of reply.

"And I," said Tchaikovsky, "will keep my ear to the ground and try to discover more about these attacks. If we pool information and resources, there's a good chance we can do something to prevent any further mass killings, and perhaps even end this campaign before it gathers momentum."

"That's the general idea," said Redlaw, disappearing off into the snow-thickened darkness.

CHAPTER FIVE

THREE BLOCKS, NO more.

That was how far Redlaw walked before he sensed he was being followed.

Someone was dogging his footsteps through the city. He was 99% sure of it.

One block further, and suspicion hardened to absolute certainty.

He didn't look back. He didn't alter his pace. He kept walking, trying not to exhibit any self-consciousness, acting natural even though it felt as if he had picked up an anchor and was dragging it along behind him. That was the trick when being tailed. You mustn't let the person tailing you know you knew they were there. That way, you gained control. You, not the other, led the dance.

Whoever it was, they were sticking to the shadows, hugging the side of buildings. Redlaw collected glimpses every now and then, casually turning his head a little and at the same time swivelling his eyes as far round in their sockets as they would go. There, at the periphery of his field of vision. A figure on the other side of the street, dim through the fizzing static of snow. Travelling at the exact same speed as him, but moving with studied nonchalance. Artless stealth. Straining with the effort of looking as if they *weren't* following.

Who?

A vampire?

Had Tchaikovsky sent one of his flock after Redlaw to keep tabs on him? To make sure he wasn't going straight to the authorities or some sinister ally to report the whereabouts of several dozen vampires?

Redlaw wouldn't have put it past him. There was something a little too slick about the shtriga, a little too accommodating. Redlaw didn't trust him, so why should Tchaikovsky trust him in turn?

He paused in front of a technology store and feigned interest in all the smartphones, e-readers and tablets on display in the window. Several of them were streaming the broadcast from a rolling news channel. The headline was 'Big Freeze Continues,' and an anchorwoman attempted to furrow her botulism-stiffened brow while she listened to a live report from beside a freeway where drivers were spending the night trapped in their snowbound vehicles.

Redlaw focused his gaze not on that but on a laptop whose webcam was relaying an image of the street outside. He himself occupied most of the screen, but past his elbow he could see clear across to the pavement opposite.

And there, lurking, was his pursuer. The person was skulking behind a Toyota people carrier, peering out every so often round the edge of the windscreen. Watching what Redlaw was up to. Waiting for him to move on.

The camera resolution wasn't sharp enough for Redlaw to make out much detail at this distance. He could see that the person was bundled up in winter wear, with a woollen watchcap drawn down tightly over the head, but the features were a fuzzy pale blur. He couldn't tell if it was a man or woman.

He carried on.

At the next crosswalk he changed over onto the same side of the road as his pursuer. He stepped smartly round the corner, out of sight. The entrance to a 24-hour grocery store beckoned, and he darted in. Loitering at a spinner rack, he perused a bewildering range of chewing gum flavours—*liquorice-watermelon?*—but his attention was really on the view through the window.

Soon enough, the person in the woollen watchcap hurried by outside, looking confused and anxious. Redlaw made a beeline for the door, oblivious to the Sikh cashier who called out from behind the grille of his bulletproof booth, "Sir? You're not buying? Is there something special you're looking for? Condoms, maybe? We have plenty. All styles and colours."

Back out in the cold, Redlaw was now the tailer, not the tailee. He followed the stranger for a couple of hundred yards, making assessments. Height and body shape said female. The posture and gait were not those of a vampire. She looked young, perhaps in her mid-twenties. Black jeans. Big clumpy boots.

He quickened his pace, intending to accost her. She, at the same time, slowed. It was dawning on her that she had been wrongfooted. Her quarry was nowhere to be seen. He'd vanished somehow, somewhere. Belatedly, she realised he must have dived into the grocery store she'd just passed. She turned...

...and there he was, a few paces behind, heading towards her with purpose.

Her face registered shock and annoyance.

Redlaw squared his shoulders.

"Right, miss," he said, reaching out to grab her shoulder, "that's quite enough of that. Who are you and why are you—?"

He heard a sound like a cricket's chirrup, felt a stab of pain in his belly, and next thing he knew, he was flat out in the snow, his muscles useless, his limbs twitching spastically.

The woman loomed over him. She had a stun gun in one gloved hand, a can of pepper spray in the other. She pointed the latter in his face.

"Okay, buster," she said. "No funny business. Try anything stupid and I'll put another three million volts through you. You even blink wrong, and I'll Mace you 'til your eyeballs bleed. Get me?"

Redlaw nodded feebly.

"Good. Then answer this. Are you or are you not John fucking Redlaw?"

CHAPTER SIX

TINA CHECKLEY DIDN'T want much out of life. Just fame, wealth and the adoration of millions. The things everybody lusted after and strove for, and she wanted them as badly as anyone, and what you desired, you deserved, right? That was the American Dream, wasn't it? To become rich and rewarded. And by wishing hard enough, working hard enough, you could make it real.

She didn't want to be a celebrity for celebrity's sake, like a talent contest winner or a reality show star, none of that fake shit. She didn't want to be lobbed into the public eye by the opinions of a panel of judges or by couch potato zombies voting with their fat backsides. Jeez, give her some credit, why don't you? Tina wanted to get to the top on her own merits, by the sweat of her brow. That, too, counted in her favour in the overall cosmic scheme of things. Made her worthier of the prize.

She was finding the struggle a lot harder than she'd thought, however. The ladder to success was a hell of a lot taller and slipperier than she'd expected. In fact, Tina was having trouble even getting her foot on the bottom rung.

She had graduated two years ago with deep debts and high hopes. Her waste-of-space parents had claimed they couldn't pay for college tuition, meaning they hadn't saved up and couldn't be bothered to get off their butts and arrange finance. She'd failed to qualify for a scholarship, either, her grades not being high enough and her parents' income not being low enough. So she had funded her education herself through food stamps, a student loan and a fistful of maxed-out credit cards which she now was busy repaying with a string of soul-sapping McJobs. Majoring in journalism, minoring in media studies, she had prepared herself for the game. Tina Checkley was going to be a TV news icon, nothing less. She was going to kick down doors and ask the awkward questions and take no bullshit from anyone, not from the hardest-bitten crooks, not from the squirrelliest politicians. She was going to crusade on hot-button topics and stand up for the rights of the little people: Diane Sawyer, Wonder Woman and Gandhi rolled into one. The world would know about Tina Checkley and sing her praises, not because of who she was, but because of what she said and did and who she helped.

At college—State University of New York, not what you might call an Ivy League institution—Tina had earned herself the nickname "Tick." She embraced it, even though it was never really intended as a compliment. She had a habit of latching onto people and using them for whatever she could get from them. Boys with money, professors who might be able to give her extra credit, anyone who appeared to have contacts that would be advantageous to her out in the world. Tina shamelessly threw herself at these people and clung to them until she had sucked them dry. It was the only way to get ahead when you came from nowhere—also known as Randallstown, Maryland—and had nothing. And a tick was tenacious. It was a thriving species. A tick was a coper and a survivor.

So yes, maybe there were a couple of trust-fund guys she'd slept with who hadn't strictly speaking been single at the time and whose girlfriends had then scrawled venomous comments about her on the walls of the women's restroom. And maybe her fling with that Eng. Lit. teacher during her sophomore year had been ill-advised—but then the bastard had said he had a friend who worked at CNN, and how could she have known that he was lying? In the final analysis, you did what you had to, and college wasn't a popularity contest, no matter what some of the snootier co-eds might think. College was a bear pit, a scrimmage, Thunderdome, Darwin in action. Like high school but with fewer handguns and slightly better dope. You got through it not by making friends, but by defeating enemies.

Degree in the bag, BlackBerry stuffed with useful phone numbers and email addresses, Tina had set to work finding herself a job. Every TV station in the state had received a copy of her résumé and a DVD showreel of to-camera pieces she'd taped while at SUNY, with a follow-up call coming less than a day later, and a further follow-up call the day after that. But the news departments at the big networks just weren't hiring. It was bounce after bounce after bounce. *Sorry. It's the economy. Advertising revenues are in the dumper. We're not taking on any new staff. In fact, we're laying off. Try again in a year's time, maybe.* Same from the locals. Even the top-of-the-dial cable channels.

At this point Tina had begun to take it personally. It must be her. Something about her. She was overeager, or not compliant enough, too confrontational, too forceful. Or could it be that her thin dark hair and slightly pinched Italianate looks—thanks for those, Grandma DiBonnaventura—didn't conform to onscreen bimbo standards?

So she'd lowered her sights and tried radio, but it was a similar story there. She'd offered to intern for free, fetch the coffee, anything. No dice. She'd even approached NPR, for fuck's sake. That was how desperate she was. Still no dice.

Well, screw that. It was the internet age. The old order changeth. You didn't have to claw your way up through the ranks any more. You could leapfrog the entire queue just by getting yourself out there in cyberspace and becoming a big noise among the geeks and trolls. The road up the mountain was long and winding, but online there lay a shortcut, like a ski lift to success.

So she'd invested in some new equipment: a hi-def camcorder with a 240-gigabyte drive, some editing suite software for her PC. To pay for this she had come to an arrangement with the landlord of her fourth-floor walkup in Astoria, with its scenic view of the jetliners landing and taking off at LaGuardia. Once a week Mr Constantinopoulos was entitled to visit her in her apartment and watch her undress and take a shower. In return, that week's rent was forfeit. "Throw in a pair of panties from your laundry hamper, maybe a jogging bra as well," Mr Constantinopoulos had said, "and you got yourself a deal."

It wasn't so bad. All she had to do was ignore him, make like he wasn't there, while he sat on the end of her bed, staring at her with his fried-egg eyes and wheezing asthmatically as he jerked off inside his baggy sweatpants. She even got a weird kick out of it. Her power over him. The look of intense, furious worship on his face that lasted at least until he came. She mightn't be the best-looking woman on the planet, but she knew she had a decent figure, a good pair of tits (and a genuine vote of thanks was due to bosomy Grandma DiBonnaventura for *them*). This must be how a stripper or a lap dancer felt, able to command total male submission simply by being in a state of undress. The feminists could go fuck themselves. If you'd got it, girl, work it.

All set up to launch herself online, Tina had only one problem. She needed a subject. If she was going to start making short filmed reports and posting them on YouTube or wherever, they needed to be dazzling, daring, juicy; if possible, controversial. They needed to grab attention. She couldn't go around doing pieces on lost dogs or flashers in public parks or sacked derivatives traders living on handouts and soup-kitchen meals. To make a name for herself, it had to be something edgy and now. Something people hadn't seen before and hadn't known they wanted to see.

The answer was obvious, really.

Vampires.

What else?

Vampires were it. Vampires were offbeat and on-trend. Vampires were the one thing guaranteed to grab an online audience. Footage of vampires always garnered huge hit totals. The stuff coming in from Europe was a ratings winner every time. America wanted to know about vampires, it wanted to learn about them, it was intrigued by them. America didn't have any of its own, at least none that it would admit to. They *were* here. Everyone knew that. There just weren't enough of them here to make most American citizens feel that they had to worry about them. The government had expressed concern, but Joe Public, though uneasy, was still basically undecided.

Well, Tina "Tick" Checkley would make Joe Public worry about vampires. She'd rub people's noses in vampires. She'd show them the truth. And then everyone would sit up and take notice.

Of the vampires, naturally.

But also of her.

TINA WAS NOW in an East Village basement bar, nursing a Jägerbomb which the man on the stool next to her had grudgingly consented to pay for.

He himself was nursing a black coffee and a sore patch on his abdomen where her stun gun's charge electrodes had made contact.

And while they sat uneasily side by side, surrounded by a half-dozen hardcore barflies and the trebly warbling of Céline Dion, Tina gave John Redlaw a potted version of her story, minus all the unpleasant bits—the unsuitable hook-ups, the naked ambition, the Greek landlord beating his kebab over her every week. A sanitised edition of the life of Tina Checkley so far, in which she came across as the plucky, redoubtable heroine, beset by circumstances but still battling on.

"The moment I saw you outside St Magnus's, I recognised you. Not many people over here would, but then I'm not many people. I took one look at you and I thought, what the fuck, I know that guy, that's John Redlaw. 'Cause I've seen stuff from Great Britain, video clips, BBC reports, phone footage, all of it. You guys have got serious vampire issues over there, but I guess you know that already; but you see, I'm into all that. Vampires are my business. You could, I suppose, call me a vampire hunter. Only I don't actually *hunt* them as such. Stalker, maybe."

Redlaw said nothing, merely sipped his coffee. Tina took his silence as an invitation to carry on.

"I stalk them because I'm fascinated by them, but also, you know, because it's my job. I'm a communicator. I communicate things. Communicating's my thing. And people in America, they really need to be educated about vampires, because like it or not, we've got vampires, and the way it's going, judging by the situation in Europe, we're only going to have a whole lot more of them in the coming years. The President keeps saying it's under control, he has a lid on it, he doesn't think it's a pressing matter. But hey, this is an election year, of *course* he's going to say that. If he 'fessed up and said, you know, 'Arrrgh, vampires'"—she waved her hands either side of her head in a parody of panic—"then the opposition candidates would jump on him and call him weak and chicken. Instead of what they're saying now, which is he's sticking his head in the sand and hoping it'll all go away, which isn't so bad as being chicken, is it? Not politically. Am I talking too much?"

Redlaw shrugged. He was being polite. Was he being polite?

"So anyways, I'm out to spread the word about vampires, the truth, because someone's got to, right? I've made it my mission. The mainstream media aren't doing their bit on that front, not really. There've been a couple of HBO documentaries, a searing exposé on Fox, but mostly it's like a war we haven't got any soldiers in. You know, it ain't happening here, it's happening somewhere else, so screw it, nothing to do with us, let's watch *Dancing With The Stars* instead. Only, it *is* to do with us, or it will be soon enough. The vampires—you people call them Sunless, don't you? You've found a nice, what's the word, euphemism for them. That's so typically British. Like 'I'm just popping off to the loo,' when what you mean is you want to take a crap. I've never been to England but I imagine you're all tipping your hats to each other and making 'cuppas' for each other all day long. I'd like to go there. See what it's like. So you work for the Sunless Housing And Dispersal Executive, right?"

"Disclosure," said Redlaw, frowning, as if he was having a hard time keeping up with her. "And it's *worked*, past tense."

"Oh, yeah. That's right. Heard about that on the news feeds. You quit."

"In a manner of speaking."

"In a manner of speaking," Tina echoed. "But you're still in the vamp game? Please tell me you are."

"Miss Checkley," Redlaw began.

"Oh, my God, I love the way you said that. Say it again. Makes me feel like I'm in a Jane Austen movie."

"Miss Checkley, I'm sitting here with you, against my better judgement, for one reason only. Bad enough that you zapped me with a stun gun, although I'm prepared to take some of the blame for that on myself. I should have seen it coming. My guard was down."

"Yeah, well, it's New York. You should know better than to paw a girl in this town."

"You could simply have called my name when you first saw me."

"I was going to, but I wanted to get a better look, make sure it *was* you, before I did. Also, you looked sort of jangled, and I didn't want to spook you by yelling."

"Instead of which, you made me think you were coming after me with hostile intent."

"My bad," said Tina with a shrug.

"Anyway, what's done is done," Redlaw said. "But now I'm having to listen to you prattle on, and no offence, but it's nearly as excruciating as being electrocuted."

"None taken." Tina felt a peculiar spasm of pleasure. Never before had she been dissed so... so *elaborately*.

"You told me, after incapacitating me, that you have something you think I ought to see. Some video footage you captured that might be of interest."

"I did, uh-huh."

"Well?"

"First, can I ask why you broke into St Magnus's? And what were you doing in there all that time?"

"I might ask you a similar question. What were you doing *out*side there?"

"I was on stakeout," Tina said. "No pun intended."

"You knew there are vampires inside?"

"I suspected it. Are there?"

"Why did you suspect it?"

"Who's interrogating who here?"

"Right now? Me, you," said Redlaw.

"Okay. Well, I suspected it on account of I hunt vampires, like I told you, and I've gotten pretty good at it. St Magnus's seemed like a likely place for them to hang. Never mind the whole house-of-God thing. Perfect cover. Who'd even think of looking for them there? But also, I saw someone go in the other night. It was, like, stupid o'clock in the morning, and cold as a witch's tit. No one else around but nosey old me. This guy just scuttled up the front and got in through a window. Quick as all hell. Damn creepy to see. Like fucking Spider-Man or something. That clinched it. I didn't get a shot of him on my camera—it was all over in a couple of seconds, I kind of didn't have my wits about me—but I've been going back there ever since, every night, in hopes that it'll happen again. Your turn. There *are* vamps in that church?"

"Some, yes," said Redlaw.

"Jumping Jesus on a bicycle! Right in the heart of Manhattan. Who'd a thunk it?"

"Please. A little less of the blasphemy."

"Sure. Sorry. You're godly, yeah? A believer? Forgot that about you SHADE types."

"And the video footage?" Redlaw prompted.

"Absolutely. I don't have it on me. It's on my hard drive at home."

"Can you describe it? Give me some idea?"

"Not really. It's kinda... murky."

"But you definitely think it's relevant to me? Something I could do with seeing?"

"Well, no," said Tina. "What I'm hoping is, given how you're you, you might be able to explain what it means. Because I sure as hell don't have a clue."

CHAPTER SEVEN

They took the subway, the N train out of Manhattan. It was the late train, the last of the night. It felt to Redlaw like the last train to anywhere. No one on it but a few drunks, a few nervy gangsta kids, and them.

The New York subway stank. The London Underground was bad, but this was worse. Human secretions, seat plastic, brake fluid, ozone. The air in the carriage had an actual taste, like something you could drink but would never choose to.

While they rocked north, then east, diving below the river into Queens, Redlaw covertly appraised the girl, this Tina Checkley. She sat opposite him, watching tunnel lights flicker past, shoulders hunched high, one leg drumming up and down. Her eyes darted around. Her gaze was never at rest. *She* was never at rest. He wondered what would result from this encounter with her. Nothing, probably. She was just some strange, jittery New Yorker whose path had chanced to cross his. Whatever she'd recorded with her camcorder, it would be meaningless, irrelevant.

But if it wasn't, then she might be a useful lead. He had nothing to lose by seeing what she had to offer.

She caught him studying her.

"What?" she challenged.

"Nothing."

"You think I'm some kind of fruit loop, don't you? I can read it in your face. But that's okay. Tell me, how many vamps have you staked?"

"We call it dusting."

"Again with the goddamn euphemisms. Like you're doing the housework. ''Ello, where you orf to, luv?' 'Just orf to do a spot of dusting.'"

"Is that supposed to be an impression of me?"

"Yes. So? How many?"

"I always tried my best to avoid resorting to terminal measures when dealing with Sunless," said Redlaw. "If I couldn't get my way through persuasion or coercion, only then would I take the next step."

"Blast 'em with wooden bullets. Stick the stake in. You still haven't answered the question."

Redlaw pondered. "Truthfully? I don't know."

"Lost count, huh? That many."

"I was with SHADE nearly twenty years. In that time, I had frequent run-ins with 'Lesses. If my personal safety was in jeopardy, if it was a case of me or them, inevitably I chose me."

"How's it feel? Dusting?"

"Why are you so keen to know?"

"Journalist. Plying my trade."

"Personal curiosity?"

"Okay, that as well."

"It feels..." Redlaw hesitated. Should he tell her? Did he even know himself how it felt? "It isn't ending a life. It's more... finishing unfinished business. Making happen what ought to have happened earlier."

"'Cause they're undead, right? Should be dead, but the vampirisation process keeps them going longer—indefinitely."

"It isn't killing, that much I'm sure of. Not the same thing at all. Because of the way they crumble, like a statue of sand collapsing away. Which wouldn't happen if they were fully human."

"But they talk. They're sentient. They have emotions."

"True, but..." He looked at his hands. "It's a grey area. What is human? How far do you have to go before you're not human? Sometimes I looked on dusting a vampire as a mercy."

"Putting them out of their misery."

"Precisely."

"Like a vet with a hypodermic."

"If less clinical."

"You sound like it makes you sad now," Tina observed.

"Put it this way," said Redlaw. "I used to think vampires were monsters. I've since discovered that there are worse monsters."

"People."

"Some. What people can do. What they're *prepared* to do."

"Care to elaborate?"

But by now the N train had reached an elevated section of track, and there were things to see outside, views, distractions, a snow-blanketed cityscape, a whitened night-time world, and Redlaw pointedly fixed his gaze on those.

*   *   *

THE LINE TERMINATED at Ditmars Boulevard, and it was a not-so-short walk from there to Tina's apartment. Redlaw's watch read three in the morning as Tina unlocked her front door. Late hours normally never bothered him. He had long been a professional nocturnal. But he felt inordinately tired right now. The time zone change was playing havoc with his circadian rhythm. Or could it be age? That was the time zone change you could do nothing about. Life lag.

Before they went in, Tina put a finger to her lips. "Quiet on the staircase. My landlord lives on the first floor, and he doesn't sleep too well and he's got ears like a fucking hawk. I'm not supposed to have male visitors in my apartment after eleven. It's in the tenancy agreement. Although," she added, with a speculative glance at Redlaw, "I don't think you count."

"Thanks."

"Not like that. You couldn't be a boyfriend, could you? More like my dad. Or maybe an uncle. Yeah. If Mr Constantinopoulos sees you and asks, you're my uncle. Uncle John from jolly old England. First Stateside visit in ages. You okay with that?"

"If you'd only stop talking, there's every chance we won't wake him," said Redlaw.

Three flights up, without having disturbed the landlord's repose, Tina ushered Redlaw into a cramped, messy set of rooms with the words, "My luxury condo." Thin rugs covered not nearly enough of the bare floorboards. Damp-stains dappled the ceilings and walls, a few of them poorly hidden behind tacked-up squares of batik. Icy draughts seeped in through several windows. Outside, the sky was burnt umber—the glare from the airport, reflected on low cloud.

Tina closed blinds and cranked the thermostat up full, muttering about how rent control was all well and fine but not if it meant the furnace was never serviced regularly. Then she booted up her computer and drew up an extra chair in front of it, sweeping empty cans of Red Bull and Mountain Dew off the seat.

"All righty, park your ass here and watch this."

She clicked open a file, and a dark, grainy image sprang to life on the monitor.

"Now, I've run this through every filter I've got, upped the contrast and resolution, unsharp-masked it, edge enhanced, gamma corrected, the works, and it still looks like shit. But I was shooting in ambient light, which there wasn't much of."

Redlaw peered. All he could see were dim irregular blocks of colour, various shades of dark blue, charcoal and black. "What am I looking at?"

"This is me just doing a bit of preliminary filming, seeing how much I could pick up without switching the camera light on. Didn't want to use it if I didn't have to."

"No infrared?"

"Take a look around you. I'm not made of money. So I'm in a subway tunnel. One of a whole bunch that aren't used any more. Over on the West Side, near Ninth. Used to be where mole people lived."

"Mole people?"

"Homeless. Had themselves a regular little sub-city neighbourhood there. All the comforts of home. Only, they had to leave."

"Why?"

"Why do you think? Somebody else moved in and evicted them."

"Vampires?"

"What I heard," said Tina. "This bum I met in Tribeca told me about it. I was digging around, making enquiries about vampires, trying to get a fix on where some might be, and who better to ask than hobos? Who knows what's going on at street level better than them? So this old guy with ratty grey dreads who you sometimes see playing a penny whistle on West Broadway, I talked to him, and he gave me a whole spiel about how he used to have this place in the tunnels. Bed, stove, storm lantern, all that. Somewhere to lay his hat, out of the weather. But then these foreigners—that was what he called them, 'foreigners'—came along and he knew he wasn't welcome any more, so he hightailed it out of there, him and all the other moles, and now he's back on the streets, freezing his ass off, tooting his whistle for spare change, probably not going to make it through the winter, yadda yadda. I gave him five bucks to make him happy."

"Did he describe the 'foreigners'?"

"Guy drinks past-its-sell-by mouthwash to get loaded. I doubt he could have described his own mother. But I got the impression they weren't *people*, you know what I'm saying? Because those moles, normally they'd defend their turf. Tooth and nail, with box cutters and broken Thunderbird bottles and whatever else they've got. And they didn't, they just ran. Anyway, that's why I went down there. To find out. See for myself."

Redlaw regarded her.

"I know!" she exclaimed. "Brave or crazy, take your pick. In the event, I didn't find any vamps. This is what I found. Keep watching. Any second now..."

Sounds first: the tread of feet, shuffling, echoing. The camera swung. Tina's voice, a whisper: "What the fuck...? Oh, God. Oh, shit. Someone's coming. Who?"

The image veered about wildly, incomprehensibly.

"That's me hiding," she told Redlaw. "There was this place beside the track, like a room at the top of some steps, a refuge for people working down there, they could sit and have their lunch in it or something."

The image stabilised again. On-camera, Tina whispered, "Oh, my God, I hope they aren't vamps. Maybe they've heard me."

"I thought the whole point was you were looking for vampires," Redlaw said.

"Yeah, but on my terms. I didn't want to get *caught* by them."

"And for what it's worth, they're far more likely to have smelled you than heard you."

"Thanks for that, Mister Expertise. I'll have you know I wash regularly."

"Makes no difference."

Now figures came into view on the screen. They were moving in a line along the track. Six, no, seven of them. Silhouettes, only just discernible in the gloom. Chunky outlines. Bulky clothing. Guns.

Tina's camera jumpily panned right to left, following them as they tramped by. The focus wavered in and out. On the soundtrack, above the marching of boots and soft clanking of equipment, frightened, shallow breaths were audible—hers.

The figures filed out of sight. The camera dipped, almost with relief. Tina's voice said, "Jesus, that was a pretty—"

And there, abruptly, the clip ended.

"I can't remember how I finished that sentence," Tina said. "'A pretty close call,' maybe. Freaked the hell out of me, as you can tell. I mean, I suppose technically I was trespassing, and my first thought was those guys might be transport employees or something. I didn't dare move for about another hour, in case they returned or there were any more of them further back along. Then I just sort of crept out. Didn't much feel like doing any more vampire chasing after that. Oh, and apologies for all the God and Jesus stuff. It just comes out. I don't mean anything by it."

"That's the trouble, no one does," said Redlaw. "Run the clip again."

She did.

"And again."

Twice more, and then yet again for good measure.

"So what do you think?" she asked. "Who are they?"

"Can't tell that much about them. Not enough detail. But they definitely look military."

"Exactly. Since seeing the playback, that's my thoughts exactly."

"Helmets. Assault weapons. That looks like military-grade body armour they have on. Ballistic vests, elbow and knee pads. But also the fact that they're going single file, evenly spaced. Smacks of training to me. Drilled-in discipline. And that's not all. Can you wind it back? Freeze-frame on the clearest shot you've got, one where you can see the whole of one individual, head to toe."

Tina obliged.

"See that?" Redlaw said, pointing to one of the silhouetted figures. "See how he walks? The way he's putting his feet down?"

Tina frowned. "So what?"

"There's something about it. It's not how a man carries himself ordinarily. No, scratch that. It's not how an ordinary man carries himself."

"I don't get."

"I wouldn't expect you to," said Redlaw. "I could be imagining it, but... If you've been around Sunless as long as I have, you become familiar with certain aspects of their behaviour. The body language, for instance. Vampires may not look like much, but they're surprisingly graceful when they want to be. They go on the balls of their feet, a bit like dancers. This fellow"— he tapped the screen—"has almost that exact same walk. All seven of them do. If only we could make out their features better..."

But the figures' faces remained hidden throughout the duration of the clip, lost in impenetrable shadow.

"What are soldiers doing down in the New York subway? That's what I'd like to know," Tina said.

"Down in the subway where Sunless are reputed to be," Redlaw added. "I need to go there and have a look for myself." He stood. "Will you show me where it is?"

"Whoa there, hoss," said Tina. "You mean right now? Do you have any idea what the time is?"

"No time like the present."

"Yeah, but we're talking the West Side. Trains have stopped running, and forget catching a cab. It's twenty below and the snow's not stopping. All the hacks with any sense have gone home. What say we leave it 'til morning, huh?"

Redlaw saw the logic in this. "Okay," he said. "So I suppose I'm crashing here. Or are you going to turf me out onto the street?"

Tina indicated a couch in the corner. It was threadbare and holed, and looked as though it had been rescued from a skip. "That's yours. I'll grab you a couple of blankets."

Redlaw made himself as comfortable as he could on the couch's pancake-thin cushions. It irked him that he had paid for a hotel room he wasn't using, but there was nothing to be done about that.

"Word of warning." Tina pointed to her bedroom door. "I'll be in there, and guess what? I sleep with my Taser and my Mace. Just saying. In case you should get any funny ideas."

"Trust me, I won't."

"You betcha you won't."

"One thing, Tina," Redlaw said, before she disappeared into her room. "Has anybody else seen that footage?"

She shook her head. "Just me, and now you."

"So you haven't put it on the web anywhere? Shown it to a friend?"

"Nuh-uh. Why?"

"Good."

"Why?" she persisted.

"A feeling, that's all."

"So it's important."

"Conceivably. I just think, for your sake, that advertising that you've got it might not be a wise move. At least not until we've investigated further, and maybe not even then."

"Fuck. Seriously?"

She didn't seem concerned at all. If anything, she seemed thrilled.

Unusual girl, Redlaw thought, and he rolled over on the couch and surprised himself by falling instantly asleep.

CHAPTER EIGHT

THE HUMMER H2—gunmetal-grey paintjob, blacked-out windows, licence plate number unknown to the DMV—pulled in at the dockyard gate. Dawn was breaking. The night's clouds had dumped their freight of snow and moved on, and a weak sun was rising over Brooklyn.

Weak, thought Colonel Jacobsen, *but enough. Any sun'll do.*

He and his team performed a quick equipment check. Face masks were clipped into position, UV-resistant goggles donned. Then they sounded off, codenames into throat mikes, all seven of them on the same frequency and fully communicado.

A night watchman waddled out his prefab hut, yawning blearily. He skirted the barrier and approached the Hummer, twirling a finger in midair: *wind down your window.* When the Hummer driver didn't comply, the watchman leaned in close and tapped on the window, trying to peer through the heavily tinted glass but seeing only his own reflection.

The driver, Red Eye Three, rammed the door open, knocking the watchman off his feet. Before he could recover, Three sprang out and spritzed him in the face with a squirt of BZ gas from a small canister. The watchman spluttered and wheezed, his face went red, and then his eyes rolled up and he passed out. He would wake up in an hour's time with a splitting headache and no recollection of what just happened.

Red Eye Three hurried into the hut and threw the switch that operated the gate barrier. Back in the Hummer, Three steered the car into the dockyard, pulling up alongside an aluminium-sided administrative building.

"Okay, we're in, let's roll," said Colonel Jacobsen, and all four doors of the Hummer opened and Team Red Eye bundled out.

It was like stepping into a blast furnace. Jacobsen could feel the sun's rays through his thick protective gear. Wintry and watery though it was, the sun was hot to him. It was trying to pierce his fatigues and body armour, get to his flesh. It wanted to consume him whole, and would if given a chance. Before joining Red Eye, Jacobsen had done tours of duty in the Iraqi desert at the height of summer, a hundred and twenty in the shade, heat that could fry a man alive and desiccate his brains. Here in subzero New York in January, now that he had become something other than a mere infantry officer, it was about as bad. The daylight glared through the goggles' polarised lenses. Had any of his skin been exposed, blisters would have erupted in seconds. Longer than that, and there would be singeing, wisps of pale smoke, first degree burns, second degree, then rapidly third.

Team Red Eye moved with practised precision, each of them with a fixed role, a set of procedures to execute. CCTV cameras were disabled and the hard drive that stored their recordings was wiped. The perimeter was secured. All alarms were put out of action. In under five minutes, the team had control of the entire dockyard, nothing able to come between them and their target.

Four of them took up prearranged lookout positions. Jacobsen, meanwhile, headed for the waterfront with Red Eye Two and Red Eye Five in tow. Wharf cranes loomed against the sky, their long necks seemingly bowing under the weight of snow. The three men moved lightly, even Red Eye Five, for all that he was toting a large oxyacetylene cylinder set on his back. Five, also known as Gunnery Sergeant DuWayne Child, was the size of an ox and, thanks to the course of treatment the entire team were undergoing, as strong as one too.

Colonel Jacobsen consulted a download of the dockyard's delivery manifest on his smartphone. He and the other two were almost at their objective. A mound of shipping containers rose before them, steel boxes the size of railway carriages arranged in a grid pattern. Serial numbers were visible on the sides. Jacobsen identified the one they wanted, the topmost of a stack of three.

"This is Red Eye One. I have visual. Target is acquired. Radio silence from here on in."

The container had arrived yesterday afternoon, offloaded from the *Star of Szczecin*, a 10,000-ton Polsteam cargo vessel outbound from Gdansk. According to the bill of lading, there were rolls of carpet and assorted items of furniture inside, and doubtless that was true. What mattered to Team Red Eye was what *else* might be inside. If their intel was correct—and the man who was funding the Red Eye initiative seemed to have access to rock solid intel—the container was home to a score of trafficked vampires. Some Russian hoods had charged the vamps a small fortune to cross the Atlantic, in accommodation that made steerage class look luxurious. Tonight, local contacts were due to come and release them from confinement. But not if Team Red Eye had any say in the matter.

Jacobsen leapt up the side of the container stack, scrambling easily from handhold to handhold until he reached the top. He undid his mask. Sunlight dug needles into his lips and cheeks. He inhaled through his nose several times, deeply, before re-covering his face.

He gestured to Two and Five below. A rapid flick of gloved fingers, beckoning them.

In no time, Jacobsen had been joined on top of the container by Child and the team's second-in-command, Lieutenant Harvey Giacoia. Child unpacked the cylinder set and the blowtorch attached to it. Jacobsen and Giacoia, meanwhile, cleared the snow off the container, brushing it aside with sweeps of their feet. Child opened the gas flow regulator on the acetylene tank, sparked up the jet with a friction lighter, slowly brought in the oxygen until the mix was right, and got busy cutting.

Up to that moment, the vampires had been staying very quiet, keeping still, hoping that whoever had climbed onto their container was there to do nothing more than conduct an external inspection. As sparks began raining down inside, alarm swiftly turned to panic. The vampires scurried to find cover amid the packing crates and pallet loads.

Child worked methodically, slicing along the upper rim of the container. Steel glowed and dripped like lava. When he had cut through one end and two corners, he halted, nodding to Jacobsen and Giacoia. They grasped the edges of the container top and heaved backwards with all their might. The top curled upwards. It was like peeling the lid off a giant sardine tin. Metal screeched and groaned as it buckled and bent.

When they had created a large enough gap, the two men leapt down into the container's interior, and Child joined them. They unshipped MP5 submachine guns.

Crimson eyes glittered furiously in the container's dark recesses. Guttural Polish curses were flung at the intruders, but this was all the vampires could do. They couldn't go near them, not as long as the three men stood in the protective aura of the sun's slanting beams. They could only cower and snarl.

"Fire at will," Jacobsen ordered, and he and Red Eye Two and Red Eye Five let rip, unleashing salvos of Fraxinus rounds in scything arcs. The vampires were pinned down by the gunfire. Bullets whittled through their flimsy shelters and makeshift barricades. Ricochets whined in all directions. One by one, shots found their mark. Vampires erupted into dust, shrieking horribly.

"I'm out," Giacoia announced, and Jacobsen and Child soon emptied their magazines as well. With the echoes of their holocaust still ringing in their ears, the three of them advanced towards the other end of the container.

A number of vampires lay wounded, writhing in agony. All had been winged by a Fraxinus, and the bullet's ash-wood content was slowly poisoning them, eating away their flesh. The Red Eyes drew sidearms and heart-shot the vampires at point blank range.

Jacobsen surveyed their handiwork. A vampire kill was a hell of a lot neater and cleaner than the ordinary kind of kill, you could at least say that for it. No gore, very little mess. It was almost like not killing at all.

And for that reason, vaguely dissatisfying.

"Good work, men," Jacobsen said. "Let's bail."

BACK IN THE Hummer, trundling northward on the Brooklyn Queens Expressway, Jacobsen got on the phone to the money man.

"You catch that, sir?"

"Every second of it," came the reply in a thick, nasal Boston accent that stretched certain vowels almost to breaking point. "Another textbook takedown. I'm as proud as can be of you fellows."

"Just doing what we're paid for," said Jacobsen. The connection was good, but there was an unusually long delay on it. The price of dense, secure signal encryption. "How many more before we've built up a persuasive argument?"

"That's for me to decide, soldier, not you."

Jacobsen hated the way the money man called him *soldier*. Only soldiers got to call other soldiers that. It was condescending and disrespectful.

He bit back his irritation, thinking of the $50,000 completion fee that was being wired to his checking account probably right this minute and the slightly smaller but still considerable sums that were making their way into his teammates' accounts. You did not lose your temper with the person employing you. That was the golden rule of mercenary work. You took whatever shit the boss dished out, and you smiled and asked for more. So, not much different from the army, then.

"Understood," he said. "Just eager to be getting on with the job."

"And that's a very healthy attitude to have," drawled the Bostonian. "Now, you and your unit toddle off back to base, get some rest, have yourselves some of that tasty human claret I lay on for you, and leave the forward planning and the strategising to me. How about that?"

Jacobsen snapped the phone shut and stared out at the East River and the sumptuous rise-and-fall span of the Brooklyn Bridge towering against the pristine blue sky. His jaw clenched and unclenched.

"How much do you hate that bastard?" said Red Eye Three beside him as she drove. Her name was Jeanette Berger, she had been a chief warrant officer in the Marine Corps, and she was as competent in the field as she was pretty—and she was exceptionally pretty. Even the bright scarlet of her eyes couldn't detract from that.

"I'd hate him if I cared about him, and I don't," said Jacobsen. "As long as his money's good, I have no feelings about him whatsoever. He doesn't annoy me in the least bit."

Berger tipped her head in amusement. "So you say." She glanced in the rearview. The five other members of Team Red Eye were lost in their own thoughts, the usual post-successful-op reveries. Even Red Eye Seven's usually ever-flapping yap was, for the time being, at rest.

Berger slipped a surreptitious hand across to the passenger seat and Jacobsen's thigh. She squeezed, fingertips brushing the bulge of his crotch.

"Yes," sighed Jacobsen, with the slightest of sly smiles. "You can try to ride Jim Jacobsen, you can try to get a rise out of him, but you won't get anywhere. No, sir."

What Berger's hand was feeling gave the lie to his words. Her touch could get a rise out of Colonel Jacobsen any time.

LATER, BACK AT base, Jacobsen came to her in her quarters.

They didn't speak much. There wasn't a lot that needed to be said. He stripped her, fell on her, *plundered* her.

"I have my period," she told him breathlessly at one point, and Jacobsen grinned as if this was the best news ever, an invitation, not a prohibition, and shortly afterwards his head was between her legs, tongue lapping with gusto.

Etiquette and discipline dictated that teammates did not sleep together.

But Berger and Jacobsen paid no heed to that.

Appetite.

Appetite was all.

MEANWHILE, THE MONEY man was on the phone again, another secure line, this one connecting him to a private mobile number that an extraordinarily small number of people had access to. In fact, there were perhaps only a dozen individuals in all of America who had the privilege of knowing it and being able to use it.

The voice at the other end was measured and urbane, a voice that had seduced millions of voters, filled them with reassurance that their problems were shared, their complaints were listened to, their concerns were important and valid.

"Ah, my Boston Brahmin," the voice said. "I can spare you five minutes."

"Is that all? In that case, I don't think I'm getting great value for my campaign contributions. Five million dollars a minute? Is that what your time's really worth?"

"I'd give you more," said the other man unflappably, "but then I'd be late for my meeting with the Chinese premier, who's somewhat slightly higher up the totem pole than you. Or maybe *you* can come and discuss trade quotas with him, and I'll go catch a movie in the White House screening room instead. Believe me, the way my schedule is these days, a couple of hours to myself with a Blu-Ray of *Citizen Kane* would be a blessing."

"Could be that one day I *will* be in your shoes," the Bostonian said.

"Nah. That'd mean you'd have to learn to be nice to people, and I can't see that happening. Besides, you couldn't handle the pay cut."

"You have me there. Well, while I have this brief window, then, I'll take the opportunity to give you a heads-up on the status of the Porphyrian Project."

"And where are we at with it right now?"

"You've watched the helmet-cam footage I've been sending you?"

"Of course."

"Then you know for yourself that it's all going swimmingly. Our operatives have exceeded expectation.

Their efficiency and prowess are remarkable. Next to them, vampires are like children, quite defenceless."

The President of the United States let out one of his warm, patrician chuckles. "That's all very well, but you're still in the field-testing phase, aren't you? How long have your people been out there, doing what they do? Less than a month. You yourself warned me there could be potential side effects from the treatments. You haven't allowed enough time for those to come to the forefront, if they're going to. The FDA spends years trialling new drugs before letting the pharmaceutical companies sell them on the open market. Same should apply to you. What if something goes wrong? What if, tomorrow, one of your guys suddenly sprouts fangs and starts chowing down on some poor, unsuspecting lab tech? You're asking a lot from me, so early in the game. You need to be a little more patient."

It took all the patience the Bostonian possessed to keep from blowing his top. "Mr President, sir," he said, "you told me last July that a government contract for the Porphyrian process was guaranteed, on condition that I could prove it could be made to work. With all due respect, I think I've done that."

"No, what I said was, I would look into securing you a government contract," the President said, with the verbal exactitude of the attorney he used to be. "I never promised anything."

"I was led to believe—"

The President cut in. "What you *chose* to believe is your lookout, Howard. I'm not responsible for how you interpreted our little informal chitchat in the Rose Garden. You seem to forget that the economy is down the toilet. We've got a fiscal debt the size of Mount Everest."

"It ought to be half as big by now, the amount of tax you take off of me."

"Stop grumbling. You billionaires are doing okay. I'm just saying that, in the current climate, I'd be hard pushed to find funding for you. Congress would need to be wooed like a Catholic virgin on prom night. And if something then went wrong, if it all blew up in my face, I'd lose all political credibility. I'd be dead in the water. I've got to tread carefully on this one."

"I'm offering you a cast-iron solution for dealing with the vampire immigration problem."

"The vampire immigration problem that we don't have."

"I know of a few senators and governors who'd disagree with you there."

"The Van Helsing Party? Those bozos make a lot of noise but nobody pays any attention. Nobody ever does, with these breakaway factions."

"Fox News does. Middle America does. You've always got to think about the fly-over states."

"Please," said the President. "You can't jump-start me into making a decision. Your scare tactics won't work. You should know better than that."

"What exactly has my twenty-five mill bought me, then?" asked the Bostonian.

"It's bought you this phone number. My ear."

"Hardly seems a sound return on my investment."

"Your donation," the President corrected him.

"Whatever. It just strikes me that, with your term running out and you being up for re-election and all, I could take a similar sum and *invest* it in one of your rival candidates. Someone who'd place a higher priority on my needs. A Van Helsing, even. That guy from

North Dakota, the Pentecostalist with the great hair and the cute charity worker wife, he's looking like a frontrunner. He killed at the Iowa Caucus and the New Hampshire primary."

"The man's an idiot."

"This is a nation that put George W. Bush in the Oval Office *twice*. We've got a track record with idiots. And the Van Helsing message is skewing pretty well with Middle American voters right now. With my cash behind him, Mr North Dakota could become quite the contender. And I know he'd be properly grateful. Unlike some."

There was silence on the other end of the line. The Bostonian had scored a direct hit.

Then the President came back on. "Sorry, distracted, missed what you just said. I've got an advisor standing beside me tapping his foot and pointing at his watch. Looks like the honourable chairman and his equally honourable wife can't wait any longer for me to come and break dim sum with them. We'll carry on this discussion at a later date, eh, Howard? When you've got a bit more information under your belt. In the meantime, keep at it. I'm far from giving you an outright 'no'. I just need more reassurance that this isn't going to be a fiasco, like that Solarville thing your pal Lambourne was involved in over in the UK. The British prime minister's career was left in tatters after that whole sorry affair. Don't want the same happening to me, do I? See you around."

And that was that, connection cut, conversation over.

The Bostonian, J. Howard Farthingale III, glared at the phone in his hand as though it, somehow, was to blame for the call not going the way he would have liked. The medium was at fault, not the message.

Very deliberately, he placed the phone on the writing surface of his vintage Art Deco desk, a massive block of macassar ebony with silver bands and Bakelite drawer handles, once the property of a Golden Age Hollywood producer. Then, just as deliberately, he picked up an ornament, a fist-sized chunk of moon rock, and smashed the phone to smithereens with it.

The act damaged both desktop and moon rock, in addition to destroying the phone. The cheap item of consumer electronics could be easily replaced. As for the other two, the desk could be repaired, the moon rock substituted, but only at immense cost in both instances. This was altogether more masochistically satisfying to Farthingale.

Fucking president. Fuck that weaselly fucking slimeball. Who the fuck does he think he is?

Farthingale opened a sliding window and stepped out onto a sun terrace that one of the caretakers had scrupulously shovelled clear of snow first thing that morning. He took in the view and tried to appreciate it, hoping this would calm the thoughts raging through his head. The downward sweep of hill, fringed by tall pines. The cliff, the beach, the jetty where his Sunseeker Predator 108 was moored, icebound, its decks sheathed in winter tarpaulins. The reach between his island and the mainland, a channel two nautical miles wide which currently looked like a stretch of the Arctic Ocean, all pack-ice and small bergs. The mainland itself, a bay, a Massachusetts fishing port town, summer homes speckled along the coastline.

Just relax. It doesn't matter.

The doctors had told him that with his condition, it was important to avoid stress. Stress could exacerbate the symptoms. It could even hospitalise him.

You can fix this. You can fix anything.

He'd been meaning to inform the President about Team Red Eye's latest operation, but that had fallen by the wayside as their conversation had unfurled. No doubt word would reach him, probably by no later than midday today. The President had a team of secret service agents working for him who were dedicated to nothing else but compiling reports of vampire activity and vampire-related incidents. He would soon be aware that Team Red Eye had conducted their first ever mission in broad daylight. How would he react? Would he be impressed? He ought to be. Or would it trouble him that Farthingale had upped the ante? Hard to say. It could be either. The Most Powerful Man In The World was infuriatingly inscrutable at times.

Farthingale's best option seemed to be to continue piling on the pressure. By escalating the scale and audacity of his team's attacks on vampires, he could apply more leverage on the President, force his hand. The President blathering on about the economy, what bullshit. He had a military black budget slush fund that was equivalent to the GDP of the average Arab emirate, and he could dip his hand into it any time he liked, without needing to seek congressional approval. The Porphyrian Project could be rolled out countrywide in a matter of months, at great financial advantage to its progenitor, Farthingale. All that was required was the presidential say-so.

"I just need more reassurance that this isn't going to be a fiasco, like that Solarville thing."

Farthingale thought of Nathaniel Lambourne. Not a friend, as such, but a close colleague, a fellow business titan. Solarville had seemed a sure thing. Too bad it had turned to shit.

That fate would not befall Porphyrian. Farthingale was convinced of that.

His eye was caught by movement below. His sister, coming out from the lower storey, onto the snow. She was wrapped up well—one-piece ski suit, mittens, fur-trimmed hat and polka dot wellingtons, all in fuchsia pink, her favourite colour. Her nurse, Rozetta, made sure Clara was always dressed in whatever was appropriate for the occasion and the time of year, and always fashionably.

Clara bent and started rolling a ball of snow. Soon she'd amassed it to a decent size, as big as one of those inflatable exercise balls people wallowed on at gyms. But she was struggling. It was too heavy for her.

Farthingale pulled on a fleece-lined waxed Barbour and went down to help. Clara was thrilled to see him. Her pudgy face lit up and she threw herself at him for a hug.

"Howie! Howie! I'm making a snowman. You wanna make a snowman with me?"

She was forty-four, two years his junior, and had the mind of a child and the body mass index of a baby. Her slanted, Down's Syndrome eyes sparkled brightly with winter wonderland delight.

"Sure, let's do that, Clara."

They spent an hour assembling the snowman and patting it into shape. Rozetta fetched all the necessary accoutrements: a carrot, some lumps of coal, and a scarf and an old felt hat she had scavenged from somewhere in the house. Farthingale felt better when it was done, when the coal eyes and smile were in place and the snowman looked like a classic storybook snowman. He watched Clara as she skipped in circles around their creation, chortling with glee and singing a song only she knew. Her happiness was consoling, contagious. Clara was good for him, in so many ways. So many ways.

CHAPTER
NINE

REDLAW HELD UP the loose corner of chainlink fence and Tina scooted under on hands and knees. Then she held up the corner for him. Side by side they slalomed down a steep embankment, like skiers without skis, and crossed an area of waste ground.

Rail tracks lay buried in snow, raised lines like surgical scars on skin. The subway tunnel yawned. Above it hulked the remains of a decommissioned industrial plant, the name of a toothpaste manufacturer still just visible in huge spectral capitals on one side.

Graffiti fringed the tunnel entrance, incongruously gaudy in an otherwise colourless place. The swarms of tags, slogans and illustrations continued inside the tunnel, but only as far as the daylight extended. As the darkness thickened, the graffiti petered out. Eventually the walls were nothing but bare bedrock.

Tina switched on the ruggedized flashlight they'd bought at an army surplus store that morning, along with a parka and gloves for Redlaw and, most expensive of all, a set of night vision goggles. She aimed the beam around, spotlighting rails, ties and concrete pillars.

"Try and hold it still," Redlaw said. "Otherwise you create false movement with the shadows."

She swung towards him, accidentally shining the flashlight in his face. His vision seemed to explode. It was like looking into a supernova.

"And keep that wretched thing out of my eyes," he snapped.

"I didn't mean to," said Tina, adding under her breath, "Jeez, chill out, why don't you?"

It took over a minute for the afterimage of the 500-lumen bulb to fade and for Redlaw's eyesight to normalise.

About half a mile in, they arrived at the place where Tina had shot the footage of soldiers.

"They were heading in this direction?" Redlaw asked, pointing back the way he and Tina had come.

"Yeah."

"Then let's carry on."

They went deeper in, and Redlaw could feel the tunnel's gradual descent. They were delving further below Manhattan with every step, and the air grew damp and stale. There was litter here, food wrappers, beer empties, fast-food packaging, all of it suggesting relatively recent human habitation. No Sunless detritus yet.

Then he spotted bones. A jumble of small white skeletons, rodents and mammals, strewn by the trackside.

A good sign.

There were more piles of bones further on, and then Redlaw and Tina came to an area where three sets of tracks converged. At least one of them was still in use, judging by the service lights affixed to pillars alongside it at infrequent intervals.

"Turn off the torch," he said to Tina. "We can manage without it for now, and those things eat batteries."

She did as told, slipping the flashlight into the rucksack she was carrying. At the same time, she produced a camcorder and thumbed its power button on.

"What's that?" Redlaw demanded.

"Duh! What does it look like?"

"I know what it is. I mean what are you doing with it?"

"I'm going to start videoing."

"Videoing what?"

"You, stupid. The great John Redlaw, on the case."

"Give it to me."

He made a grab for the camcorder. Tina was too quick for him, stepping aside and pulling it back so that his fingers just missed.

"What the fuck are you on?" she yelled. "What's up with you?"

"You can't record this."

"And why not?"

"Because I say so."

Her laughter was scornful. "You need to give me a better reason than that."

"Because I'd prefer you not to."

"Same difference. Uh-uh. Don't you dare." Redlaw had braced himself to make another lunge for the camcorder. "Try that again and I'll kick you in the balls. I know self-defence, too. Hapkido moves. I can have you on the floor with a thumb lock, crying like a baby."

"If you believe that'll happen, you're sorely mistaken," said Redlaw. He took a deep breath. "Tina, please put the camera away. I can't be in any footage you shoot. I just can't."

"Well, tough, because you're a story, *my* story, and I'm getting you down on disk whether you like it or not."

"For what purpose?"

"To show the world what you're doing."

"I really don't want the world to know what I'm doing," said Redlaw. "Couldn't we have discussed this beforehand? You never even asked my permission."

"Would you have given it?"

"No."

"That's why I didn't ask for it," said Tina. "What's with the camera-shyness anyway? You're not that bad-looking, if that's what you're worried about. For an old guy, I mean. You're in okay shape. Still got most of your hair. Your eyes are pretty scary, but apart from that..."

"For one thing, it'll be distracting having you pointing a camera at me the whole time. For another, I like to maintain a low profile. I'm... I'm not in this for publicity."

"And that's it? Nothing else? No other justification?"

"Absolutely none."

He could see she was sceptical. She knew she wasn't getting the whole truth. How could he tell her that the last thing he needed was SHADE finding out where he was? Khalid would have search bots scanning the cybersphere for the slightest mention of his name.

"Well," she said, "then we have ourselves a problem, Mr Redlaw. 'Cause I only took you down here on the understanding that I could film you at work."

"An understanding you never actually voiced."

"I thought it was obvious."

"It was not."

"You saw me pack my camera as we were leaving the apartment."

"No, I didn't."

"You should have been watching more carefully, then," she said. "It's not my fault you weren't paying attention."

Aggravating little...

Redlaw reined in his temper. "Tell me," he said, "what are you planning on doing with whatever you film here? Upload it onto the internet, presumably."

"Hey, check out grandpa, all hip with the modern computer jive! Yeah, I'd edit it down, post teaser clips on Facebook and wherever. YouTube, of course. Various other places, all linking back to me. I've got my own website, see. Well, the stub of one. Tick Talk's what I'm calling it. Tick's my nickname."

"But why?"

"Because it'll be cool stuff," she said simply. "And it might well help me get my dream job, working for one of the big networks."

"Ah. Right. Self-interest. Of course."

"I live in the real world. And I think you do too, in your way. I'm helping you, aren't I? Why would I even be here, if I'm not? So, fair's fair, you help me in return."

"By being your story."

Tina made a quiz show *ding-dong* sound. "Kee-rect. Quid pro quo. Something for something."

She had appealed to his sense of morality.

Damn her.

"Look," Redlaw said, "I could agree to you videoing me—"

"Yay."

"—but on one condition."

"Like what?"

"You don't upload, post, share anything, not one frame, without my approval."

"Okay. Participant's consent. I can get with that."

"And," said Redlaw, "none of it appears anywhere 'til after I'm done and gone."

"Which'll be when?"

"I don't know. How long is a piece of string? I don't even know what I'm getting myself into here. It may be nothing. What I'm saying is, shoot what you like, and when we're finished—and I'll tell you when we're finished—the footage can see the light of day, but not before then."

"Hmm."

"Oh, and you pixellate my face, or whatever it's called," Redlaw added. "Blur it so that I'm unrecognisable. And bleep out my name whenever it's mentioned."

"What would be the point of that?" Tina fumed. "The footage will mainly be of interest because of the subject matter—the star of the show, you."

"It's negotiable, I suppose," Redlaw conceded. "We'll see. But my other conditions stand. Break them, and I break you. Clear?"

Her expression was mulish, but Redlaw could be obstinate too, and he meant every word he said. His threat was genuine, and she knew it.

"Grumpy much?" she said.

"Dead serious, that's all. And I'm not a man you want to cross."

"Yeah, yeah. You've made your point, Huffy the Vampire Slayer. Now we know whose dick's bigger, can we get on with this?"

Redlaw fixed her with his sternest, most forbidding stare, then nodded.

THE TRACKS DEVIATED, the lit one continuing on a level course to some unseen station further up the line, both of the others plunging into pitch blackness. Redlaw wavered between the latter two, then plumped for the left-hand one. It was instinct as much as anything. The tunnel was the steeper of the pair; it went deeper, therefore seemed to afford greater protection, better shelter.

He had commandeered the flashlight off Tina, and with its beam he soon found confirmation that he'd made the correct choice of tunnel.

"Shit," said Tina.

"Precisely. Sunless faeces. Roughly a week old."

Tina dollied in with the camcorder, capturing a close-up image of the long, black-red turd. "Just laying on the rail like that. Aren't these vamps, like, housebroken?"

"It's a signpost," Redlaw said. "For the benefit of other vampires. I'd say this one was deposited by an adult male, judging by the calibre."

"You can date it. You can tell whether it came from a man or a woman. You're like a Navajo tracker, only with vampire poop."

"If I'm not mistaken, there'll be more nearby. A couple of dozen yards further along... Ah yes."

The flashlight's ring of brightness targeted another clump of faecal matter, a much smaller one.

"It's known as a secondary marker," Redlaw said. "It points the way."

"Ugh," said Tina, although she sounded as much fascinated as revolted. "So the biggie says 'here we are' and the little one says 'keep going'."

"That's more or less it."

"This is good shit. That's not a joke. I mean as in good material."

Redlaw ventured on, Tina following with the camcorder held up before her face, her features ghostly in the moonglow of the screen.

A soft scuffling sound ahead brought Redlaw to an immediate standstill. He whipped his Cindermaker out.

"Whoa," said Tina. "What's up?"

"Could be nothing."

"Mighty big piece of artillery you've got yourself there, if it's nothing."

"Just a precaution." Redlaw trained the flashlight along the tunnel, pointing the barrel of the Cindermaker alongside. The beam extended fifty yards before beginning to lose brilliance and definition. Streaks of moisture glistened on one wall, where a water main or a sewer above was leaking through. Some kind of moss or fungus flourished in a semicircle beneath, forming a thick spongy mat that covered half the tunnel floor.

"This is so fucking creepy," Tina whispered, just loud enough for the camcorder's mike to pick up. "We're about one mile underground, I'd guess, and we're on the trail of vampires. That man there is John Redlaw, who used to be with London SHADE, a.k.a. the Night Brigade. Nobody even knows we're down here, so if anything goes wrong, we're—"

"Shh!" Redlaw hissed.

"I'm narrating."

"Well, don't."

"But you've got to narrate," she protested. "It adds to the general atmosphere."

"No, all it does is annoy me and make it hard to listen out."

"So I should shut up."

"Ideally you should be somewhere else entirely, but since we can't have that, shutting up would be great."

"Okay," Tina pouted. "I'll tack on a voiceover later, then. Won't be the same, but what the hell."

Redlaw advanced slowly. All at once, a rat popped up from behind one of the rails. It blinked in the light, whiskers fibrillating madly. Another rat appeared behind it and started grooming the first's fur, nibbling with its incisors and combing with its claws.

"Hmm," Redlaw said. "That's pretty telling."

"Aw, Mr and Mrs Rat are in *lurve*."

"They're comfortable. They're not scared. Which implies that there aren't any predators around. Any 'Lesses that were here, they're gone, so the rats feel it's safe to be out in the open."

"You are just a mine of useful vampire information, Mr Redlaw."

"Come on."

Not much further on, their destination came into view—a huddle of very basic living accommodations. There were sticks of furniture, little cubicles divided from one another by blankets or sheets of plywood, loose newspaper pages lying everywhere, and a few rudimentary creature comforts such as books, board games, kerosene lanterns and rusty camping stoves. Everything was tattered and broken, riddled with holes, overturned, strewn. Clearly there had been some semblance of order once, and then something like a hurricane had come tearing through.

Redlaw bent into a crouch. "Look," he said, indicating the ground directly in front of him. "What do you see?"

Tina adjusted focus with the camcorder, zeroing in on what he was pointing at: a glinting expanse of small round objects littering the track, like an army of dead metal cockroaches.

"Those are bullet casings, right?" she said.

Redlaw picked one up and examined it closely. "Fraxinus. Nine millimetre. See?" He showed her the "FRAX-9" stamped on the cartridge case head around the primer. "But also..." He sniffed the small copper cylinder and held it out to her. "Yes. Not just cordite. There's a distinct smell to a spent Fraxinus round. Burnt wood, like a bonfire or a hearth." He straightened up. "And that there..." He gestured at the wreckage. "That's been shot to pieces. This is where your homeless man's 'foreigners' were living, until someone came along and raked the place with gunfire and wiped them out."

He strode five paces and bent again. He dabbed his forefinger into what appeared to be a thick scattering of dust, then held it up.

"Ash," he said of the gritty grey coating on his fingertip.

"You mean to say that's..."

"Vampire remains."

"So gross."

He pinpointed several other mounds of dust with the flashlight beam. "Must have been around twenty of them. A mid-size nest. The question is, who did it? Who dusted them? Who's responsible?"

"Those soldiers."

"Seems logical. You obviously caught them on their way out, after they'd completed the task. Overall, I'd say you were pretty lucky, Tina. Had they spotted you, I imagine at the very least they would have confiscated your camera, but at worst..."

He saw her shudder. Good. He wanted her to be frightened. It would stop her treating everything like a game.

"Jesus," she breathed. "I mean, not Jesus. Buddha, Allah, L. Ron Hubbard, someone else. You really think...?"

"I think we're talking about some well-organised and well-equipped people, ruthless, with a very specific agenda. I've no idea who they are, but I do know that they're easily a match for the quarry they're hunting. There's no indication that any one of them was hurt during their attack. No blood at the scene, no scraps of torn clothing, no suggestion that the vampires gave as good as they got and went down fighting. Your footage backs that up. Nobody in it looked like they were limping or injured in any way. It was a massacre. A one-sided, cold-blooded massacre of vampires. And I don't mind admitting I'm really quite unnerved. Even a squad of seven SHADE officers couldn't have pulled off something like this, not without taking casualties."

"So what's the plan?" Tina asked. "What do we do now?"

Redlaw deliberated. She was using him as documentary subject matter. He didn't like it, but there wasn't much he could do to change it now. He might as well get something in exchange and use *her*.

"Film," he told her. "Film everything. Gather evidence. Make sure it's all recorded for posterity. If anyone wants proof of what's going on, we can supply it, proof aplenty. Get it all into your camera, Tina Checkley."

Tina didn't need any further prompting. She fired up the built-in light on her camera and set to work.

CHAPTER TEN

"TEA," SAID REDLAW, gazing morosely at the murky brown liquid in the mug in front of him. "You'd think, this being the world's last remaining superpower, the cradle of liberal democracy and free-market economy, and all that, that Americans would have the nous to be able to brew tea properly."

Tina held up a finger. "One. We're in a diner in Hell's Kitchen. I think you're raising your hopes a little high."

"They certainly got the name of the place right," Redlaw muttered.

"Two." A second finger rose to join the first. "We chucked crates of tea into Boston harbour to show how much we hated your British asses. You think we're going to make an effort with the stuff now?"

"You're saying this abomination I'm drinking is a calculated insult?"

"Call it a historical tradition. A protest. Don't take it personally."

"Well, it's just not my cup of tea." Redlaw shunted the mug aside and scooped up a mouthful of scrambled eggs instead.

The diner was steamy hot, its windows fogged with condensation. Lunchtime patrons filled every booth, some hunched over tabloid newspapers, others over laptops, many consulting their phones. The waitress barked at the short order chef, she enormous and Jamaican, he tiny and Vietnamese. His response every time was to curse her in his native tongue, to which she simply rolled her eyes and gave a talk-to-the-hand gesture. They wore matching wedding bands.

A wall-mounted TV set added to the general hubbub. The news was on, and yet again the weather was the lead story. "Forecasters predict no end in sight, as the Big Freeze enters its nineteenth day," intoned an immaculately coiffed anchorman. "Last night's fresh snowfalls will be followed by blizzard conditions this evening, lasting well into tomorrow morning. Already it's being called the worst winter in living memory, and the battered economy is taking a further pounding as industry and commerce all along the East Coast grinds to a halt, with workers struggling to make their daily commutes."

"Missing home, then?" Tina said to Redlaw.

"Somewhat. Certain aspects of it."

"So why'd you leave, again?"

"It's personal."

"Yeah, only, the thing is, I've just remembered something about you. Vaguely. Am I right in thinking you got yourself into a spot of bother back in the UK?"

"This isn't bacon, either," Redlaw said, intent on trying to spear some with his fork. The rasher shattered into a dozen pieces. "Bacon's meat, not this brittle nonsense."

"Wasn't there some kind of scandal? I'm pretty sure there was. You were in the headlines."

"And a jug of syrup on the side? With the main course?"

"Avoid the subject all you like. I've got my BlackBerry. I can do a search and have the full story at my fingertips within seconds. Whyn't you save me the effort and just tell me yourself? Give me your side."

Redlaw put down his fork with a heavy sigh. "It's simple enough. I uncovered a plot to eliminate Sunless. It was a Final Solution affair, concentration camps by any other name. I blew the whole conspiracy wide open. Stopped some very bad people doing a very bad thing."

"For which you were hailed as a national hero," said Tina.

"For which I was vilified, accused of murder, and obliged to go on the run."

"Well, I wasn't *so* far off. Have you considered there might be some way of clearing your name?"

"So you believe me?"

"Why wouldn't I?"

"You hardly know me. All you've heard is my account of things, and you take it at face value. Don't journalists need to double-check their facts?"

"From what I've seen so far, you're a straight kind of guy. I may not be a professional journalist—yet— but I've got the instincts. Some people are fakers. Some are lying fucks. Some people you shouldn't trust any further than you can throw them. You're not any of those. You act like you've nothing to be ashamed of. And whistleblowers always, *always* get screwed over.

It's like…" Her shoulders rose and fell. "I don't know, a law of nature. The bastards are in charge. Anyone who crosses them or challenges them comes off worst. Sucks, but that's the way it is."

"Doesn't mean one should stop trying," said Redlaw. "Jesus defied the authorities all his life. He stood up to the money lenders, the Pharisees, the Romans…"

"Yeah, and look how he ended up. You want to martyr the fuck out of yourself, go right ahead. That's your prerogative. But this thing we're doing, this investigation or whatever it is, don't you see that ultimately it could be your way out, your ticket back to respectability? I'm providing you with a platform here, a public forum where you can defend yourself and show that you're fighting the good fight. It's a chance to state your case, somewhere where nobody can mess with you or shout you down. A chance to put John Redlaw's point of fucking view."

"You swear an awful lot."

"Point of fudging view." Tina gripped his hand on the tabletop. "Redlaw, I'm willing to be your Woodward and Bernstein, all in one charming half-Italian, half-Baptist package. Together, we can stick it to the twenty-first-century Nixons. We can… Redlaw? Are you even listening?"

But Redlaw's attention had shifted abruptly to the TV, where a report was being filed live from a Brooklyn dockyard. A reporter with chapped pink cheeks stood in front of a stack of shipping containers, the topmost of which appeared to have been broken into from above.

"…still baffling NYPD," she was saying. A caption identified her as Molly Chan, Home Affairs Correspondent, and stated that she was broadcasting from the East River docks, Brooklyn. "The container has been extensively vandalised and there are reports, as yet unconfirmed, of large quantities of shell casings and spent bullets being found inside."

"Turn up the volume, please," Redlaw asked the waitress.

She either failed to hear or chose to ignore the request.

"Yo!" Tina bellowed across the diner. "Lady! Man wants to listen to this. Turn it up."

The waitress sucked her teeth, but complied.

"Most puzzling of all," Molly Chan said, "is how the culprits were able to open the roof of the container. They clearly used cutting equipment and possibly crowbars, but we're talking half-inch steel. To bend that, you'd need to apply more pressure than an ordinary person is capable of. One theory is that a 'jaws of life', the device firefighters use to cut accident victims out of wrecked vehicles, was involved. However, that doesn't account for the strange 'curl of butter' effect that you can see behind me."

The cameraman zoomed in over her shoulder to the container. On it stood a pair of police officers who were gazing down at the peeled-back roof. They looked appropriately mystified.

The anchorman in the studio asked, "Molly, what can you tell us about the possibility of an alleged vampire connection with all this?"

"Dale, that's one of the many rumours that are swirling around right now, but detectives investigating remain tight-lipped on the subject. The container came from Poland and supposedly was being used to transport furniture destined for a well-known chain of department stores. However, since its point of origin is eastern Europe, some kind of vampire element to the crime cannot be completely ruled out."

"Thanks, Molly. We'll give you more on this breaking story as we get it. Now, over to Kevin Weingarten with the latest from the stock exchange. Kevin?"

"It's them," said Redlaw firmly. "I know it is."

"You think?"

"Same *modus operandi*. A military-style infiltration. A hail of bullets. I bet you anything those are Fraxinus rounds in that container. I bet you anything there are piles of ash in it, too, like in the subway. The police just aren't telling us that yet."

"But the report was mostly supposition," said Tina. "That skinny little bitch with the bad nose job was inferring and sensationalising. She didn't *know*."

"Shipping containers are ideal for Sunless who want to travel overseas. Sealed so no light gets in. Like giant steel coffins. The things get ferried around from A to B to C and nobody ever looks inside, not until they reach their final destination. The number of 'Lesses who've been sneaked into Britain that way—it beggars belief. We didn't have enough manpower in SHADE to put a stop to it, and we found it hard to persuade customs officials to do more than just glance at the container manifests and wave them through."

"Not exactly club class, is it, though?"

"Usually there's no alternative. Sometimes the vampires can manage unaided, slipping into a container when no one's looking, but more often organised crime's involved. Gangs can make a bundle out of smuggling them across borders. The 'Lesses scrimp, save, steal, use cards from the wallets of their victims, until they've got the money together to pay for their passage. It invariably costs a small fortune. But worth it, to be transported to a new land where there's room to roam and no vampire overpopulation problem." Redlaw quickly finished up his meal. "I want to visit that dockyard. Brooklyn, it said. Can you get us there?"

FINDING THE RELEVANT dockyard was easy. It was where police cars and outside broadcast vans were parked in droves. Getting beyond the crime scene tape, however, proved impossible. Back in London, in the good old days, Redlaw could have waltzed past with just a flash of his SHADE badge. But this wasn't London, and the days were neither good nor old. The cop stationed at the gate was turning away everyone who didn't have a legitimate excuse to come through. He was also flatly refusing to answer queries. "No comment" was all he would say. To anyone. About anything.

Redlaw had to be content with joining the throng of gawkers and rubberneckers on the wrong side of the perimeter fence. There was little to be seen but the damaged container in the far distance and, nearer by, a couple of CSU officers in pale blue coveralls conferring together and several of New York's finest standing around drinking coffee from cardboard cups and looking robustly officious.

"This is a waste of time," Tina said. "We could stand here all day freezing our tits off. No way are we going to see anything interesting."

"I disagree. This is all very revealing."

"How so?"

"Look. Police crawling all over the place. No effort's been made to disguise what happened here.

There's been no attempt at a cover-up. The attack was incredibly bold. Brazen, even. Out in the open where everyone can see."

"Meaning whoever's responsible has clout."

"Or cast-iron self-confidence. Also, they're starting to swagger. Which makes them even more dangerous. They've made a big splash, so now they may well be tempted to make an even bigger and splashier one. There's somebody I need to warn about this."

Redlaw about-turned and started walking.

"Who?" Tina said, following.

"You're going to insist on tagging along, aren't you?"

"Uh-huh, sure am. I'm sticking to you, Redlaw, like a... Well, like a tick to a bulldog."

"How flattering. For both of us."

"Come on, we're a team now, aren't we? Partners."

Partners? Redlaw neither wanted nor needed a partner. In the past, it hadn't worked out well. Twice, indeed, it had ended with a death.

But he couldn't deny that he owed Tina Checkley something—a debt of gratitude, perhaps. And she had her uses.

"Well," he said, "I suppose I'm lumbered with you for the time being. For better or worse."

She linked her arm through his. "Then cheer up. I'm good news. Without me, you're just a surly old Grinch who doesn't know his way around and can't handle the natives. With me, you've got vigour, class, and sass. Plus, I'm a font of local knowledge, Google in a g-string. Together, we can kick ass and change the world. Anything's possible."

"That's exactly my fear," Redlaw said dryly. "Anything's possible."

Tina playfully punched him on the shoulder.

It was his bad shoulder, the one that had been torn up by a vampire a few months back, and her blow left it smarting horribly for the next hour. But Redlaw bore the pain as he did so many things: with grim-lipped stoicism. He was, all said and done, a long-suffering man.

CHAPTER ELEVEN

"It's time, Clara," said Farthingale.

She was in the den, lolling on a beanbag, engrossed in the TV.

"Awww," she griped. "But it's *Transylvanian Families*. It's only just started. Sit and watch with me, then we'll do the transfoodlum after."

Farthingale had a reasonable fund of patience, especially where his sister was concerned, but he drew the line at a kids' television show—even one that was produced by a studio he owned and aired on a network he owned, with most of its licensed merchandise manufactured by a toy company he had a controlling stake in.

"No," he said gently but with resolve. "It's this time every week, you know that, Clara. It's just what we have to do. And I have calls to make afterwards, important ones that can't wait."

"Come along now, Clara," said Rozetta. The stocky little Filipina nurse placed her hands on Clara's shoulders. "It'll only take a moment, and when it's done I'll sit with you and we'll watch whatever you want."

Farthingale could see Clara's posture tightening, her face beginning to scrunch up. He knew the signs. They were in for a tantrum if they weren't careful. An apocalyptic meltdown.

"But it hurts," she complained. "The needle always hurts, and I don't like it."

"I know, darling, I know," Rozetta soothed. "But remember how it helps your brother. Poor Howie's sick, and without you he would get even sicker. You keep him nice and strong and healthy." In anyone else's presence, Rozetta would refer to Farthingale as Mr Farthingale. Only when Clara was around was he Howie.

"Get off me!" Clara snapped. "You're not my mommy. Don't talk to me like you're my mommy."

Rozetta looked helplessly at Farthingale. Both knew they mustn't push Clara. When cornered or intimidated, she was apt to go berserk, often biting herself until she drew blood or hitting herself until she was black and blue.

Farthingale stepped in front of the TV, squatting so that his eyeline was level with his sister's.

"Clara," he said. "Lovely Clara. You know how much I love you."

She nodded, her lower lip jutting.

"And you love me too, don't you?"

Again a nod, and Clara tried to peer round him to get a better view of the animated adventures of the vampire clan, the Fangers, and their neighbours, all of whom were residents of a village in the Carpathian mountains and were undead and monstrous in one way or another. The most popular character in the show was the youngest Fanger child, Felix, whose life was a neverending quest to find the next helping of his favourite form of nourishment, "red juice".

"And because you love me, you do this thing for me. Once a week, you give me some of your blood. Because without it, I might die. And you wouldn't want me to die, would you, Clara? You wouldn't want your big brother Howie to die."

Stiffly she shook her head.

"Because what would happen to you if I did die, Clara? Who would take care of you? Where would you live?"

"Rozetta would," she replied. "And I'd live here, in our house."

"But not if I'm not around to pay for everything."

"You're a billionaire. That means you have lots of dollar bills. Billionaire. And I'll inherit it all. So *I* can pay for everything."

Sometimes she was more perceptive than he gave her credit for. She might behave like a child, she *was* a child in most ways, but a child with forty years of life experience. It was never wise to underestimate her.

"I'm in your will," Clara went on. "You told me so. The lawyers wrote it and you signed it and if you die I get all the money. And first thing I'll do is I'll paint the whole house pink. And next I'll buy a pony, which you won't let me have because you say I'll fall off, only I won't. And I'll have ice cream for every meal, even breakfast. And I'll ride my pony every single day, who's called Mr Truffles, by the way. With a big plastic hat on, to be safe."

"Wills can be changed, Clara. I could have the lawyers fix it so that you inherit nothing at all. How about that? Would you like that?"

"But you wouldn't."

"Why not?"

"You love me," she said. "You just told me. So you wouldn't leave me with no money, because that wouldn't be what someone who loves someone would do."

She had him there.

J. Howard Farthingale III was CEO of eighteen different blue-chip corporations. He had a diverse and formidable business portfolio with interests in fossil fuel exploitation, entertainment, publishing, retail and technology. Nearly all of his companies were ranked in the *Fortune* 500. He made decisions every day that involved millions of dollars and affected the lives of a workforce numbering in the hundreds of thousands. He habitually negotiated deals with some of the sharpest and hardest-nosed tycoons alive, men and women who would not only sell their own grandmother but charge extra for the dentures and artificial hip. He swam with ultra-rich sharks and was far more often the biter than the bitten.

And he had just been outsmarted and outmanoeuvred by a girl with a chromosomal birth defect and severe learning impairment.

There was no alternative, then, but for him to sit down cross-legged next to Clara and find out what scrapes Felix Fanger and his best pals Dread Ursula and Zebedee the Zany Zombie would be getting into this episode. When Felix let out his trademarked catchphrase cry, "Red juice! Red juiiiice!" Clara chorused it along with him, and Farthingale showed willing by doing so too.

* * *

THAT ORDEAL OVER, Farthingale, Clara and Rozetta filed downstairs to the medical suite.

The house, Far Tintagel, was made up of interleaving and overlapping single-storey sections, like a pile of books slotted together with artful casualness. Some of the floors extended out into cantilevered balconies and terraces. Others sheltered beneath shallow pitched roofs with long eaves. A few of them were half buried in the hillside they perched on, protruding from the ground like monolithic tongues. Limestone bricks and slabs of reinforced concrete were the predominant structural materials, their blockish rectangles and right angles softened indoors by plenty of dark wood panelling. In all, the interior of the house covered nearly 10,000 square feet, with broad, banisterless staircases linking the various different levels and light coming in through a combination of skylights and French and clerestory windows.

Far Tintagel had been built three years ago, at a cost of some $20 million, and its design paid homage to Frank Lloyd Wright and in particular Wright's two masterpieces, Fallingwater and Taliesin. Farthingale was of the belief that the inter-war period had been a golden era for American business and, not uncoincidentally, American architecture. As huge profits were reaped by bankers, brokers and industrialists, even during the Great Depression, so there were significant quantities of private capital going spare, and some of that money went on erecting beautiful buildings that spoke of growth, aspiration and modernity. Of these, Wright's creations were the epitome. Even his lower-budget suburban 'Usonian' homes had a kind of boundless optimistic expansiveness to them.

Now, with the world seemingly slumping into a second Great Depression, it was all the more important for the tradition of vanity property to be carried on. Farthingale was one of the select few who were flourishing while most other people went to the wall, and Far Tintagel was a clear and unambiguous statement of pride and self-esteem. It and the island it perched on were his private fiefdom, separate from the rest of the nation, splendidly and grandly aloof. Nobody came here who was not invited or needed, but all were welcome to view—from a distance.

In the main hall, the little parade of three passed beneath an oil portrait of Josiah Farthingale, J. Howard's and Clara's great-great-grandfather. The famous railroad magnate, depicted here with glowering eyebrows and thick muttonchop whiskers, was the first Farthingale to make serious money, obscene amounts rather than merely colossal. He was also a Grand Imperial Wizard in the Klan and a staunch advocate of racial eugenics. It was he who had devised the family motto, *sanguis ordo est*—blood is order—which could be seen in the painting, picked out in brass on the flank of the 19th-century 4-4-0 steam locomotive that raced across the background. Josiah Farthingale had been fanatical about the purity of his own bloodline, to the point where he was adamant that none of his three sons could marry a woman who was not some sort of relative, however distant. J. Howard Farthingale III often wondered if his forebear's beliefs weren't ultimately responsible for Clara.

In the medical suite, just off the hall, a pair of steel-frame hospital daybeds stood side by side, with blood transfusion equipment on a trolley nearby. Farthingale and Clara lay down. Farthingale rolled up a shirtsleeve, while Rozetta did the same for Clara, then busied herself unsealing a venous cannula from its wrapper and attaching it to the end of a tube. She fastened a rubber tourniquet round Clara's upper arm, tapped the crook of her elbow to raise a vein, swabbed her skin with an antiseptic wipe, and expertly inserted the trocar needle. Clara screeched, as usual.

"You always say it's just a little scratch," she protested to Rozetta. "But it's not a little scratch. It's a big owie one."

"Clench your fist now, darling," said Rozetta. "That's it. And again. Good girl."

Bright red blood began to nudge its way down the transparent tube, spurting in short bursts into a bag that was suspended off the bed's side-rail. Once the bag was full it would be hooked on a drip stand, and another cannula would be attached to the outlet tube that ran from its base and the needle installed in Farthingale's forearm. Gravity would take care of the rest.

It wasn't just that Farthingale had a rare blood type, although he did, AB Rhesus negative NS HP1, a permutation of proteins and antigens found in a vanishingly small proportion of the population, something like 0.00002%. There were matches available, and with his wealth and resources it wouldn't have been difficult to ensure the supply of the pint per week that he desired.

Farthingale came from a good family, however. American nobility, a long line of wealth creators who could trace their roots all the way back to the *Mayflower*. He was an unabashed blueblood, and it seemed to him that he could not contaminate what ran in his veins with replacement plasma from just anyone. Not if he didn't have to, and thanks to Clara he didn't have to. She was of the same stock as him, with the same breeding, the same basic genetic code. They shared a blood type, but more, they shared parentage and ancestry. Clara was the only person a man like him could reasonably be expected to take donated blood from on a regular basis. Anything else would be unacceptable, unthinkable.

Sanguis ordo est.

All the doctors he had consulted had told Farthingale that having this weekly transfusion was not necessary. It wouldn't make any difference. It wouldn't alleviate his condition in any meaningful way.

But what did they know? It was *his* body, *his* medical problem, and he would tackle it however he saw fit.

He'd first become aware that something was amiss with him a couple of years ago, shortly after Far Tintagel was completed and he and Clara moved in. He'd begun experiencing dizzy spells. They could come on at any time, for no appreciable reason, and go just as mysteriously. Farthingale was no hypochondriac. He'd put it down to overwork, fatigue, and carried on as normal, believing it was a temporary glitch and would pass.

Then bruises started appearing, sizeable purple-black swellings on his hands and legs. They were painless and there was no obvious cause for them. He hadn't become unusually clumsy all of a sudden. He wasn't bumping into things without noticing.

Around the same time, he noticed pink streaks in the toothpaste he spat out after brushing. His gums were bleeding. Also, a rash of tiny scarlet spots appeared on the inside of his wrists.

James Lovegrove

He searched medical websites and found his symptoms all pointed to one terrible, heart-stopping conclusion: leukaemia.

But after his physician put him through an extensive battery of tests, he was referred not to an oncologist, thank God, but to a haematologist, who diagnosed something Farthingale had never heard of, ITP. Idiopathic thrombocytopenic purpura, to give it its full name. An autoimmune blood disorder which manifested as an abnormally low platelet count. Basically, as the incredibly expensive haematologist explained, Farthingale's immune system had gone haywire. His antibodies were mistakenly identifying his platelets as hostile organisms and were destroying them faster than his bone marrow would produce fresh ones. He was at war with himself, fighting a bogus enemy within, and the result of the severe platelet depletion was that his blood no longer clotted the way it ought to.

The condition was very similar to haemophilia but, the haematologist assured him, far less hazardous to the health and with a much better prognosis. There was a small risk of spontaneous, uncontrollable bleeding in the brain, and Farthingale would need to be more careful now about accidental nicks and cuts, which would heal far more slowly than before. He should also avoid being in a car crash if at all possible and do his best not to get stabbed or shot. "Steer clear of dark alleyways and muggers. Always buckle up. Shave with care." The haematologist chuckled at his own little joke.

What had brought it on, Farthingale wanted to know.

In answer, the haematologist could only point to the "I" part of "ITP"—idiopathic. The word was doctor-speak, he said, for "nobody knows." Just one of those things. The human condition.

Which, roughly translated, meant *shit happens, bad luck, get over it.*

There were remedies—a course of steroids, an intravenous immunoglobulin infusion, even a platelet transfusion in extreme circumstances—but they were quick fixes at best, were not at all pleasant, and came with no guarantee of success. There was no surefire, permanent cure. Learning to live with the condition was your best option. ITP was inconvenient but, all things being equal, not life-threatening.

J. Howard Farthingale III, however, was not someone who put up with inconveniences. To him that smacked of compromise, and only weaklings compromised.

The solution lay to hand: Clara. Her blood was wholly compatible with his, perfect in every respect. He had had it tested. Her platelet count was 275,000 per microlitre, well above the median, in fact near the top of the range. It was safe, too. He had checked on that. Down's was not contagious, not some virus you could catch.

With her blood, Clara could make up for what he lacked.

Sanguis ordo est.

He looked across at her now. The daybed's adjustable mattress was propped up at the head end at a 45° angle, and Clara reclined, staring miserably down at the cannula and the nearly full blood bag. "Red juice," she murmured softly to herself, "red juiiiice."

His sister was, objectively speaking, a spectacularly ugly creature, yet there were visible hints of the woman she might have been, had fate not so cruelly spiked her DNA. She had splendid blonde hair, same as their mother had had, and her eyes were a deep cerulean blue-green, just like their father's. But for the presence of an extra 21st chromosome, she would doubtless have become a highly accomplished woman and be a great beauty, wearing her age well as their mother and both grandmothers had. Perhaps she would have been an equestrian, a showjumper or polo player, in early adulthood, or maybe a concert pianist. Certainly she would have had children of her own by now, and her husband would be some respectable ex-Harvard-Law type, senior partner in a top Boston practice, and they would have a large house on Beacon Hill and a beach home in Kennebunkport, or possibly up in Ogunquit, for weekends and the summer. Perhaps, in that case, freed of the burden of Clara, Farthingale himself would have had the opportunity to find a spouse and produce offspring, an heir...

But Farthingale did not like to dwell on might-have-beens. There was no point. What mattered was the here and now, the actual rather than the hypothetical. He had chosen to look after Clara as soon as he was old enough to. He had made it his duty to see that her needs were catered for and her life was a good one. Their parents had never done so, at least not to the same degree. Their mother in particular had scarcely been able to look at Clara without wincing, as if incredulous that *that* could have sprung from *her*. Throughout her childhood and adolescence she had been treated as an embarrassment to the family, something to be ignored, shunned, seldom mentioned. She had been relegated to a set of rooms above the triple garage, rarely allowed to visit the main house, certainly not when guests were over. There'd been caregivers, a stream of well-paid and well-meaning nurses and nannies, but Deborah Martinborough Farthingale had done little actual practical parenting of Clara, and J. Howard Farthingale Junior none at all. The less the two of them saw of their daughter, the happier they were.

Even as an adolescent, Farthingale had known this was wrong, known this was not how it ought to be. Taking Clara under his wing had been his way of making a point. A kind of retaliation, even. That which his mother and father had rejected, he embraced.

The blood bag was full. Rozetta withdrew the needle from Clara's arm and stuck a plaster and absorbent pad over the tiny entry point. She transferred the bag to the stand and plunged a cannula into Farthingale's forearm.

It was only fair, Farthingale mused as his sister's lifestuff flowed into him, that Clara should return the favour he had done her, repay what she owed him in whatever way she could. A reckoning had fallen due, and the fee was all she could afford—blood.

IT WAS NO accident that the weekly "transfoodlum" preceded the weekly teleconference with Yukinobu Uona. Farthingale invariably felt invigorated with a pint of Clara's blood inside him. A doctor would no doubt say this was psychosomatic. Farthingale would beg to differ. Enriched with Clara's platelets, he was pumped up, full of energy, raring to go—and he needed to be, because Uona was a slippery customer. A colleague, yes, and an equal, but as devious a man as any Farthingale had met, and frighteningly clever, too. You had to have your wits about you when dealing with him.

As the call connected, the Bostonian put his game face on.

"Yukinobu!"

"Howard. How goes it?"

Uona was slim, trim, smooth-skinned, in excellent condition for a man pushing sixty. The only real indication of age was a slight silvering at his temples, which he could have covered up with dye but preferred to leave untouched, perhaps to emphasise how youthful he appeared otherwise. Behind him, his high-rise office window revealed a sweeping panorama of Tokyo. There was the massive Izumi Garden Tower, there the knifelike Dentsu building, and there the brilliant illuminated Christmas tree of the Tokyo Tower. A red sun was coming up over the city skyline, drenching everything in its ruby glow.

"You know," said Farthingale. "Getting by, surviving."

"Yes. And how is your beloved sister?" Uona asked.

There was no chance he was unaware of the transfusions. Uona knew everything, every truth, every secret. The enquiry, which seemed so polite and casual, was his way of showing that.

"Clara's well."

"Clara. Clara's well. Excellent." Uona's countrymen might have struggled to pronounce the name, but he made a point of demonstrating his facility. Everything Uona did was a calculated act. "It's vital to look after family. Family should always come first. Without the love and respect of our kin, all that we do, all that we achieve, is nothing."

Thank you, o Zen master, Farthingale thought to himself. "So," he said, "I imagine you'd like to know how Porphyrian's coming along."

"I've been keeping abreast of the situation through my various sources," Uona said. "Impressive so far. But the crucial question is, has your President taken the plunge?"

There was no point in lying. Uona most likely knew the answer already, or had a strong inkling. "No. Not yet. We're close to a sale, but he's hedging. He wants more time. More proof."

"You must push him."

"I am. But it's an election year, and the man is covering his ass with both hands and a trash can lid."

They discussed a few other business ventures that were of mutual benefit to the both of them, or had the be potential to be. Then Uona said, "It feels odd to be having this conversation without a certain third party present."

"True. We're shy of a Musketeer, aren't we?"

The Japanese man looked wistful, although not for long. "Nathaniel let us down. He was insufficiently astute in his choice of allies. But on the bright side, he did at least leave the two of us materially advantaged in the end."

In the wake of Nathaniel Lambourne's death there had been a feeding frenzy in corporate circles as investors and executives made moves on the various companies he'd headed. The share prices had gone into freefall, the stock at bargain-basement levels, and everyone had wanted a piece. Farthingale and Uona, however, had been informed of their colleague's demise several hours before the news leaked out to the media, and that gave them a crucial head start. After a period of grief and mourning, which lasted approximately a minute, they had set to work cherry-picking the very best of

Lambourne's business portfolio for themselves, steadily increasing their holdings in the assets they co-owned with him until they effectively owned them outright, and leveraging loans to perform buyouts on the assets they had no pre-existing interests in but fancied the look of. That left only the scraps—the start-ups, the underperformers, the runts—for everyone else to fight over. Both men were sure that this was how Lambourne would have wanted it.

"Although," Uona added, "it wasn't only treacherous allies who brought about his downfall..."

"Sure, if you're talking about the bastard who slit Nathaniel's throat," said Farthingale. "John Redlaw. Piece of work he is. Thanks to him, we lost a partner *and* a promising project. He's vanished, though, hasn't he? Last I heard, he'd completely dropped off the radar."

"Three days ago he was found and cornered in London."

"No shit."

"Yes shit. He managed to evade arrest, but resurfaced again almost immediately." Uona's expression turned sly. He loved to know what others didn't, and to rub their noses in their ignorance. "Can you guess where?"

"Enlighten me."

"In your neck of the woods, as it happens."

"Oh?"

"Yes. I have a man inside Interpol. In their international terrorism department."

No surprise to Farthingale. Uona seemed to have "a man" everywhere, fingers in innumerable pies.

"I employ him to keep tabs on customs databases worldwide for me," Uona continued. "Not a single international passenger arrival or departure occurs—

airport, seaport or rail terminus—that he can't have access to, and through him I can find out where almost any individual is, at any time. John Redlaw's name was one of those he's flagged at my request. It pinged up the day before yesterday. He was aboard a Heathrow-to-JFK flight."

"Redlaw is Stateside?"

"So it would appear."

"Why?"

"Isn't it obvious, Howard?" said Uona. "He's coming for you. He started with Nathaniel. You're next on the list."

Farthingale's voice went hoarse. "You're kidding."

"Of course I am. My guess would be, the United Kingdom has become too 'hot' for Mr Redlaw and he's hoping to lose himself in the vastness of your great nation. He's on your doorstep, however, that's the thing, and it would seem sensible to take advantage of the fact."

"Take advantage." Farthingale felt a prickle in his gut. He knew what Uona was insinuating. "I don't know. I mean, clearly something needs to be done about the guy. No question on that front. You don't kill a man like Nathaniel Lambourne and expect to get away with it scot-free. But..."

"Do you not have the stomach for revenge?"

"It's not that. I just don't see where the profit would be in it."

"There are some things that matter more than money."

"I can't believe you just said that, Yukinobu."

"I mean it," Uona shot back sternly. "There are principles at stake here, Howard. Thwarting the schemes of one of us is bad enough, but murdering one of us in cold blood? That cannot be allowed to stand. Think of the message it sends to the little people. Think of the encouragement it gives them. Soon they'll be sneering at us and showing us disrespect. They'll get the idea that violent death is something we somehow deserve, and they will try to emulate Redlaw's example. We're gods, not pariahs. We're special, *exceptional*, and nobody must dare believe otherwise."

"But there's the police, the justice system, the courts, due process," said Farthingale. "Society can deal with John Redlaw. We don't have to."

"Society has failed in its obligations. Taking a more proactive approach is our only recourse."

"I see that, but—"

"Or are you forever that slick little prep-school boy who was lucky enough to be bequeathed millions and made the money grow without ever really having to get his hands dirty?"

"No..."

"Then I shall leave it with you," said Uona. "You know what's expected of you. I only hope you don't disappoint."

Uona leaned forwards to strike a key, and the connection was cut.

Farthingale stared at the empty teleconference window for several minutes before clicking it shut. A part of him wanted to believe that Uona had only been joking. This was some kind of test, a provocation. Uona wanted to see how far he was prepared to go in order to prove his ruthlessness, that was all. He surely didn't expect him actually to follow through on the idea.

Did he?

The more he thought about it, the more Farthingale had the impression that his Japanese associate was in earnest.

Deadly earnest.

SHORTLY AFTERWARDS, AN email popped into Farthingale's inbox. It was from Uona.

"FYI," it read, "Shinobi Eternal has just pinpointed another nest for you. GPS co-ordinates below. It's a large gathering, by all accounts, at least fifty. Perhaps this could be the one that finally convinces the President that he has a significant and pressing problem on his hands, with the benefit to us that that entails."

He wrote back thanking Uona. The reply came almost instantly: "Glad to be of service."

Farthingale didn't know much about the Shinobi Eternal programme. It was one of Uona's vampire-related pet projects and Uona was remarkably shy— bordering on shifty—when it came to divulging details about it. The two men still considered themselves a consortium, just as they had been when Lambourne had made up the third of their triumvirate, but they had an agreement not to pry into or interfere with one another's business affairs. There were firewalls of discretion and deniability between them, the only criterion for this arrangement being that each should profit mutually from the other's efforts. So far, with the exception of the Solarville débâcle, it had worked out fine.

What Farthingale did know about Shinobi Eternal was that it unfailingly provided accurate intelligence about vampire locations. How—by what means—he had no idea, but then it wasn't his place to enquire. Gift horses and all that.

He cross-referenced the GPS data. Downtown Manhattan. Virtually on Team Red Eye's doorstep.

A populated area.

Very public.

A statement that couldn't be missed, or misread.

Just the ticket.

His hand went to the phone.

CHAPTER TWELVE

Dusk over St Magnus's. The church's steeple lanced sharply upwards against a field of black, swollen clouds. They reminded Redlaw of necrotic flesh. A few tiny snowflakes were wisping through the air. They were precursors, feather-light flecks that heralded the coming storm.

The padlock and chain had been reattached to the door. Redlaw pounded, hearing echoes reverberate within.

"Tchaikovsky. I know you can hear me. We need to talk. Let me in."

Tina, beside him, stamped her feet to keep warm. "Tell him it's Domino's. Nobody keeps pizza delivery waiting."

"Thanks for the advice. Very helpful."

"Are you always this snarky?"

"Are you always this annoying?"

"Yes."

"Then yes." Redlaw pounded again. "Tchaikovsky! It's urgent. I have information you need to hear."

"You sound like my mother's voicemail messages," Tina said. "She pretends she's calling about something really important but she refuses to say what it is so I have to call her back. Only it's bullshit. She's bored, is all."

"Please," snapped Redlaw. "Unless you have something useful to contribute, keep your comments to yourself."

"Oh. So how about I *don't* tell you that I just saw a face in the empty window up there?"

Redlaw glanced up at the paneless circular aperture. No face.

"You sure?"

"There and gone, just a moment ago. I swear."

Redlaw kept looking. All at once a hand appeared. It threw out a small object that pinwheeled down, plopping into the snow at his feet. He dug it out. A key.

Moments later, he and Tina were inside the building.

"Holy cow," Tina breathed, looking at the stately, cobwebby decay around them. "This is awesome. Super eerie."

She fished out the camcorder. Redlaw pointedly shook his head.

"Oh come off it," Tina said.

"It's a delicate situation. Vampires are easily antagonised. We need to be cautious and diplomatic, not go about waving cameras in their faces."

"I can be diplomatic."

"You? I don't think so."

With a snort, Tina stowed the camcorder back inside her rucksack.

"Tchaikovsky," Redlaw called out into the barren vastness of the church.

No answer. But the shadows were full, as they had been the last time he was here, and busy. Bodies on the move. Crawling. Peering.

"Tchaikovsky. Show yourself."

From the darkness, as though from another world, came the priest's rich, Russian-inflected baritone. "Redlaw. Back so soon. And I see you've brought a friend."

"Her name is Tina Checkley. I can vouch for her. She's a neutral party, nothing to be afraid of."

"Unless you fuck with me," Tina chipped in. "Then I'm your worst nightmare."

"Not helping," Redlaw said out of the side of his mouth. To Tchaikovsky he said, "Just a bit of bluster, that. She's harmless. We need to discuss things, you and I. The attacks on Sunless nests are getting more overt and reckless. That's dangerous for—"

"You bring a stranger," Tchaikovsky interrupted, "unannounced, into our home?" The menace in his voice was clear and unmistakable. Up in the rafters and high on the walls, his vampires whispered and hissed in sibilant discontent. "You dare?"

"I told you, she's nothing to be afraid of. She's of no consequence."

"Hey, thanks," Tina said.

"Do you want to live?" Redlaw asked her.

"Uh, yeah."

"Then shut. Up."

Meekly: "Okay."

"Why?" Tchaikovsky demanded. "Why is she here? We barely know each other, Redlaw, and already you jeopardise my security and the security of my flock by dragging along some random girl into our place of hiding, our sanctuary. You I can just about tolerate, but she—she is a trespasser. And trespassers are not welcome."

The priestly shtriga emerged into a patch of dim gloom, his cassock flowing around him. His gaze was fixed on Tina, eyes ablaze with hostility.

"I apologise," said Redlaw. "I thought we had an understanding."

"What next? The police? The army? Maybe some of your old Night Brigade cronies. You think this is acceptable? You think this is something I'm going to allow to go unpunished?"

Redlaw turned to Tina. "I think you should get ready to make a run for it."

"What?"

His hand moved several inches towards his Cindermaker. "My fault. I should have been firmer with you. Should have forced you to stay behind."

"Oh, God. We're in serious shit, aren't we?"

"I'll do my best to cover you. When I say go, head for the door and don't stop. Find the nearest sunlight, if there's any left, and stay in it. I can buy you a minute or two at best. Don't hesitate. Don't, whatever you do, look back."

"Redlaw..." said Tina.

"Oh, Redlaw," said Tchaikovsky. "Shame on you, lying to her like that. You know there's no way she's getting out of here alive. I am shtriga. My vampires are legion. Try your hardest, and she still won't make it to the door. Why give her false hope?"

"Then do me a kindness," Redlaw said. "Let her

leave, unharmed. You can have me. I don't matter. I won't resist. A trade. Her life for mine."

"How noble. But the fact is, my children are hungry. So very hungry. So many mouths to feed, and I can't keep fobbing them off with animal blood. Not when there's only one kind of blood that can truly placate and satisfy."

"Mine. Take mine."

"One man's? When there are two of you? When you've so obligingly supplied an extra body, filled to bursting with delicious hot blood? Yes, this is the best solution for all concerned. You've presented yourselves to us on a plate, as it were, and we shall make the most of it."

All around, the vampires were showing themselves, slinking between the pews and, spider-like, over them, making for Redlaw and Tina. The church resounded to sighs of joy and hideous moist slurps of lip-smacking relish.

Tina was trembling, her knees starting to buckle. She gripped Redlaw's arm, digging her fingernails in so hard that it hurt, even through the parka sleeve's thick lining. "Jesus, Redlaw, please, stop this, make it not be happening..."

A single shot, Redlaw thought. *Hit Tchaikovsky in the head. Might kill him. Might startle the others enough so that we can make a getaway.*

It was a Hail Mary, a desperate ploy.

God, hear me.

They were as good as dead anyway. What other chance did they have?

Guide my aim, O Lord.

He drew the Cindermaker, lightning fast. The gun boomed.

But Tchaikovsky was not there. Quick as Redlaw had been, the shtriga, inevitably, was quicker. He sprang into the air, leapfrogging over the Fraxinus round's trajectory. A split second later he came down on top of Redlaw, feet on his shoulders. The impact drove Redlaw flat onto the church flagstones, winding him. The last thing he saw before blacking out was Tchaikovsky's fist as it lashed at his face, a blur of flesh and bone. The last thing he thought was *I failed her*, followed by *God failed me*.

CHAPTER THIRTEEN

COLONEL JACOBSEN WENT round the basement levels, rousting Team Red Eye from their quarters.

"Up you get. Up and at 'em. New mission. This is not a goddamn drill."

He hammered on Red Eye Seven's door.

"That means you, Abbotts. Switch off the gay porn, wipe down your dick, be in the parking garage in ten. Hustle, hustle. Now, now, now."

"Screw you, asshole," came the reply from Abbotts's room.

"Screw you, asshole, *sir*," Jacobsen retorted.

Eleven minutes later, Private Chris Abbotts stumbled into the garage, securing the last of the Velcro straps on his protective vest. He folded himself into the narrow back-row seat of the Hummer H2, next to Red Eye Six, PFC Kyle Larousse.

"Hey, bud."

"Hey."

The two men had plenty in common. Both were the youngest and lowest ranked on the squad, both were southerners—Abbotts from Birmingham, Alabama, Larousse from Corpus Christi, Texas—and both were just a beer and a paycheque away from being hopeless white trash. Abbotts could boast the distinction of having spent a total of fifty-seven days in the stockade for a string of disciplinary infractions throughout his career, including gross insubordination and brawling while drunk and disorderly, leading to an Other-Than-Honourable Discharge. Larousse's military record was, on the face of it, clean, but thanks to a good-time reputation and a lack of respect for authority he had never been likely to progress further than the lower ranks.

Jeanette Berger started up the Hummer and the giant car rolled up a ramp to the garage door, which retracted automatically. All at once, Team Red Eye were out on East 84th Street, having emerged from beneath an impressive midtown townhouse. The building was, to all intents and purposes, a grand, single-occupancy home with little to make it unusual other than that its owner had not long ago done what a lot of the super-rich were doing with their urban residences: extended underground. Workmen had excavated down below the basement and out beneath the street to create an extra pair of floors, each of which was larger than the house's ground footprint. There was the garage now, and a network of rooms, guest suites mostly, along with a gym and recreation complex and a dining area. This had augmented the property's overall square footage by a good 50% and its market value by as much as 75%.

Turning left onto Lexington Avenue, the Hummer cruised south. Snow chains gave the car a firm grip on the icy roadway, and its laden weight, nearly 9,000 lbs, added further stability and traction. Still, Berger drove with care. It was the other traffic she was worried about. The Hummer could survive any collision almost intact, but a crash would bring unwanted attention and complications, and of course there was the potential for a fatality among the occupants of any vehicle that ploughed into it or it ploughed into.

"Okay, listen up, people," said Jacobsen. "Here's the deal. You want the good news or the bad?"

"Good first," said Gunnery Sergeant Child.

"The good news is that we don't have to travel at all far this time. We should be hitting the op zone in about ten minutes."

"Well, hallelujah," said Abbotts. "It's okay for the rest of you guys, you got comfy seats, but me'n Larousse back here, we ain't got legroom fit for a midget. Any longer than a quarter-hour journey, I start getting cramp in my thighs like you wouldn't believe."

"And already the moaning starts," said Red Eye Four, Justin Lim, lately a corporal in the Green Berets.

"Hey, fuck you, convenience store," said Abbotts sharply. "How come you ain't sitting back here anyway? What are you, five-three? Five-four, tops? This seat was made for your Korean ass."

"'Convenience store,'" sighed Lim. "Racial profile much?"

"Matter of fact," Abbotts went on, "why don't we have two of these cars 'stead of one? Seems crazy. Ain't as if the guy bankrolling this whole deal is short of money. What's an extra Hummer to him?"

"Think about it," said Lieutenant Giacoia. "Two of these things driving around in convoy, that stands out.

It gets noticed. One, on the other hand, just looks like some Russian oligarch or rap artist taking his wheels out for a spin. Does the word 'covert' mean anything to you?"

"I don't know much," said Abbotts, "but I know a pimp ride like this is anything but covert."

"Sure it is," said Lim. "Maybe not in Redneckville where you come from, where a rusty pickup's a limousine, but here in the civilised world, we're blending right in."

"Oh, now who's stereotyping? Guess you'd like me to put on a wifebeater and fetch out my banjo so's we can all—"

"Enough!" barked Jacobsen. "I'm not getting paid to listen to you bitch and bicker like a schoolroom full of little girls. Minds on the job. Don't any of you want to know what the bad news is?"

"Kinda not," said Child, "but tell us anyway."

"This is going to be the largest nest we've tackled yet, by a wide margin. Estimate puts it at fifty vamps, maybe even more. So we do not take any chances. We stay sharp and play it by the book."

"That's the best guess we have?" said Larousse. "Up to fifty?"

"I'm sorry, is that a problem?"

"How are we even getting hold of this intel? Where's it coming from? Enquiring minds need to know."

"No," said Jacobsen, "all you need to know, Private Larousse, is that you're part vampire, you have all of a vampire's strengths and pretty much none of its weaknesses, you have guns that destroy vampires and body armour that makes you impervious to their teeth and talons, you are, in short, superior to a vampire in every meaningful way, and your purpose in this world is to be pointed at vampires and blow their undead asses to hell. Anything more than that is above your pay grade and no concern of yours."

Twisted round in the front passenger seat, Jacobsen stared down Larousse until the latter looked away.

"That's settled, then," he said. "If the working conditions don't suit, you can always quit, any of you, and kiss a cosy retirement goodbye. Otherwise, brain in neutral, zip lip, engage training."

Jacobsen had to keep reminding himself that his team, like him, had volunteered to be subjected to the Porphyrian process and that this was not an official military unit; this was private enterprise. Hence, he was prepared to cut them some slack.

At the same time, discipline and the chain of command could not entirely be dispensed with. That would be inviting disaster.

THEY ARRIVED.

Jacobsen had earlier carried out a preliminary reconnaissance of the op zone via satellite image and Street View. Eyeball reconnaissance confirmed that his theoretical plan of attack was valid and viable.

With the Hummer parked out of sight in a back alley, seven masked and armed figures scurried up fire escapes to the tops of the buildings immediately adjacent to the target. They leapt from flat roof to sloping roof, from asphalt to tile. Then, with the utmost stealth, they crawled into position and, crouching, awaited the 'go' command.

CHAPTER FOURTEEN

RÓISÍN LEARY HAD never been one to mince her words.

"What in the name of the Pope's holy ringpiece were you thinking, Redlaw?" she thundered. "Are you truly as daft as you look? The poor girl has about as much experience of vampires as you have of hot rampant sex, and you drag her right slap bang into one of the biggest vamp shindigs you can find! If my mother were here she'd give you a smack upside the head, and frankly I want to, too. It's the least you deserve."

"I had no idea," Redlaw protested. "I didn't mean for it to turn out this way. She followed me. She was so insistent."

"Ah, and you couldn't have told her to feck off?" said Leary, cocking one eyebrow. "What does she weigh, eight stone? Slip of a thing. And you're big, rough, tough John Redlaw. You really mean to say you couldn't have stopped her coming with you if you'd wanted to? Punched her cold, maybe? It's what I'd have done."

"I'm not into hitting women, not unless it's absolutely unavoidable. Besides—"

Leary overrode him, as she was wont to. "Your thing is, boss, you like having a sidekick. You pretend you don't. You make out you're Mr Self-Sufficient, don't need anyone, Redlaw the loner, the hard man who always works solo. But you're at your best with someone beside you, preferably a gobby female. You'd never admit it, but deep down you know it's true. And that's why you didn't turn this Checkley girl away, even though you know you ought to have."

"She deserved a chance to prove herself."

"So you take her to a church teeming with vampires?"

"Vampires under a shtriga's control," said Redlaw.

"Still, she's a civilian." Curiously, Leary's accent was slipping, morphing from a Dublin brogue into something more clipped and angular. "Not versed in the ways of the Sunless. It was like leading a sheep to the slaughterhouse, old bean. Very poor show."

It was odd, Redlaw thought, how alike Leary and Illyria Strakosha looked. He'd never noticed that before. The one was practically indistinguishable from the other. With just a slight blurring, a squint of the eye, his former SHADE partner could easily become the Albanian-born shtriga.

"Yes, I can't say I'm not disappointed in you, Redlaw old thing," said Illyria in her peculiar speech pattern that hybridised European intonation with 1930s upper-class slang. "Innocent filly like that, hardly out of short trousers, wot? And now, thanks to you, she's going to die. None too pleasantly, either."

"But the shtriga..."

"Not all shtrigas are like me. A shtriga's only loyalty is to their vampires. Anything else is just incidental.

Remember when we first met? I nearly threw you off a balcony. And I would have, in a heartbeat, if I'd felt it necessary in order to protect the vampires in my care. Don't go thinking that just because you and I became chums, every other shtriga is going to want to have tea and crumpets with you. That would be a mistake. Shtrigas are spiffing fellows, but ruthless too. We take our responsibilities very seriously."

"Tchaikovsky isn't like you."

"He's *exactly* like me!" Illyria declared, baring her perfect fangs. "In every respect. He will kill anyone to preserve what's his, and he won't even hesitate about it. And right this moment, old bean, he's going to kill me, and I need your help."

Now Illyria's accent was shifting, too. Her imperious cadences were becoming frantic, panicked, almost a scream.

"You have to wake up, Redlaw. Redlaw! Wake up! They're going to kill me. Please, wake the fuck up."

Illyria would never swear like that.

"Wake the motherfucking fuck up."

It wasn't Illyria talking any more. It was Tina.

"Oh, please, oh goddamn Christ, someone please do something!" Tina begged.

Redlaw, surfacing from unconsciousness, opened his eyes.

He was in the church, St Magnus's. He was groggy. His head was aching, pulsing, feeling like an overstuffed rubbish sack about to burst.

He blinked. It was hard to focus.

There was Tina. She was surrounded by vampires and they were dragging her towards the bare stone altar. There was something ceremonial about the way they all moved along the aisle. It had the air of a ritual procession, Tina being led, struggling, like some unwilling bride to her nuptials.

Or a human sacrifice.

And behind the altar, waiting, presiding, was Tchaikovsky. His hands were clasped at his solar plexus, like those of someone about to pray. His face was calm, but his eyes gleamed with avarice.

"Place her there," he ordered the vampires, and they hauled the resisting, shrieking Tina onto the altar and held her down, two to a limb.

Redlaw got to his knees and tried to stand. The action seemed to demand an inordinate amount of strength and coordination, and he wasn't even able to complete it. Taloned hands clamped down on his shoulders, pushing him remorselessly back into a kneeling position. Two vampires were standing sentry over him, one on either side. A further three stood directly behind, in case those two weren't up to the task. The Cindermaker lay on the floor a few yards away, alongside Tina's rucksack. The gun was tantalisingly close, and yet, given that Redlaw's guards would never give him a chance to reach it, it might as well have been a mile away. Tchaikovsky didn't want Redlaw going anywhere or doing anything. He wanted him to remain put, powerless, until it was his turn to be stretched out on the altar.

"We have been provided for," Tchaikovsky said. "God has smiled on us."

He had to raise his voice to be heard above Tina's grunts of effort and shrieks of protest.

"We have been offered succour in our hour of need, manna in the desert, a blessing from on high. Some call us damned, but we are not damned. We are merely beings whom the Lord, in His infinite wisdom and grace, has allowed to become different. He has refashioned us, re-created us, and now our needs are not those of mortal men, but we must acknowledge them and we must answer them, for that is how we have been made. This girl..."

He gestured along Tina's bucking, writhing form.

"This girl carries within her everything that we require to survive, and not just survive but prosper. Her veins throb with that which gives us renewed life. Let us partake of her now. Let us take, eat of her body, drink of her blood, which she will shed for you."

"Noooo!" Tina wailed at the top of her lungs, and then she spat in Tchaikovsky's face, with remarkable accuracy. "You fucking undead fucker, you scumbag son of a bitch!" She was pinned down, helpless, about to die, but she was fighting to the end, with hellcat spirit.

The shtriga priest wiped the spittle off his cheek indifferently and carried on with his grotesque parody of the communion catechism. "Let us sip of her, each unto fulfilment but no further. Let us share her bounty evenly, and that of the other, Redlaw, in order that we may be replenished and enjoy continued health and vigour."

Tina turned her head. Her gaze locked on Redlaw. Her eyes bulged with horror and pleading.

Tchaikovsky extended a forefinger. "With this first incision, I will begin."

Redlaw yelled, "This is blasphemy! This is not God's way!"

Tchaikovsky, even if he heard, didn't pause. His talon lowered towards Tina's neck. "I will take the first taste."

"Tina!" Redlaw said. "Listen to me. The Lord is waiting for you. This will be over sooner than you think. There is eternal life. Trust me. There is a hereafter. Don't be afraid."

How could he make her believe it when he wasn't sure he believed it himself?

That didn't matter, as long as his words brought her comfort in her final moments. It wasn't much, but it was all he could do.

The talon came to rest on Tina's carotid, and Tina went silent and still, resigned to the inevitable like a rabbit in a wolf's jaws.

At the rear of the apse, the crucified Christ looked down benignly on the scene. It was as if He just didn't care.

A miracle, thought Redlaw. *Right now, a miracle. Please. I implore you.*

The Redeemer of All Mankind didn't seem in any hurry to supply one.

But then...

TWO OF THE windows at the church's narthex shattered, blown inwards by plastique charges. A split second later, grey cylinders the size of soup cans were lobbed through. They landed, disgorging billows of yellow smoke.

The smell hit Redlaw's nostrils. An aerosolised suspension of allium sativum. Garlic gas.

The vampires recoiled. Covering their faces, they backed away from the spreading clouds. They choked and spluttered, repelled as a human would be if the stuff were tear gas. A couple of them fell to their knees, overcome with retching and gagging.

People followed the smoke bombs into the building, swinging in through the hollowed window frames on ropes. Redlaw saw them only dimly through the wreaths of gas, but he recognised their silhouettes, their uniforms. The paramilitaries from Tina's subway footage.

They abseiled to the floor and fanned out, taking up positions behind pillars and overturned pews. The vampires were milling about in panic. They were barely aware of the intruders in their midst, just desperate to get away from the stinging smoke.

Redlaw took advantage of the chaos. His guards were momentarily distracted. He clobbered both of them in the groin. 'Lesses might be hardy creatures, but they had physical weak spots just like anyone. A scrotum was a scrotum, tender and vulnerable, no matter who it hung from.

As the two vampires bent double in pain, Redlaw scrambled over to his Cindermaker.

An indignant Tchaikovsky bellowed at the soldiers, "You dare invade our sanctum? You dare interrupt our service of sacrament?"

The response was a barrage of gunfire from machineguns and assault rifles.

Vampires howled and sprang for cover. Fraxinus rounds whipped and whined through the air, slashing the yellow smoke to shreds.

Tchaikovsky sprang into action, making for the enemy by a circuitous route, from pulpit to window ledge to rafter, leaping to avoid the strafing onslaught.

Redlaw, meanwhile, scuttled on all fours in the opposite direction, over towards the altar where Tina lay. He had the gun in one hand, her rucksack over his shoulder. Tina was in a state of dull-eyed shock, still anticipating the death-by-draining that had seemed so inescapable. She was oblivious to the soldiers' arrival and the sudden reversal of fortunes that it had brought.

No time to be elegant or gentle. Redlaw threw himself at the altar, scooping Tina up as he slid across it and tumbling down behind it with her. They lay in a tangled heap in the lee of the stone structure, shielded from the hailstorm of bullets, for now.

"Redlaw, what's... what's going on?" Tina asked bewilderedly.

"Salvation's come, in the nick of time. Although I don't think a rescue's on the cards."

He peeked round the side of the altar. The soldiers were advancing in two groups, covering one another's progress with sprays of bullets. They were coming this way, driving the Sunless before them through the transept and towards the apse, funnelling them into a confined space where it would be easier to dispose of them en masse. Every now and then a Fraxinus round struck home and a vampire collapsed, dissolving as it fell.

Where was Tchaikovsky?

There.

Redlaw spotted the shtriga high in the rafters, limbering along upside down like some humanoid insect. It occurred to him that Tchaikovsky might be fleeing. He appeared to be making for the broken windows. Was he shirking his responsibility? Abandoning his flock to their doom?

No. Merely seeking a vantage point. High ground from which to counterattack. Tchaikovsky halted, canted his head back and peered down. He was directly above one of the soldiers.

Go, Redlaw willed him.

Tchaikovsky was a dangerous lunatic. He had been on the point of slicing Tina open for her blood, and would have done the same to Redlaw. Redlaw wanted nothing more than to see him reduced to ashes, wiped off the face of the world.

Except...

At this moment, Tchaikovsky was the vampires' best and only hope of survival. And, by extension, Redlaw's and Tina's too. No one else had the wherewithal to take on these marauders. Their massive firepower gave them a tactical superiority that could not be compensated for or defended against—save, perhaps, by a shtriga.

Tchaikovsky dropped from his perch, plummeting headfirst towards the soldier. Redlaw assumed the man was unsuspecting, heedless of the possibility of assault from above.

But the soldier looked up and stepped smartly back. It was as though some sixth sense had warned him he was being ambushed.

Tchaikovsky twisted in midair like a cat, landing awkwardly on the spot where the soldier had been standing. He'd hoped to hit him and crush him. Instead, he found himself confronted by an opponent who not only appeared to have reflexes equal to his but was toting weaponry.

Tchaikovsky naturally went straight for the gun. He ducked under the barrel, grabbed it and wrenched the rifle upwards. But the soldier responded with a brutal kick to the ribs that sent Tchaikovsky hurtling backwards.

The shtriga was back on his feet in a flash and springing sideways to evade a volley of bullets. He rebounded off a wall and flew at the soldier's flank, colliding with enough force to knock him over.

The soldier was quick to recover and retaliate, throwing Tchaikovsky off him with a single fierce shove. He must have emptied his rifle's magazine with that last burst and there was no time to reload, so he tossed the gun aside and unsheathed a combat knife. He lunged at Tchaikovsky with it. The blade was a good ten inches long and matt black. Carbonised ash, was Redlaw's guess. Like a Fraxinus round. Wood toughened and tempered by controlled exposure to heat until it became diamond-hard.

The soldier slashed at Tchaikovsky, who danced warily out of range and slashed back with his talons. The to-and-fro of their struggle was almost too swift for the eye to follow, feints and thrusts conducted at a speed no mere human could match. Tchaikovsky was the first to draw blood, ripping a hole in his opponent's thigh. The soldier answered almost immediately, gashing open Tchaikovsky's forearm.

The shtriga howled, more affronted than in pain. Redlaw had no doubt, though, that the injury hurt. Ashwood was lethal to vampires, its touch corrosive, like a mix of neurotoxin and acid. Perhaps a shtriga, being a higher order of vampire, was not affected to quite the same degree, but judging by the way Tchaikovsky favoured his arm from then on, he was not immune either.

The fight continued, but Redlaw no longer had the luxury of watching it. There were more pressing concerns. The rest of the soldiers were nearing the altar, behind which several vampires were now cowering alongside himself and Tina. Tina shrank away from them, pressing herself close to him.

"Can't we surrender?" she said over the clattering

cacophony of the guns. "You and me? We're not vampires. They'll see that. They'll let us go. They've got to."

Redlaw didn't share her optimism. "In the heat of battle we're likely to get shot if we show our faces. Besides, I don't think these people are the type to show mercy. Especially not to eyewitnesses."

"Then we're fucked. Just as fucked as before." Her voice fractured with despair. "There's no way out of here. We just wait 'til they get to us and blow us away."

"There is a way out," said the vampire nearest to Tina. Redlaw recognised him from his previous visit to St Magnus's. He'd seen him speak to Tchaikovsky. The Latino. What was his name? Miguel.

"Go on," he said.

"The crypt," said Miguel.

"The crypt's a dead end, surely?"

"Not exactly. Our shtriga, he foresaw that we might need an escape route, in case of emergency."

"You can get out through it?"

"Maybe," said Miguel, adding, "Maybe we all can."

"If you help us, I promise I'll not harm you," Redlaw said. "There'll be no comebacks for what Tchaikovsky tried to do to us just now."

"And if I don't help you?"

"I think you want to. I think you know that we're in this together. And I think you know that you stand a better chance of making it to safety with me than without me."

Miguel acknowledged this with a nod.

"Wait, what?" Tina said. "Not five minutes ago these bastards were going to eat us. Now suddenly we're best friends?"

"We're not best friends," Redlaw replied. "But we're all going to die unless we can get away from those soldiers. I'd say we have more in common now than we do dividing us. Allies in adversity. Miguel, lead the way."

"I would," said Miguel, "only..."

He pointed.

The doorway to the crypt lay some thirty yards distant, over by the west wall. Between it and the altar there was a stretch of open floor, exposed ground, no cover, nothing to hide behind.

"Shit," said Tina. "We try to cross that, we'll be ducks at a shooting gallery. They'll pick us off."

Redlaw nodded grimly.

"Any bright ideas?" she asked in quavering tones, hopefully.

"You do have a gun," said Miguel.

Redlaw glanced down at the Cindermaker. A full clip. Thirteen rounds.

"I do."

He adopted a crouching stance, braced like a sprinter on the starting blocks.

"All of you," he said to Tina and the vampires. "Follow me. Full tilt. On my mark. Three. Two. One. Now!"

And he sprang from cover.

And they ran.

AS HE RAN, Redlaw let loose with the Cindermaker. He fired wild, looking ahead towards the crypt entrance while directing his shots sideways, aiming roughly where he knew the soldiers to be.

He was betting on them not having anticipated return fire. As far as they were concerned, vampires didn't carry guns. The Cindermaker gave him an element of surprise. The thinnest of edges, but better than none.

His gamble paid off. The soldiers were startled to be met with incoming. Instinct took over and they threw themselves flat to the floor or hid behind pillars. For a few brief, precious seconds, bullets were flying the other way across the church interior. The soldiers were on the receiving end rather than dishing it out.

Vampires followed Redlaw in a straggling line, perhaps ten of them in all, plus Tina. As they neared the door, one of the soldiers poked his head out from behind a pew. Redlaw sent a bullet his way. That deterred him and his cohorts for a little while longer.

The door was stiff, hard to budge. Redlaw leaned back and heaved. Miguel assisted and effortlessly drew it all the way open.

"Move!" Redlaw barked, and the vampires charged past him and down the spiral staircase. He, meanwhile, scanned the church, watching for the soldiers. He'd been keeping count of his shots. Three rounds left before he'd need to reload.

He glimpsed an arm, an elbow, poking out from round a pillar. He took aim and scored a direct hit. Expecting a howl of agony, all he heard was a muffled curse. He must have struck armour. Damn.

Rifle fire came at him from another corner of the church. Redlaw slammed himself flat behind the door. Bullets *whumped* into its thick oak panels. He felt the impacts through his back.

The last vampire hadn't quite reached the crypt entrance, and caught several shots from behind. His scream went unfinished, cut short. Some of him came through the doorway, in the form of an avalanche of fine, ashy dust.

There might be other vampires still out there in the church, but Redlaw could do nothing for them. None stood a chance of even getting near the crypt entrance. He could save only those he could save. He loosed off another bullet around the edge of the door, his second to last, then hauled the door shut. There was a heavy iron key in the lock. He turned it, knowing it wouldn't hold the soldiers back for long, but any delay, however small, was welcome. Then he headed downstairs. The stairwell was unlit, and he negotiated it by touch, one hand on the curving wall, his feet judging the position of each step by the previous one.

The crypt itself had a bare low-wattage electric bulb which afforded just enough light to see by. Tina seized Redlaw's arm as he appeared at the foot of the stairs. She clung on, scared to let go. The vampires were clustered in the middle of the crypt, crouching down, frantically busy. They were dismantling a section of the floor, where the stones were loose rather than mortared in place. Redlaw had not registered this fact the last time he'd been here.

As the stones were cleared away, a steel trapdoor was uncovered. It was scuffed and discoloured, but looked to have been installed relatively recently. Miguel threw a bolt and raised the trapdoor, revealing a vertical shaft with the diameter of a swimming-pool flume. A stink arose from the hole, as did a sound: the faint hiss of rushing water.

Miguel stuck his legs into the shaft and dropped out of sight. One by one the other vampires followed suit.

"Does that go where I think it goes?" Tina said.

"The sewers," Redlaw said with a nod.

"Oh, ick. Must we?"

An explosion rumbled and rattled overhead, the blast wave reverberating down the staircase.

"They've blown the door," Redlaw said. "They'll be here in moments. If you have a better plan..."

"Clearly I fucking don't." Tina peered into the shaft. "I don't see the bottom. How far are we going to fall?"

"Bend your knees. Brace for impact. The vampires seem to have landed safely."

"Yeah, but they're, like, super us."

"Tina, jump or die. It's your choice."

She shot him a truculent look, then flattened her arms against her sides and jumped. As she disappeared down the shaft she let out a cry, which ended abruptly two seconds later.

Redlaw dug out the army-surplus night vision goggles out of his pocket and strapped them on. They emitted a high-pitched whine as they powered up. Before pulling the goggles down over his eyes he smashed the lightbulb with the butt of his Cindermaker, plunging the crypt into darkness. Then he immersed himself in the phosphorescent emerald world of light enhancement.

Footfalls on the staircase. Cautious. The soldiers had learned that there was an unforeseen factor in play. One of their foes was packing a gun, and if one was, might not others be? They were no longer quite so gung-ho as before. The mission's risk level had been upped. This was not a turkey shoot any more.

A preliminary burst of gunfire raked into the crypt. From the angle of fire, the shooter was some ten or eleven steps up the staircase.

A smoke bomb tumbled down in the wake of the bullets, jetting out garlic gas.

That was Redlaw's cue to make a hasty exit. Once the smoke thickened, a full-on assault on the crypt would commence.

He slid halfway into the shaft, grabbing the trapdoor with one hand. Shunting himself off the edge, he fell, yanking the trapdoor shut.

It was a slithering, hurtling descent. Redlaw was scraped and buffeted by the rough-hewn walls of the shaft.

Then he was plunging through empty space.

Then he struck the ground jarringly, splashing shin-deep into water. He lost his balance, sprawled, and scrambled upright.

He was half-soaked. His trousers and coat sleeves stuck to his skin, dripping wet. His knees throbbed, protesting at the amount of kinetic energy they had just had to absorb. At their age! In their condition!

Redlaw peered around, taking stock.

He was in a circular sewage tunnel, perhaps ten feet high at its apex. The water flowed along a central gully, churning and bubbling. Lumps floated in it, objects whose nature and origin he didn't care to speculate about, some pale, some dark. The stench was nauseating.

Nearby, Tina stood. She peered around, wide-eyed, looking shivery and lost. She couldn't see anything. It was pitch black.

The vampires waited a little way further off, in a huddle. Unlike Tina, their vision in these conditions was perfect.

Redlaw waded over to her. "Tina."

"Thank fuck." She groped for him. He took her hand. "We're up to our asses in human waste, right?"

"I don't think it's that bad," he replied.

"It smells that bad."

"Better get used to it. We have to keep going. Those soldiers won't give up easily. They're thorough and they haven't finished the job. Hold on to me. I have my goggles on. I'll guide you. I can see for both of us."

"Knew I should have got myself a pair of those things," Tina said, hooking an arm round his waist.

"Tell you what. If we get out of this, I'll buy you one. My treat."

"You sure know how to spoil a lady, Redlaw."

"Miguel," Redlaw said, addressing the Latino vampire. "Which way now?"

"I don't know," Miguel confessed. "The *padre* never said. If we ever had to use this escape route, it was assumed he'd be with us."

"We can't leave Father Tchaikovsky behind," said another of the vampires, a plump woman whose hair retained the vestiges of a bad perm and who was dressed in a dirt-stained fleece embroidered with the logo of a supermarket chain. A name badge on her chest said *Hi! I'm PATTI. How may I help you today?* "We'll stay put until he comes for us. He'll lead us out of here."

"There's no saying he *is* coming," Redlaw said. "When I last saw him, he was fighting one of those armed men. He was defending you, buying you time to get to safety. We can't presume he'll be catching up soon—if ever."

Whimpers of dismay from the vampires. The shtriga priest's hold over them was strong, so strong that they were lost without him. To them he was part shepherd, part drug. They feared and adored him.

"Now, pay attention," Redlaw said sternly. "Those people back there have one objective only, and that's to destroy you. They're going to keep after you until they've turned you all to dust. You can't stop them. The only thing you can do is run. If death's what you want, fine, stay here. They won't be long. But if you have any desire whatever to survive, you'll move, right now."

The vampires looked at one another.

Redlaw raised the Cindermaker, which had just one round left. "Put it this way. If they don't shoot you, I will."

He saw them weighing things up. They weren't to know the gun was almost out of ammunition, and even if they suspected it, it didn't matter. He could target any one of them. Nobody wanted to be the unlucky victim, the one who got singled out.

"But... we don't know where to go," said Miguel forlornly.

"I'd suggest that direction," said Redlaw. "The way the water's going. It must decant somewhere, some outflow pipe, maybe even into the river."

The vampires set off, hesitantly.

Redlaw recalled something Illyria had told him: *They are like dogs in many ways. They simply need to be shown who's boss.* Well, he'd done that. The role of shtriga meant imposing your will on other vampires and reinforcing your dominance by means of threats and, when called for, violence. Being leader of the pack, in other words. Alpha vamp.

"We're heading that way, too," he told Tina. "Stick with me."

"Sticking," she replied. "Like glue."

He waded through the sewer water, Tina stumbling along beside him. He went as fast as he could while making allowances for the fact that she was effectively blind. The vampires remained a few paces ahead but kept checking back to reassure themselves that Redlaw was still with them. He, in turn, looked over his shoulder at regular intervals, expecting the soldiers to appear at any moment.

Sure enough, a helmeted head emerged from the shaft opening in the ceiling. A soldier had clambered down and was reconnoitring, getting the lie of the land. The fact that he was upside down suggested he was braced against the sides of the shaft, holding himself in an inverted position. That was some feat of athleticism, and once more Redlaw found himself wondering what sort of people these soldiers really were. Were they even people?

He debated whether to open fire. But it was a tricky shot—a target the size of a football at fifty yards with a handgun—and he couldn't afford to waste the last bullet. Refilling the clip took a minute, time he currently didn't have.

Instead, he redoubled his pace, almost hauling Tina along now. The vampires sensed his urgency and sped up too.

The sewer trended downward. The water grew shallower, its rush more hectic. Ahead, in the distance, Redlaw glimpsed an end to the tunnel. Behind him, meanwhile, the soldier had lowered himself out from the shaft, uncurling, dropping lithely to the floor. A second soldier eased out after him. They began to prowl along the sewer, dogging their prey.

The tunnel disgorged into a huge chamber, a nexus where a dozen sewers of various calibres met and emptied. Streams of water cascaded into a frothing, boiling central pool, whose contents were funnelled into a broad channel leading underground. Iron bars formed a grille across the channel's exit, too narrowly spaced for a person to fit through. Redlaw wouldn't have contemplated taking that route anyway. The water was a coursing torrent and there was scant headroom. Drowning was all but guaranteed.

There was a way out, though. Had to be. Tchaikovsky wouldn't have designated this an escape route otherwise.

He spotted a ladder on the far side of the chamber. It hugged the wall, rising to an aperture near the ceiling. There for maintenance purposes, presumably. Municipal workers must come down here from time to time to inspect for leaks and blockages.

Acutely conscious of the two soldiers breathing down their necks, Redlaw indicated the ladder to Miguel and the other vampires. They sprang down from the lip of the sewer into the pool.

"Tina," Redlaw said in her ear, "we're going to jump. It's a drop of about five feet, no more. Then we're going to swim. You first. I'll be right behind you."

He thought she would object. It seemed that there was nothing straightforward with Tina Checkley, nothing she wouldn't argue about first. But she surprised him by nodding assent and taking a shuffling step forward. She plunged feet first into the pool and surfaced straight away, spluttering. Redlaw launched himself in after her, on his back, spread-eagling himself so as to distribute his weight out. The night vision goggles were water-resistant but not waterproof. If the mechanism got wet, they might short out and stop working.

He managed to hit the pool without going completely under. The goggles were splashed but not soaked and remained functional, allowing him to thrash over to Tina and guide her across the pool towards a platform around the base of the ladder.

The vampires were already there and shinning up the ladder at inhuman speed, like monkeys up a palm tree. Redlaw heaved himself out of the bitterly cold, noxious-smelling water. He helped Tina out too. Then he turned, just in time to see the two soldiers arrive at the mouth of the sewer, their guns unshipped. They scanned around, searching for the vampires. One spied them on the ladder and pointed them out to the other. Both trained their rifles, curling their fingers inside the trigger guards.

Redlaw steadied the Cindermaker with both hands and aimed at the soldier on the left. It was unlikely he could kill the man, not with that body armour on, but the kick from the bullet impact might put him out of action. At the very least he could draw the soldiers' fire, giving the vampires a few extra moments to make it to the top.

God, really, if you're listening, I could do with a little divine intervention.

He squeezed the trigger.

He hit the soldier in the dead centre of his body mass. The man reeled, his finger tightening convulsively on the trigger. A volley of rounds pumped from his rifle into the soldier on the right, who was hurled backwards as though yanked by an invisible rope. His body struck the edge of the sewer mouth a glancing blow, then fell flailing into the pool, bellyflopping with an almighty splash and disappearing below the surface.

The first soldier, winded by Redlaw's shot, slumped against the sewer wall. He clearly couldn't quite believe that he had just fired on his comrade at point blank range.

Regaining his senses, he staggered to his feet and leaned out over the pool. No sign of the other man. He was clearly wracked with indecision. The vampires had, nearly all of them, scaled the ladder. They were getting away. But a fellow soldier was down, injured, in danger of drowning...

With a grunt of thwarted anger, the soldier leapt into the pool and dived under.

Redlaw grabbed Tina and hustled her over to the ladder. He clamped her hands on one of the rusted rungs.

"Up," he said. "Don't think about it. Just climb."

"But I can't see a damn—"

"Doesn't matter. It's a ladder. One rung after another. You could do it blindfolded."

"What about you?"

"I'm coming. Right behind you."

As Tina fumbled her way up the ladder, Redlaw ejected the Cindermaker's clip and snugged fresh rounds into it from the box in his pocket. He rammed the full clip home and racked the slide.

All the while, the soldier continued to scour the pool for his comrade, breaking surface every so often to take a breath.

Redlaw kept an eye on him as he himself began his ascent of the ladder. The rungs were slimy and corroded. The ladder creaked alarmingly, rusty bolts juddering loosely in crumbling sockets.

At the top lay an access duct just large enough to stand upright in. The vampires had again halted, awaiting instructions. Redlaw ushered them forward. "We can't be far from the surface," he said. "There'll be a door, a manhole, something."

As the vampires moved off, he took Tina's wrist. "Come on now. Last stretch."

"It better be."

Instinct made him turn. The soldier had abandoned the pool and mounted the ladder in pursuit of them. He was clambering into the duct, about to bring his rifle to bear.

Redlaw emptied five rounds into him. Tina shrieked as the Cindermaker flashed and boomed in the confined space. The soldier was pounded backwards by each bullet, the last knocking him clear off the ladder. He toppled out into space, and a moment later there came the heavy slap of a body hitting water.

"Is he...?" Tina said.

"I don't know. Let's not hang around to find out."

A couple of hundred yards on, there was another ladder, this one leading up to a manhole cover. Miguel shoved the iron disc aside as though it weighed nothing, and everyone climbed out into the middle of a road and the teeth of a blizzard. Snow raced sideways, driven by a knifing northerly Atlantic wind beneath a black sky. It came not in flakes but in cotton-ball-sized clumps that landed thickly and clung. Redlaw felt his damp clothing begin to stiffen and freeze. Tina was already shivering, and even the vampires, less susceptible than humans to extremes of temperature, looked uncomfortable and unhappy.

"Shelter," Redlaw said, deactivating the goggles and pulling them off. "We're not going to last ten minutes out in this. Tina, where are we?"

She peered around, trying to get her bearings. "Beats me. Can't see shit in this weather. I think—is that trees down that way?"

"Could be."

"Then that's probably Battery Park."

"What's Battery Park near?"

"Nothing. It's kind of at the ass end of Manhattan. Catch a ferry to Staten Island from there, see the Statue of Liberty in the distance, that's about it."

Redlaw thought. "How far are we from the subway tunnel? The one we explored this morning?"

"What are you talking about?" Tina said with a scowl. "Let's find the nearest chain hotel and check in. We don't have to share a room. Long as it's somewhere close by, it's warm, and it's got cable and a mini bar. We can ride out the storm there."

"It isn't just the two of us, Tina."

"What the—? Oh, you cannot be serious." She jerked a thumb at the vampires. "Them, too? They can take care of themselves, surely."

"We've got to find them a place of refuge," Redlaw said. "While that paramilitary death squad is around, no Sunless is safe."

"Yeah, don't know if you noticed, but you and me, we're not vamps. We don't have to worry. We can blend in, disappear. Those guys won't come looking for us."

"You can disappear if you want to. In many ways, I'd prefer it if you did." He handed over her rucksack. "Me, though, I'm taking charge of these 'Lesses. Point me in the general direction of the tunnel entrance. I'm sure I can find it if I try. And be quick about it, would you? Before we die of hypothermia."

TINA RUMMAGED THROUGH her rucksack, stalling for time. The bag's canvas had a rubberised inner layer, so the outside was sodden from the plunge into the sewage pool but the interior was more or less dry. She took out her camcorder and switched it on. It powered up as normal.

"Looks okay," she said. "Damp but not ruined."

"Tina, please."

"One second, all right? I'm thinking."

Tina was, in fact, asking herself several hard questions. She had just been through a harrowing ordeal. She had been violently manhandled, almost ended up as a living juice bar for vampires, been shot at, been dragged along shit-stinky tunnels—she was altogether convinced that pursuing this vampire story was, after all, a very bad idea. She hadn't bargained for quite this level of personal risk and suffering. It made sense to give up. Quit while she was ahead. Quit while she *had* a head. It could have been blown clean off her shoulders any time during the shootout in the church.

If she bailed now, however, she might not be able to hook up with Redlaw again. Lose track of him, and she'd lose the best chance she'd ever had of getting her work noticed and her name known. Some of the footage she had shot while with him was primo stuff, and if she stuck around she was likely to get more, of even better quality. Redlaw was the story really, as much as vampires.

And not forgetting the fact that here, right in front of her, was an actual group of vampires, and she was with them, alongside them, and nobody she knew of had ever gotten so close to the creatures before, no journalist or reporter. The word *embedded* sprang to mind, like those intrepid souls who bunked down with troops during a war, sending home filmed packages and blog updates from the front line. Tina could see herself getting embedded with vampires. She could see the value of it. Unprecedented access. Vampires up close and personal, like never before. The exclusive to beat all exclusives.

God. She'd be crazy to stay with Redlaw, but crazier still to let an opportunity like this slip through her fingers.

Who was she? She was Tick Checkley. And what did ticks do? They fastened on until they had drunk their fill, got what they needed.

"No," she said firmly to Redlaw. "You haven't got a hope of making it there by yourself. I'm coming with you. It's the only way."

"Fine." He was less grateful than she'd expected. But she guessed that with Redlaw it was all about what was expedient. "Let's crack on, then. Miguel. All of you. I'm no shtriga, but for the time being I'm your best hope. I think I've proved that already. I have a plan, and if you're wise you'll follow it."

The vampires deliberated amongst themselves, but not for long.

"Okay, we'll put ourselves in your hands," said Miguel. "For now. But we ain't going to trust you. Mostly because we know you can't trust us."

"Can't argue with that logic. Tina? What are you waiting for? There's no telling when our attackers might reappear."

Tina set off at a fast pace, head bent against the snow, which patted her face with a soft, insistent beat. Not far away, sirens were howling and wailing. The sound was undoubtedly coming from the direction of St Magnus's. There would have been reports of gunfire, summoning the emergency services. She mapped out a route in her head, one that steered well clear of the church.

Her thoughts, however, were mostly on the bravery of her decision and what she might get out of it.

She didn't have visions of a Pulitzer Prize medal in her hands, not quite, but almost. She'd nearly died tonight, and now she was throwing in her lot with the same vampires who'd been on the brink of sucking her dry. By some cosmic law, ballsy persistence like hers must surely be recognised and rewarded.

Cowards never prospered.

Do or die.

Dare or beware.

CHAPTER FIFTEEN

COLONEL JACOBSEN STUDIED the creature in front of him, the vampire in priest's clothing. Giacoia and Child were gripping the vampire by the arms, holding him upright. He couldn't stand unaided. Jacobsen had made sure of that by stamping on his thighs until both femurs snapped.

"What in hell's name are you?" Jacobsen said.

The priest vampire sneered. "I could ask the same of you. You're neither one thing nor the other, neither fish nor fowl. Human, essentially, but tampered with. Augmented."

"All you need to know about me is I'm the one doing the interrogating. Your life is in my hands."

"Forgive me if I don't cower and grovel," said the vampire. "I don't tend to do that to my inferiors."

Jacobsen took a swing at him, landing a roundhouse that would have shattered an ordinary man's skull.

The vampire shook off the blow, grinning fiercely. "I

am Father Rudi Tchaikovsky. I am a hundred and fifty years old and counting. I have lived two lifetimes and met far worse than you. I do not fear you."

"You should," Jacobsen growled, "because I'm the guy who's going to turn you to dust unless you start cooperating."

"And I am shtriga," Tchaikovsky retorted. "I could tear you apart with my bare hands."

"Could, but can't."

In fairness, Jacobsen thought, Tchaikovsky's threat wasn't entirely an empty one. It had taken three Red Eyes to subdue him. They had had to wrestle him off Corporal Lim and pin him to the floor, Child using his considerable bulk to secure him in place while Jacobsen got busy breaking his legs in order to disable him. The average vampire wouldn't have presented anywhere near as much of a problem to the team—but then they would have just eliminated an average vampire, whereas this one seemed worth capturing because he was so unusually *above* average.

"Shtriga, huh?" Jacobsen went on. "That would explain it. Kind of an *über*-vampire, right? Well, you gave Four a run for his money, that's for sure." Lim had in fact been in danger of losing his fight with Tchaikovsky until his comrades came to his assistance. "But against all of us? Crippled as you are? Really, I'm not worried."

"I say we waste this scumbag right now," Lim chipped in. He was nursing a sprained arm. Tchaikovsky had all but dislocated his shoulder trying to wrench the combat knife off him. "Cops'll be on their way. We can't hang around."

"Noted, corporal," said Jacobsen. "But I want some answers."

"As do I," said J. Howard Farthingale III in Jacobsen's ear. "Who is he?"

Jacobsen lowered his voice. "That's what I'm trying to ascertain, sir."

"No, not the shtriga. The other man. The one who shot at your team."

"I don't know, but Red Eye Six and Seven are in pursuit. I'm sure they have him by now."

"And I'm sure they don't," Farthingale said. "I'm monitoring all your feeds, remember? And I've lost contact with both Six and Seven. Their helmet cam signals are down. All I'm getting from either is dead air. Who is he? Ask."

Jacobsen turned back to Tchaikovsky. "There was someone else here with you. He had a gun. Friend of yours?"

"What's it to you?"

Jacobsen kicked him in the gut. Were Tchaikovsky human, inner organs would have ruptured.

Tchaikovsky coughed up a black tarry substance that might once have been blood.

"Why are you so interested in him?" he said. "Am I not enough of a prize?"

"Just tell me about him."

"He's eluded you, hasn't he? That must make you very displeased. I saw him take several of my flock with him. Survivors. Loose ends. How aggravating for you."

"Sir, I'm hearing sirens," said Berger. "We've not got long."

"Please give me permission to cut off this bastard's head, then we're good," said Lim.

"The man's name," Farthingale insisted in Jacobsen's ear. "Ask him if it's John Redlaw."

"Redlaw," said Jacobsen. "John Redlaw. That name mean anything to you?"

Tchaikovsky gave a crooked smile. "If you already know who he is, why are you bothering to enquire?"

Farthingale started cursing and ranting. "I knew it! I knew I recognised him. Goddamn cocksucker limey bastard. Fucking with us *again*..."

Jacobsen tuned his voice out as best he could. "You and this Redlaw are in cahoots?"

"I wouldn't say that," said Tchaikovsky. "But if he has helped some of my flock escape, as I'm assuming he has, then I have much to thank him for. I only wish, with hindsight, that I had treated him a little more charitably. I undervalued him. I mistook him for just another brainless piece of human cattle, a convenient source of nourishment. I see clearly that he is better than that." He heaved a rueful sigh.

"Sir?" said Lim. His knife was drawn. Even with his dominant arm out of action, there was no question he would be able to behead Tchaikovsky with ease. A single left-handed slash, that was all it would take.

"Go on, do it," said Tchaikovsky. "I've done all I can. Some of my flock will live to see another day. My duties have been discharged."

"Aargh!"

It was a cry of pure fury, from the direction of the crypt entrance. Red Eye Seven—Private Abbotts—staggered out from the doorway. He strode across the church, clothes sopping, leaving a trail of water splashes behind him. His helmet was a ruin, cracked in several places, camera unit dangling off on its cable. His face was ragged and bleeding.

"Seven," said Jacobsen. "What the fuck?"

"Shot me," Abbotts raged. "Shot me in the face. And killed Larousse."

"Who shot you?"

"Who the fuck do you think? White-haired guy who was leading those vamps, the one you sent me and Larousse to deal with. Motherfucker got Kyle, nearly did for me too."

Tchaikovsky started chuckling. "Oh yes, I did undervalue Redlaw. How I regret that now. He is sincere in wanting to protect vampire-kind. I thought it a pretty pose, mere words, but it seems not. He is as much God's agent as I am. Truly the Lord does move in mysterious ways."

"You can shut your mouth and all," Abbotts snapped. "Stop that laughing. Friend of mine's dead. Only one on this team who was worth a damn, only one who'd give me the time of day."

Tchaikovsky just laughed louder.

"I said shut your mouth, bloodsucker!" Abbotts bellowed. "Enough of that jibber-jabber of yours!"

Tchaikovsky had no intention of complying. His throaty guffaws echoed to the rafters. "Oh, this is rich," he said. "One man thwarts you. One lone man kicks the legs from under you. So much for your weapons and your armour and your unnatural strength. So much for your programme of assassination. One mere human makes a mockery of—*grrkkk!*"

Abbotts grabbed him by the jaw and neck and, before anyone could stop him, twisted hard. Tchaikovsky's head rotated with a crackle of vertebrae parting, cartilaginous discs popping. His tongue shot out between his fangs. His eyes bulged.

Abbotts shifted his grip and pulled upwards. Skin ripped, muscle and sinew split, tendons were torn asunder. Tchaikovsky's entire head came free in the soldier's hands, and Abbots raised it aloft like some grisly trophy. The decapitated body sagged, now just so much dead weight for Giacoia and Child to support. They dropped it, and almost immediately it started the process of rapid atrophy, losing cohesion and becoming hot dust. The head Abbotts was holding did likewise, separately but simultaneously, and he cast it aside. It rolled along the floor, flinging off powdery clouds of decomposing matter, whittling to nothingness as it bounced and spun.

"That's better," Abbotts said, brushing dust off his gloves. A grin distended his ravaged face. "Now we can hear ourselves think again."

Sirens skirled and honked outside, far off but getting louder.

"Get out of there," Farthingale instructed Jacobsen. "Cut your losses and return to base." He sounded deeply disgruntled, but nowhere near as disgruntled as Jacobsen himself felt.

"Everyone, quitting time," Jacobsen said, circling a hand above his head.

The six remaining members of Team Red Eye began scrambling up the walls, making for the broken windows. Lim, with his bum arm, needed help from Child. Berger, too, had an injured arm, her elbow bruised from where she had been shot by Redlaw. Jacobsen offered her assistance, but she refused.

Jacobsen was last to exit the church. Outside, as he catapulted himself up over the eaves and onto the roof, he saw whirling flashes of red and blue light between two rows of nearby buildings. Police and fire crews, doubtless a SWAT unit as well. The vehicles were moving in a slow convoy, lightbars ablaze. They would have arrived a lot sooner if the driving conditions had not been so atrocious.

One man down, Jacobsen thought bitterly to himself as he ran across the snow-padded tiles. *Three hurt.*

And the mission itself had been compromised, its full remit not achieved.

Whoever this John Redlaw was, he had just gone straight to the number one spot on Colonel Jim Jacobsen's shit list.

And that was not a good or wise place for anybody to be.

CHAPTER SIXTEEN

TINA THREW ANOTHER piece of wood on the fire. Sparks arose, disappearing as they helixed towards the ceiling.

Around her, the vampires huddled. They sat singly or in pairs and their eyes gleamed a horrid crimson in the fireglow.

Redlaw was off by himself in a corner, arms folded across his chest, chin sunk to breastbone. Fast asleep. Snoring ever so slightly.

Old man needed his nap-nap. Tina couldn't sleep, herself. Too much going on in her head. She was buzzing, a blare of nerves and exhilaration.

Plus, of course, the vampires. Eight of them, one of her, and it wasn't so long since they'd been lining up to suck her blood. Redlaw had assured her that that had all changed. He was in charge of these vamps now. They wouldn't dare attack her because she was associated with him.

But Redlaw wasn't awake right now, was he? And some of the looks that were coming Tina's way seemed distinctly *avaricious*. Or perhaps she was imagining it. The fire's uncertain flicker. The dance of shadows across faces.

The group had taken refuge not in the subway after all, but above ground. Redlaw had changed the plan at the last minute. As they were approaching the tunnel entrance he had spotted the derelict old toothpaste factory and proposed setting up camp there instead.

"It's a more defensible position," he had said. "More access points and, crucially, more egress points. More options for retreat than being in a tunnel."

"And so much cosier than a Holiday Inn," Tina had said.

"I gave you the chance to quit, Tina. You chose this. Suck it up."

"Hey, I can still gripe, can't I?"

"No, you can't. Not on my watch."

Behind his back Tina had snapped off a salute at him and muttered, "Aye-aye, cap'n."

"I heard that."

"You were meant to."

The factory dated back to the 'thirties, the halcyon era of production lines and mass manufacturing. The interior was cavernous; you could easily picture overall-clad workers manning giant machines that churned out thousands of tubes of toothpaste per hour, dreary toil to create bright smiles. The roof was more or less intact, but wind whistled through cracks and missing panes in the high narrow windows, sending ripples across the puddles on the floor. Pigeons roosted on the ceiling joists, cooing and fluttering. Why no one had demolished the place and built condos, Tina wasn't sure. She assumed some arcane piece of zoning regulation forbade it, or else campaigners had sued to preserve the factory as an example of heritage architecture or some such. Either way, the legal system, through inaction, had allowed it to fall into rack and ruin.

Several side-chambers adjoined the main central space, formerly offices for management and a cafeteria for the workforce, now stripped bare, débris-strewn. Redlaw had selected a room that was large and windowless and that had a back door which led directly outside, for a quick getaway if necessary. He'd got a fire going, using strips of wallpaper as kindling and slats from rotten pallets as firewood. He'd also instructed the vampires to blockade the factory's main entrances with cinderblocks, rubble and a few leftover hunks of old rusting machinery. The vampires had done his bidding meekly and eagerly. Tina had had no idea how submissive these creatures could be. It helped lessen her fear of them, if only somewhat.

The more she looked at the vampires, the more fascinated she became. They were a mixed lot, a cross-section of the populace, all ages and ethnicities. One was little more than a child, and the man with her, who acted like her father but wasn't old enough to be, was a puddingy Goth in a frock coat with frilly shirtcuffs and round blue-tinted spectacles. There was a woman whose Dior party dress and Louboutin slingbacks must have been gorgeous when new, although they were now as ragged and filthy as anything a bag lady might wear. There was a black guy whose slim-hipped figure and elaborate way with a gesture positively screamed *gay*. In so many respects they seemed like just normal people. Yet they weren't, not any more.

As a means of distracting herself, Tina took out her camcorder and set about filming. Being behind the lens divorced her from the immediate situation. It provided the illusion of distance. She became objective, someone observing rather than participating.

Slowly she panned round the room, left to right. A rather neat establishing shot, she thought, showing the vampires' faces, their hunched bodies in a circle round the fire. Capturing the atmosphere of respite and reprieve. Something almost primitive about it, a snatched moment of warmth in a cold, cold world.

"What are you doing?" one of them challenged. The Latino.

"Uh, videoing you guys."

"You some kind of reporter?"

Tina almost said no, but then she thought, *Fuck it, yes I am.* She undoubtedly felt more like a reporter than she ever had before. If this wasn't reportage—the gathering of facts to be relayed to others—then nothing was.

"Uh-huh," she said. "I hope that's not a problem. Redlaw's cool with it. That's why he's letting me tag along. I'm kind of a documentarian. About you guys. Telling your stories. You've got a story—Miguel, is it?"

The Latino vampire nodded. "Miguel."

"You've got a story, yeah? You all have. What it's like being what you are. How you came to be that way. Who you were before. It wasn't always like this for you—skulking, hiding from humans and daylight, living on, y'know, blood. You were people. *Are* people. You want to talk about that? Now you can. Into this." She pointed at the camcorder. "To me."

"Why should we want to talk?" Miguel said, but she could tell his interest was piqued. Whose wouldn't be? It was a camera. The modern confessional. An opportunity to be recorded for posterity, to unburden yourself to the public, to be someone rather than no one—a view aired, an opinion heard.

"Put your side of things," Tina said. "Everyone's scared of vampires. I know I am. But we're scared of you because we don't know you, don't understand you. Maybe if we did, it wouldn't be so bad. Maybe it'd help your cause, help people accept you."

Maybe it'd make you think of me as something more than just a potential dinner.

"This is Tina Checkley," she said, louder this time, narrating for the soundtrack. She would edit out the previous stuff and cut in right at this point. "I'm holed up currently with, like, ten actual, living, breathing vampires. Well, not living or breathing. That's just a figure of speech. One of them, this guy you can see right now, his name's Miguel and he's—How old are you, Miguel?"

"Thirty-six," said Miguel. "Least, I was two years ago when I got bit. I've been thirty-six ever since, I guess you could say." A brief, wry smile. "Never going to have to turn forty. Never going to have to handle that. No midlife crisis for me."

"So let's do this," Tina said. "Interview with a vampire. Several vampires. Tell me all about yourselves."

And for the next hour, one after another, the eight of them did.

And Tina forgot herself, forgot the state that she was in—bedraggled, chilled to the bone despite the fire, her clothes and hair smelling like ass—forgot everything and focused exclusively on the job at hand. Collecting narratives. Gathering raw footage. Asking questions. Coaxing. Prodding. Prompting. Being a journalist.

This, for sure, was what she'd been put on earth to do.

*   *   *

MIGUEL DOMINGUEZ. USED to be a school bus driver. Loved the job. Loved the kids and their ways, their noise, their smiles. Precious cargo. He used to drive that bus like he had fragile porcelain aboard. That was what he missed most, those kids. He had looked on them as though they were his own, the family he didn't have— would never have.

PATTI MARSDEN. MARRIED, mother of two. She'd been working a late shift at the grocery store one night last summer. She lived in a good neighbourhood. Walking back home was normally safe at any time of day or night. Sure, some dogs had been disappearing lately, there'd been an item in the local paper about it, but everyone assumed it was just a freak event. There'd been rumours of coyotes in the hills and it might have had something to do with that. What actually happened, as she made her way to her apartment that night, she still wasn't sure. It was a permanent blur in her memory. She was passing the park. A figure leapt down from the trees overhanging the sidewalk. She could remember thinking, *God, those teeth!* Then pain. Then a period of foggy emptiness, of not knowing who she was or where she was supposed to be, knowing only that she must never see her husband and kids again. For their sake.

DIANE BERTORELLI. SHE'D been a girl who liked her luxuries. Her shoes, her shopping, her cocktails, her pamper sessions at the spa. She went out only with men who could give her those things, meals at the best restaurants, trips to the Hamptons for the weekend, skiing in Aspen, yachting off Cabo. No shame in that. What she was now, this wasn't her. These old raggedy worn-out clothes, the things she had to eat to survive... This wasn't her. And do you know what the worst thing was? The sun had become a deadly enemy. The sun she used to love. The sun she used to lie out in whenever possible, get that tan, look healthy...

ANU AHMED, SECOND-generation Muslim American. His father ran a dry-cleaning business. Anu had been at medical college but still helped out his dad at work during the vacations. The plan had been to become a doctor, an oncologist maybe, and earn enough money so that Dad could sell the store and retire and Anu could look after him and Mom. A good son. But not any more. He didn't know what he was any more—except an unclean abomination.

MARY-JO SCHAEFFER, and you know what? This reminded her of an AA meeting. "I'm Mary-Jo and I'm a vampire." She'd done the twelve step. Done it so many times it was more like the twelve hundred step. Relapse after relapse. And so she guessed it was poetic justice that she'd been drunk, out back of a bar in Danbury, Connecticut, throwing up, when she got attacked and vampirised. Punishment from above or something, maybe. The higher power she was supposed to trust in had got a sick fucking sense of humour, that was all she could say. Making her trade addiction to one kind of liquid for addiction to another kind.

DENZEL LOMAX, THOUGH that was only his stage name. Theatre actor, scraping a living, just. Once, fresh out of drama school, he trod the boards with Pacino, doing Shakespeare on Broadway. Only a couple of lines in the same scene, but still. "You can call me Al," Pacino said during rehearsals, but Denzel never did. Too in awe. It was always Mr Pacino. And then, coming home late one night after a show, he'd got pounced on. Thought it was an animal, some kind of rabid feral dog. He'd fought back, but... And so now he had another role. A part he had to play. Forever. It was the only way to think about it—that being a vampire was a guise he wore, something he was pretending to be—because otherwise, if he didn't, he might go mad.

ANDY GREGG, AND this kid with him, this little girl, her name was Cindy. Andy had turned Cindy. According to the lore, this made him her sire, her his get, and so it was his responsibility to care for her and look after her. Andy used to love reading about vampires. His favourite vampire novelist was Anne Rice, although he liked King's *'Salem's Lot* and George R.R. Martin's *Fevre Dream* well enough. But not *I Am Legend* by Richard Matheson. Too scientific, that one. No magic in it. Because vampires are supernatural creatures. They can't just be reduced to facts, biological rationales, viruses, allergies and the rest. Where's the thrill in that? The horror?

*   *   *

CINDY NEWTON. NINE years old. She missed her mom and dad, missed them bad, but she'd gotten used to the idea that she would never be able to see them again. Andy was her mom and dad now. She had her favourite bear with her, Jingle Ted. He used to have a bell inside him, that was how he got his name, only it had stopped making a noise for some reason. She liked the smell of Jingle Ted's fur. He smelled of how she used to smell, and how her parents used to smell. Sometimes, when she was feeling sad, she'd hold him up to her face, like this, and breathe in. The smell of home.

"THANKS. THANKS, ALL of you."

Tina switched off the camcorder, dizzy, even a little breathless. She turned round to find Redlaw at her shoulder.

"Been busy?" he said.

"You betcha. Filled up half the memory with just talking heads, but it's all quality material. Want to see?"

"Another time. I've rested, so I think I should go out on patrol. Check the perimeter."

"You reckon those soldiers could follow us here?"

"I don't know. The snowstorm should be covering our tracks. But it's best not to take any chances." Redlaw turned to the vampires. "I'd like one of you to come with me. A vampire's senses are far sharper than mine. You." He clicked his fingers at Denzel Lomax. "You seem an alert sort of bloke. Up you get."

Denzel Lomax followed Redlaw out of the room, and Tina stowed the camcorder away in her rucksack, no longer thinking of it as a mere item of electronic equipment. It was far more than that now. What she had in the can was something the world had never seen before. Vampires speaking about themselves, voicing their regrets and anxieties. Beneath the monstrous looks and appetites, they were still human. More than just vestiges of their old selves remained. They were dead but had lives.

Earlier, when she'd told Miguel that vampires were people, she hadn't exactly meant it. It had been a white lie, blowing smoke up his ass to get him to open up to her.

It seemed, though, that it might actually be the truth.

And it was a truth the public ought to hear, and Tina could hardly wait to get it out there.

CHAPTER
SEVENTEEN

REDLAW AND THE vampire walked the perimeter of the factory site.

"Anything?" Redlaw asked. "Soldiers? Danger?"

The vampire shook his head. "Nothing, so far as I can tell. We're the only ones for a ways around."

"Good. It's Denzel, isn't it? I caught your name when I overheard you talking to Tina—to her camera."

"Dennis, actually," said Denzel. "Dennis is the name I was christened with. But Denzel's way cooler, and besides, there's already an actor out there called Dennis Lomax. I checked with Actors' Equity. TV guy. Done character roles, bit-parts in a few shows, nothing you'd have heard of. We don't look a thing like each other, on account of he's old, fat and white and I'm not. He'd never be mistaken for me or me for him. But union rules are union rules."

"Tell me, Denzel. Are you scared of me?"

"Well, that's a question, isn't it? I don't know. I mean, you're our shtriga now..."

"Am I?"

"I guess. You keep saying so, and you're helping us, and you boss us about. Aren't you our shtriga?"

"Maybe. I'm still adjusting to the idea. Trying it on for size. Would it bother you if I told you I used to police Sunless and hunt and dust rogue ones? Would it make a difference?"

Denzel gave it some thought. "I've always believed you should judge someone by their present actions, not their past sins. Otherwise, nobody'd get along with anybody ever."

"What about this?" Redlaw tugged out the crucifix around his neck. He held it up. "Does this bother you?"

The vampire drew back, squinting, as if a bright light had been shone in his face. Then his frown cleared.

"Not so much," he said. "We lived in that church a while. Desensitised."

Redlaw tucked the crucifix away. "Yes, must be that."

Or my crucifix has no power because there's no faith behind it. Not any more.

What did that make him then, he wondered? An apostate? Lapsed?

How could he be? He still felt instinctively, with every fibre of his being, that there was a God and that He had a plan for John Redlaw, as He did for everybody. Redlaw might not be able to fathom the nature of that plan, but faith meant he wasn't supposed to. He was just supposed to accept that a plan existed and that it was for the greater good. As Job had done. And Abraham. And Paul. And even Jesus. The Bible was a litany of examples of people who did as the Lord bade and were loath to query His will, whatever sacrifices or suffering it entailed.

Why should John Redlaw be any different?

He recalled a conversation he had had with Father Graham Dixon, one of their get-togethers in the vicarage at Ladbroke Grove. Redlaw had been drinking tea, Father Dixon pale ale, alcohol being his one priestly vice. This was after Father Dixon's term as visiting SHADE pastor had ended, when the two men realised they had gone beyond being priest and penitent and were friends. Their get-togethers had become an occasional, informal substitute for confession and also a chance to enjoy each other's company and chat.

"The absolute all-time bummer," said Father Dixon, "is you're never going to get a firm yes or no. About anything. Not 'til after you die. Life is a bizarre one-sided game show, all questions, no answers. The Almighty Quizmaster fires off riddles and conundrums at us and expects us to work them out for ourselves. Occasionally He'll give us a hint, a nudge, a clue, a sign, but mostly we're on our own. You, John, want to know if Sergeant Leary's death has meaning. That's what's preying on your mind."

Róisín Leary had been killed by vampires less than a month earlier, and the wound of her death was still raw and festering, with Redlaw still nowhere nearer fathoming a divine rationale for it.

"And I can't say if it does," Father Dixon went on. "That's got to be for you to figure out. You're angry that Róisín's dead because it seems so senseless and because you weren't there to protect her. Fair enough. We're allowed our regrets and self-recrimination, especially when we're grieving. 'But how can I carry on?' That's what you're asking yourself. She was dear to you, we all know that."

"She was an over-talkative pain in the you-know-what," said Redlaw.

"She never shut up, did she? I'm glad I'm C of E and never had to take *her* confession. That would have been a long haul."

"And for a woman educated by nuns, she certainly didn't stint on the expletives."

"Exactly. Róisín was crude and earthy and vivacious and everything you're not, and you'd never have put up with her as your partner if she hadn't been special to you, and she likewise wouldn't have endured being with a grumpy old fart like you if she hadn't been able to see the decency that's intrinsic in you, even if you keep it buried deep down. And now she's dead and you're thinking, 'Where's the justice in that? Good people, people who are important to us, shouldn't die. Only scumbags should.' But if God only picked off the scumbags... Well, the world would be a better place, wouldn't it? But He doesn't. He's indiscriminate. He's tough and arbitrary. He makes us work hard for what we've got and He kicks the legs out from under us time and time again. It's what He does, it's all He does, and He absolutely will not stop, ever, until you are dead."

"That's some sort of quotation, isn't it?"

"You need to go to the movies more, John. Would it kill you to rent a DVD every once in a while? Be like the rest of us, us ordinary mortals?"

"So the good are allowed to die while the, as you put it, scumbags flourish," said Redlaw. "Is that it? You're fine with that? That's perfectly acceptable in your world?"

"I never said they flourish."

"They seem to. There's evil all around, sin on every street corner, and nobody seems too bothered by it. God certainly not."

"Ah, and that's the paradox, Captain Redlaw. The great unresolvable." Father Dixon took a long, deep pull on his beer. A thin strip of froth adhered to his top lip. "Why does God allow evil to exist in the world, when it's surely in His power to stamp it out? The thing is, evil isn't fixed or quantifiable. Evil people aren't aware that they're evil. To them, committing foul or harmful deeds is of no consequence. They've somehow squared it morally with themselves. They feel no more guilty about it than I do about having this beer. Which is to say, slightly guilty but not to the extent that I'm going to stop. Same with you and your peccadilloes. If you have any. Come to think of it, you probably don't."

"I have my moments."

"I doubt it. God, at any rate, has given each of us free will to decide whether to do good or bad. It's His greatest and also most perplexing gift, in that it pre-empts Him—the New Testament version of Him at any rate—from ever taking action against malefactors. It's our responsibility to be good, He's telling us, not His. It's all down to us."

"Regardless of that, evil is wrong and should be punished."

"Oh, no argument here. Transgressing man's laws, never mind God's, is a bad thing. Luckily we have fine law enforcement professionals such as yourself to apprehend and bring to justice anyone who does."

"So where does that leave vampires?" Redlaw asked.

Father Dixon looked calculatingly across the room at him. "Unequivocally evil. I'd have thought that was obvious. Monsters. Abominations. Things of the pit. That's why men and women of faith are required to police them. Stands to reason. Men and women of faith armed with Holy Water bombs and whacking great handguns. Are you not so sure about that, John? Even after what's just happened to Róisín?"

Just then, before Redlaw could frame a reply, the vicarage phone rang. A parishioner in need. A mother whose infant son had a life-threatening brain tumour and who was in the depths of despair and seeking pastoral counselling.

"No rest for the non-wicked," said Father Dixon as he grabbed his coat and bicycle lock. "We'll resume this discussion another time, I trust."

But the subject hadn't come up again. Redlaw had been reluctant to revisit it, and Father Dixon had sensed his reticence and, the soul of tact, let the matter lie.

FATHER DIXON'S CHUCKLE. The beer froth on his lip. The moment faded in Redlaw's memory. Father Dixon was dead too. Shot by Lieutenant Khalid, having taken a bullet meant for Redlaw. Another good person gone to their reward. Another profound loss. Another body-blow to Redlaw's faith.

Redlaw and Denzel Lomax circuited the factory perimeter one more time, trudging through their own footprints in the snow. One of them left white vapour puffs behind him as he breathed, the other did not.

"If I am to be the shtriga of your group," Redlaw said eventually, "I may not always go easy on you. But it will always be for your own good."

Denzel considered this, then grinned. "Long as you're looking out for us, that works for me."

Vampires—unequivocally evil?

Father Dixon had been right on many counts, but in this one instance, where he had been at his most dogmatic, he had also been at his most mistaken.

CHAPTER EIGHTEEN

JACOBSEN WAS ALL in favour of heading right back out into the field and hunting down Redlaw and the remaining vampires. Time was wasting. The longer the delay, the greater chance of losing them. America was a big place. Hell, *New York* was a big place. There were a million and one little nooks and crevices the vamps could hide in, and even Farthingale, with his uncannily accurate source of intel, might not be able to pinpoint their whereabouts.

On arriving back at Red Eye headquarters, however, he had to acknowledge that his team was in no fit state to turn and burn. They were all exhausted and, in the cases of Berger, Lim and Abbotts, in pain as well. They could hardly be expected to go haring off on another mission straight away. The first order of the day—or rather, of the night—was rest and recuperation.

Technicians were ready for them in the basement levels of the house on East 84th. The remedy for Team

Red Eye's fatigue and injuries was a fresh course of treatment—another dose of the Porphyrian process. In a large, antiseptic-smelling chamber, all six soldiers stripped to their underwear and allowed themselves to be strapped to gurneys by means of Kevlar restraints round their wrists and ankles. The restraints were as much for the techs' benefit as the soldiers'. Things could get pretty wild once the treatment was under way. Wild and potentially hazardous.

Each of the team was injected with a solution containing the active ingredient known as PP-66, the successful end-product of the sixty-sixth attempt by Farthingale's research scientists to extract vampire DNA and make it compatible with that of humans. Or, to put it another way, weaponise it.

Jacobsen wasn't any too clear on the specifics. He knew some kind of vector was involved, a modified retroviral pathogen which carried the PP-66 round the subject's body and installed it at a cellular level, like an infection. He knew also that the vampire DNA had been tweaked in order to tone down many of a vamp's less desirable characteristics, though not all of them. Some, such as vulnerability to sunlight and a taste for human haemoglobin, could not be completely edited or excised. They were too fundamental, it seemed, too intrinsic a part of vampirism.

Beyond that, it wasn't Jacobsen's business to enquire too deeply. A good soldier never asked questions. The process worked, that was all he needed to know.

It hurt, too.

The techs beat a hasty retreat, locking the chamber door behind them, and Team Red Eye waited for the PP-66 to take effect. Jacobsen cast a rueful glance over at the empty seventh gurney where PFC Larousse ought to have been. Then he looked briefly at Berger, catching her eye. She responded with a grim smile. They all knew what was coming next, and none of them was looking forward to it.

The pain hit. At first it felt like a fever. A sharp rise in body temperature. Sweats. Muscle cramps. It rapidly blossomed from there into a grinding, marrow-deep ache, as though a million maggots were boring tunnels inside your bones. This sensation grew and grew until it was unbearable.

And that was only the beginning, the initial phase. Soon Jacobsen was lost in a long, seemingly endless continuum of agony. His conscious mind fought to blot out the pain but couldn't. It was like trying to contain a volcanic eruption. All the pain management techniques the army had taught him, the mental tricks for withstanding torture, were useless. They meant nothing when your veins were channels for molten lava and your flesh was on fire.

There was screaming and groaning all around him. He glimpsed Abbotts gibbering, frothing at the mouth. Child wept and sobbed like an infant. Giacoia was bleeding from the nose and eyes. Lim was nothing but a writhe of tendon and sinew, bucking and thrashing so hard that at times he rose clear of the gurney, bent almost double, his spine a perfect arch.

On it went. At most, the treatment lasted three quarters of an hour. But it was such a hellish three quarters of an hour that time became irrelevant. It might as well have been eternity. The digital clock on the wall was no help. Jacobsen could look at it but make no sense of the numerals. They warped and shifted until they resembled Hebrew script, or a mocking robotic face, or just empty black orifices outlined in red.

It was only when the clock's numerals settled down and became intelligible once more that Jacobsen realised he was through the worst of it. The pain ebbed. Now and then it would rise to a peak again, but the intervals between these spikes widened. He clenched his jaw and rode them out, sinking blissfully into the increasingly long lulls.

Soon he was almost at normal. A sense-memory of the ordeal lingered, like a scorch mark in his psyche, but otherwise he felt good. Not just good—great. Reinvigorated.

And thirsty. Oh, so thirsty.

His whole self cried out for just one thing. He looked round at his comrades and they were full of what he craved. Their bodies were ripe to bursting with it, like succulent juicy fruit. He was desperate to rip them open and gorge himself on the crimson nectar inside. The urge was so strong, it nearly overwhelmed him. If not for the restraints he might have given in to it.

The technicians entered, and they brought with them large plastic squeeze-packs of human blood, which they distributed among the members of Team Red Eye. The restraints had just enough slack in them to allow the soldiers to uncap the squeeze-packs and guzzle the contents. As the blood slithered down his throat Jacobsen's thirst abated and the haze of *need* in his head cleared. His thoughts became entirely his own again.

Before any restraints were undone, the techs asked each soldier to give name, rank, serial number from time of service, and social security number. The checklist determined whether or not they were in full control of their faculties.

Jacobsen reeled off the data without pause or error, and was released. He stood and stretched. The overhead fluorescent striplights were harshly bright and buzzed like swarming bees. The sound of Velcro parting as Child was freed from his restraints was as loud as firecrackers. One technician's cologne was cloyingly sweet, another's underarm odour repellently pungent. Jacobsen could even smell Berger's pussy, and he divined that she was in a state of mild arousal, which in turn made him feel very randy indeed.

This was what made the forty-five minutes of pain worthwhile, this incredible flowering of the senses, this renewed surge of power and vitality. The Porphyrian process wasn't permanent. It started to wear off within twenty-four hours and so required constant re-application. It was a boost to the system, vampiric Viagra, which the human metabolism couldn't tolerate for long and invariably rejected in the end. It was a genetic fix, not a mutation.

That was fine by Jacobsen. If the alterations had been irrevocable, he would never have agreed to undergo the treatments in the first place. He was no idiot. Who would want to be a quasi-vampire for the rest of their days? Whereas to have the best vampiric traits for just a while, to experience superhuman levels of strength, speed, stamina, agility, sensory awareness...

A commotion to his right. Jacobsen spun round to see Abbotts with his hands around a technician's neck. Abbotts was clawing at the man's throat, apparently trying to tear it open with his bare fingernails.

Jacobsen sprang across the room. He thrust his arms up inside Abbotts' and levered them apart, breaking the private's grip on the tech. Then he rammed Abbotts down on the gurney, pinning him in place.

"What the fuck, private?" he roared.

"Blood!" Abbotts cried. "I feel so hollow. I want more. I want *his*."

"Stand down, Abbotts. We do not do this. We do not attack civilians."

"I want... I want..."

Abbotts resisted with all his might, straining to be free. Child appeared at Jacobsen's side and joined him in keeping Abbotts in place. Together they wrestled the Alabaman back into the restraints. Abbotts mewled and snarled. His eyes were bright with wanton greed.

Jacobsen snatched up a spare squeeze-pack and emptied it down Abbotts's gullet. Abbotts nearly choked, but managed to swallow most of the blood. Gradually he calmed.

"I'm sorry, sir. I'm sorry. I just... I couldn't control it, you know?"

"No," said Jacobsen, "I don't know."

"Let me up. I'm okay now. It won't happen again."

"I don't think so." Jacobsen glanced at the technician, who was being comforted by his colleagues. There were raw red weals on the man's neck. He looked—understandably—very shaken. "You're going to stay put for the next couple of hours, Abbotts."

"But colonel..."

"No fucking arguments. Until I'm sure you're safe to be around again, you aren't going anywhere. Understood?"

"But—"

"Is that understood, private? Because, believe me, the way I'm feeling right now, I'd happily pound your brains to oatmeal."

Abbotts, with his torn, disfigured face, looked surly but resigned. "Yes, sir," he murmured, adding, "Ain't as if *you* just watched a friend drown or anything."

"No, but a soldier under my command is dead," Jacobsen retorted, "and you'd be sorely mistaken if you think I take that lightly." He turned to Giacoia. "Oversee this, lieutenant. Two hours tied to that table, so's he can learn a little self-discipline. The rest of you, to your quarters. Grab some sack time."

Jacobsen stalked out of the chamber.

He went to his own quarters and sat on the bed flicking through a copy of *Stars And Stripes* which he'd borrowed from the rec room.

The newspaper reminded him how he used to have a cause once, a vocation. He had stood for something until, at the age of forty-one, he'd become aware that he was considered too old to stand for it any more. He had been faced with accepting an administrative post or a job training recruits. Neither appealed. Better to get out altogether than continue as a shadow of his former self, a ghost soldier, washed-up, pointless, army surplus.

His restlessness deepened. He tried to distract himself with a game of Angry Birds, but couldn't seem to make any progress through the levels. There was a nagging itch in his brain. A compulsion. An urge.

Finally he gave in to it. He got up and made his way to the ready room, where he donned battle fatigues and body armour and gathered a selection of weapons, as much ordnance as he could carry in one load. He deliberately didn't take a helmet. No camera, no comms. No one looking over his shoulder.

Shortly after that, he was at the wheel of the Hummer and heading back out into the city.

The car growled along, windscreen wipers struggling to fend off the continual assault of snow. Jacobsen drove slowly, with some impatience, peering out into a world of whirling white. He had the roads virtually to himself—here and there the occasional cab or police car, tyres caked with ice, struggling for grip, and a few snowplough trucks and grit spreaders vainly trying to subdue the snow, about as successful in their efforts as King Canute holding back the tide.

If it wasn't for the integrated sat nav unit embedded in the dashboard, Jacobsen might easily have become disorientated and lost. One snowy street was all but indistinguishable from another, and most of the street signs were frosted over and unreadable. The blizzard seemed to be erasing everything, as though God had grown sick of His creation and was rubbing it out and starting again.

Eventually, St Magnus's. A section of the street was cordoned off by police tape and sawhorses. Jacobsen rolled past at the crosswalk. Cops, firefighters, paramedics and forensics experts were tramping in and out of the church. Blue and red lightbars rippled like fairground illuminations.

Jacobsen continued round the block and commenced his hunt. With the driver's side window wound all the way down, he cruised the neighbourhood, halting every now and then to lean out and inhale deeply through his nose. The air was laden with scents, mostly vehicle exhaust particulates and the peppery aroma of Portland sandstone, New York's principal construction material. The falling snow deadened the scents, making them less potent, but Jacobsen nevertheless breathed them all in and assessed them. Vampires had a distinct odour. Old dried blood, poor personal hygiene, a faint undertone of decay. Once you knew it, you couldn't forget it or mistake it for anything else. And a group of vampires would leave a significant trail.

An hour passed, Jacobsen methodically exploring the area around St Magnus's in a widening spiral. A number of times he got out of the Hummer and stood on the running board, the better to catch the air currents. There was a chance that this search was futile, he knew, but he had to try. The vampires weren't going to get away from him. They certainly weren't going to get away with Larousse's death.

He was outside the car, being bombarded by snow, when his phone rang. Farthingale. Jacobsen hit the Accept Call icon. He had been expecting this.

"At least you've got your cell with you," the Bostonian growled. "You haven't gone completely incommunicado."

"Sir. Rather busy right now. Can we hurry this up?"

"Five minutes ago, colonel, I was woken up by a call from one of the Red Eye technicians. He informed me that the Hummer wasn't in its garage and you weren't in your private quarters."

"Which tech, sir?"

"Does it matter?"

"One of them was attacked this evening, that's all. By Red Eye Seven."

"How unfortunate," said Farthingale. "Well, it may have been him, but his motives in contacting me were purely honourable. One of my employees has gone off the reservation, and that's something I ought to know about. So we pinged the Hummer's onboard GPS and apparently it and you are on the West Side. Can this be true? And if it is, can you kindly tell me what the hell you're up to?"

"I'm furthering the mission."

"I beg your pardon, you're what?"

"Looking for the vampires who gave us the slip."

"Alone? Without my say-so?"

"With all due respect, sir, I didn't think permission was required. Our original objective was to take out all the vamps at St Magnus's, am I right? So I'm seeing that through to the end."

"I'm not sanctioning this," said Farthingale. "While I applaud your thoroughness and your initiative, Colonel Jacobsen, I can't have one of my employees going off on a jaunt, working independently. What's got into you? Does the chain of command mean nothing?"

"I feel the rest of Team Red Eye deserve a break," said Jacobsen, "and all I'm doing is trying to locate the vampires while I still can, before they get too far. That Brit as well, if he's still with them, Redlaw or whatever his name is. I can move quicker and easier by myself."

"This is highly unprofessional of you."

"Mr Farthingale, a professional gets the job done, and that's me. I've just had a Porphyrian treatment. I'm at optimum efficiency. It's now or never, really."

"You didn't think to run it past me first?"

"Do you or do you not want those vamps found?"

"The vampires I don't care about so much. There's more where they came from."

"And Redlaw?" Jacobsen asked carefully, pointedly.

"That's another matter," said Farthingale. A note of dawning comprehension entered his voice. The sound of the penny dropping. Many, many pennies, Jacobsen hoped. "Are you... are you offering to deal with him for me? Is that what this is all about?"

"Depends on what you want done with him, sir. I'm prepared to consider any and all possibilities. I gather you have a beef with the man, judging by how you reacted when that shtriga priest confirmed his identity. If I locate the vamps and take them down and there happens to be a little collateral damage..."

Jacobsen could hear Farthingale mulling things over, cogs turning in that billion-dollar brain.

He continued, "What I'm thinking, sir, is that I can resolve the issue for you. I'd want something in return, of course. A little extra on the side."

Farthingale stayed silent for a while longer, then said, "How much extra?"

"My going rate for an op is fifty k. Treble that."

"That's plenty extra."

"Your choice," said Jacobsen. "Tell you what, I'll make it easy for you. Just say nothing. If you do, I'll take it as a 'go' command. Call it moral deniability."

Farthingale said nothing.

"Then we're agreed. Leave it with me. Pleasure doing business with you."

"You know, I never pegged you as such a mercenary, colonel," said Farthingale.

"Then you pegged me dead wrong, sir. Quit the infantry and keep soldiering, what else are you? Mercenary's the only name for it."

Jacobsen cut the connection and climbed back into the Hummer. He had played that pretty well, he thought.

He'd got his own way *and* secured the prospect of a handsome bonus for his pension pot. He'd pitted himself against a world-class wheeler-dealer and won. Score one for GI Joe versus The Man.

He resumed the hunt.

FARTHINGALE STARED OUT of the picture window of his study. The lights of the mainland were invisible, obliterated by frantic flurries of snow. A keening gale howled across the reach, buffeting Far Tintagel's walls like a besieging horde.

Well, it was done now. He thought about contacting Uona to inform him. No. He'd leave it until confirmation came that Redlaw was dead.

Redlaw, dead.

He had just commissioned the termination of a human life. Somehow the fact that there was a price tag, a hundred and fifty thousand dollars, made it more palatable. It turned it into a financial transaction, much like any other. You purchased a service, paid for it, let someone perform it on your behalf. Simple. Mundane, even.

So why were his hands trembling?

Farthingale nearly picked up the phone to call Jacobsen again and rescind the arrangement.

Then he thought of Nathaniel Lambourne. He thought of Uona, who had said, "You know what's expected of you. I only hope you don't disappoint."

The phone stayed put.

It might not be trepidation, Farthingale realised, that was making his hands shake.

It might be excitement.

*   *   *

AT LONG LAST—vampires.

A clear strong vamp scent in the air, like a thread begging to be followed.

They were a mile distant, maybe less.

Jacobsen parked the Hummer, loaded up with weaponry from the trunk, and hurried onward on foot. It was the small hours. Nobody around, nobody but him. The blizzard had cast a spell over New York, putting the City That Never Sleeps to sleep. All good folk were abed, blinds drawn, snug and warm, out of the storm. Nobody to see a heavily armed soldier moving westward through New York City, keeping low, hugging the shadows, a ghost amid the snow.

Soon he was near Manhattan Island's edge, close to the frozen Hudson, the river's leaden smell strong in his nostrils. He glimpsed a hulking edifice, some kind of factory.

Yes.

In there.

CHAPTER NINETEEN

THE COLONEL ENTERED the factory via one of the high windows. Vandals had smashed out almost every one of its panes, leaving a rotted skeletal frame. A segment of transom and mullion more or less crumbled to pieces in his hands. He slipped through the opening and found himself on a steel gantry which ran the length of a space roughly the size of a football field. The gantry was precariously rickety and let out a worrisome low creak when he shifted his weight. He vaulted the handrail and landed on the floor twenty feet below, noiselessly as a cat. He listened out. Sounds came at him from every direction: the dripping of water, the fluster of pigeon wings, breezes hissing and sliding. The darkness was not darkness at all. His eyes saw everything with pinpoint clarity, in a myriad shades of grey. The nocturnal world was, to him, a black-and-white movie.

He moved with his assault rifle at the ready, stock cradled against shoulder, eye lined up along the sights.

The gun was a modified Colt AR-15 semi-auto, adapted to take 9mm Fraxinus ammo. He trod warily, his trailing foot occupying the spot just vacated by his leading foot. He recalled the house-to-house sweep-and-searches he had carried out in Baghdad and Fallujah, rousting insurgents from their lairs. The trick was to keep your wits about you, never drop your guard, always assume that a hostile lurked round the next corner or behind the next door, and never presume that there was any such thing as a friendly or a noncombatant. Vampires were insurgents, in a way. An enemy within. Ostensibly human but driven by powerful inner impulses that made them alien and unpredictable. Jacobsen felt no sympathy for them, nor even empathy, for all that some of their own genetic material was currently cycling round his body, enhancing him. He had always had the ability not to identify with his foe on any level. Even as a raw recruit, taking part in Operation Desert Storm, he'd understood that there was *us* and *them*, clearly demarcated opposites, and it was a mistake to believe there was any overlap between the two.

He approached a slightly ajar door and nudged it all the way open with the barrel of his gun. A short corridor. A half-dozen more doorways. He tried each in turn. Changing rooms. Restrooms. Broken pipes, shattered basins, partly dismantled toilet stalls. Faint lingering traces of vampire presence. They'd been here but weren't here right now. Elsewhere in the building.

He retraced his steps and moved on.

He couldn't help thinking about the money—the bounty on Redlaw's head. It was a breathtaking figure. Hard *not* to think about. His service pension was decent but barely kept level with the soaring cost of living.

That $150K, on top of the other sums he was earning as Red Eye leader, promised him a more comfortable future than he could ever have imagined. His sister lived in Florida, just outside Boca Raton. Her husband ran a boat charter firm down there, based in Pompano Beach, and was doing well for himself, taking tourists out whale watching and sports fishing. Several times he'd invited Jacobsen to go into partnership with him. He was looking for someone willing to invest a little capital in the company so that he could expand and diversify further. Despite the economic downturn it seemed like a good bet, and Jacobsen was jealous of his brother-in-law's lifestyle. Not just the income, but the pleasure of sun-kissed days out on the ocean waves, cruising the Keys, cold beers in the fridge, tourist-friendly business hours. Idyllic, it seemed. Hardly work at all.

And maybe he could persuade Berger to join him there. He didn't know if what he and she were having was just an office romance or something more. Possibly it would sputter out as soon as the Red Eye job was done. They would go their separate ways, fun while it lasted, over now, no harm no foul. But he kind of liked the idea of carrying it on with her. Berger was smart and feisty and took no shit from anyone. Great in the sack, too. Best he'd ever had. Him and Jeanette Berger, in Florida, together in a beachfront apartment, living the good life...

Focus, said a voice in his head. It sounded a lot like his one-time drill instructor at Fort Benning, chewing out the cadets. *Head out of ass!*

Jacobsen neared another door. There was a strong whiff of vampire emanating from behind it. He snicked off the safety on the AR-15 and caressed the trigger with his index finger. He reached out with his other hand and depressed the door's lever handle, gently, slowly.

Acquire targets. Assess individual threat levels. Eliminate highest-value opponents first.

The door swung inward.

In the centre of the room there were the embers of a dying fire, glowing fitfully.

Beside the fire knelt a child. A girl. She looked to be no older than nine or ten. She was a cute thing. In her hands was a teddy bear and she was tugging affectionately at one of its tufty little ears.

She turned and looked up at Jacobsen. Unafraid.

"Mister?" she lisped. She held out the bear. "This is Jingle Ted. Do you want to play with him?"

Jacobsen knew she was a vampire. *Knew*. And he knew he was going to pump her full of Fraxinus rounds. He had to.

But for a fraction of a second, he hesitated.

A girl.

Just a kid.

Even in Iraq, you didn't shoot kids. You had orders to—anyone, any age, could be a suicide bomber—but you didn't.

A fraction of a second.

Then something hit him from the side, with sufficient force to knock him off his feet. He fired his rifle, a triple burst, but the shots went wild, raking the ceiling. Hands grabbed him. The gun was wrenched from his grasp. He became the nucleus for a frenzy of heavy hammering punches. Then the butt of a handgun loomed in his vision, swinging towards him.

The black-and-white world went purely black.

CHAPTER TWENTY

SOME TIME LATER, the soldier came to.

He was bound tightly. Redlaw had made sure of that. Chains, ropes, lengths of copper cable, whatever could be scavenged from the factory site, all wrapped round his body and secured without an inch of slack, virtually mummifying him. No chances were being taken.

The body armour and weapons lay in a pile nearby. The soldier had only his battle fatigues on. No boots or gloves.

Redlaw watched him struggle against his bonds, applying all his considerable strength. Finally the soldier seemed to accept that it was futile. He was helpless. Trussed up and going nowhere.

"Neat trick with that vampire kid," he said to Redlaw. "You got me, all right. I should have blown her away the moment I set eyes on her. Wish I had now. Then you'd never have all been able to rush me."

Cindy Newton hugged Jingle Ted to her stomach

and swung her hips from side to side, looking coy but pleased with herself. Andy Gregg slipped a protective arm around her and planted a proud paternal kiss on the crown of her head.

"Cindy did well," said Redlaw. "She was very brave, agreeing to act as a decoy. Child vampires can be... problematic, even for the most hard-hearted of us. Not easy to reconcile what they are with what they appear to be. I know that from experience. Now, questions. Who are you? Who are you with? My guess is, not the regular army. You people are some sort of non-official paramilitary force. Supremacists, perhaps? Right-wing extremists?"

"Shows how ignorant you are, dickwad."

"But there's also the vampiric aspect to consider," Redlaw went on, unfazed. "You're not human, not as such. A kind of hybrid. Someone's been tampering. I suppose it was inevitable."

"I'm not telling you jack-shit," the soldier said. "You better go ahead and shoot me now. It'll save you time. I'm not going to beg for my life or spill the beans or any of that shit. You've caught yourself the wrong trooper if that's your game."

"Really?" Redlaw turned to two of the vampires beside him. "Miguel? Denzel? Let's take the gentleman outside, shall we? See if we can't make him reconsider."

The two vampires grabbed the soldier by the feet and hauled him like a sack of coal out through a doorway into the night.

Only it wasn't night, not quite, not any more. The snow was still bucketing down but, to the east, the sky was brightening. There was a crack in the darkness, clay-grey light peeking through.

The soldier flinched at the sight of this. Just a tiny bit, but enough to tell Redlaw that his conjecture was correct. The soldier shared the Sunless's inherent antipathy to the sun.

Miguel and Denzel hurried back indoors to safety, leaving Redlaw alone with the soldier.

"Dawn's coming," Redlaw said. "Five minutes, ten at most, the sun'll be breaking the horizon. Even through the overcast, its rays will reach us. I won't feel a thing. I wonder if you can say the same."

The soldier's mouth tightened. "I've been looking a little pasty lately. Could do with getting some colour in my cheeks."

"I suspect it's more than colour you'll be getting. Do you really want it to end like this? I've no desire to see you suffer. I just want some answers."

"This is bullshit," said the soldier. "You Limeys don't have the balls for this type of thing. America's always had to keep coming over and saving you guys' asses when you get into a jam. You don't have what it takes to get the job done. You're a pissant little nation that can't get over the fact that it doesn't have an empire any more and lives with its head up its queen's skirts, sniffing her butthole like a dog."

"What a charming image," said Redlaw. "But you'll have to try harder than that to antagonise me."

"Who's antagonising? I'm just telling you stuff. A few home truths. If you choose to be antagonised, that's your lookout."

"The bravado is impressive. But this isn't just any old 'Limey' you're talking to. Where I come from, I have a reputation."

"Yeah, as some kind of limp-dick faggot, no doubt."

"As a man who doesn't mess about or compromise," said Redlaw. "Look into my eyes. Look deep. Do you see someone who's bothered about leaving you out here when the sun comes up? I'm perfectly happy to stand back and watch you burn. You kill vampires. You kill them systematically and ruthlessly. That's a crime, in my book, and I see no reason why it should go unpunished."

"Yeah? You love the bloodsuckers that much?"

"Whether I love them or not, they're God's creatures as much as you or I, and they don't deserve to be treated as subhuman. No one does."

"So you're a radical Christian wingnut. Woo-hoo. Good for you."

"Just tell me who's paying you to do all this. Somebody must be."

"You don't reckon I'm in it simply for the fun of it?"

"No, I do not," Redlaw stated firmly. "That equipment of yours can't come cheap. Not to mention whatever's been done to you to make you part-vampire—someone poured funds into the research and development on that. This is an extensive, well-bankrolled operation, and you don't strike me as a man who renders his services for free. You don't have the look of an ideology-driven fanatic. Just a worker on a wage."

The brightness in the east was silvery now. The soldier blinked snowflakes out of his eyes. Redlaw could tell he was doing his best not to look towards the dawn. He didn't want to know how much longer he had.

"Why did you come here alone?" Redlaw continued, trying another tack. "Why not with the others? A little freelancing on the side perhaps? Bet you're regretting it now. You thought it would be straightforward. You were overconfident. Vampires are so disorganised, aren't they? Not prone to co-operating with one another. Pick them off one by one. Easy meat. I know the score. But all it takes is somebody to give them a little direction, and that's when a group of them can become a force to be reckoned with. You weren't anticipating that, and hence your downfall."

"Oh, just fuck you, buddy," the soldier snapped. "Fuck. You."

"Do you owe your employers, whoever they are, this much loyalty? Are you really prepared to give your life for them? I doubt they would ever return the favour, if the roles were reversed. You're disposable. One of your teammates died in the sewers, and if your superiors are mourning his loss I'd be astonished. You're nothing but robots in uniform to them, machines that do their bidding, and should one of you get broken, oh, well, never mind, they can always find anoth—"

"For crying out loud!" the soldier butted in. "I'd rather burn than have to listen to you jabbering on for another minute with that stupid accent of yours. Aren't you sick of talking yet?"

"I'll tell you what I'm sick of," Redlaw said, leaning over the man. "I'm sick of people like you and your employers treating vampires as if they're of no account. Just murdering them and thinking it's okay. It's *not* okay, and I'm here to make sure that point gets across."

He spun on his heel. Daylight was sneaking across the waste ground that surrounded the factory, creeping fingers of dull light reaching towards the soldier. The man was obstinate. Redlaw knew his sort. He'd met plenty of them during his days as a copper, before he joined SHADE. Crooks who wouldn't give up the tiniest scrap of information, anything that might incriminate them or their associates. However hard you sweated them, however doggedly persistent you were in the interview room, they clammed up and stayed that way right to the bitter end. All you could do was walk away and hope that, at the last moment, they would crack. They seldom did.

The daylight touched the soldier.

"You bastard!" he yelled out at Redlaw. "You goddamn bastard! Whatever you do to me, my team will do back to you tenfold. That's a promise. You will not get away with this. You hear me, Redlaw, you fuck? You hear? You're a dead man."

Redlaw turned, frowning. "How come you know my name? I never introduced myself."

"Oh, I know who you are," the soldier said. "I know who you've pissed off, too. It's the kind of guy who doesn't let things lie. The kind to hold a grudge. He's got a real hard-on for you."

"Name?"

"He's called Your Mother Is A Syphilitic Whore."

"Give me his name and I'll pull you inside, into the building," Redlaw said.

The soldier's face had begun to redden. At first Redlaw thought this was from the effort of shouting, but then he realised it was inflammation. Sunburn.

So the soldier wasn't vampire enough that the sun's rays would destroy him in a matter of seconds.

They were going to cook him instead. Slowly.

"Do you honestly want this?" he said. "To be roasted alive like a joint of beef? Is that how you want to die?"

"I'm not... giving you... anything," the soldier gasped. The red deepened, flaring to an angry carmine colour.

Blisters popped up on his face, and flakes of skin began to peel away.

"Give me a name," Redlaw insisted. "I can stop this before it goes too far. Just tell me who has a grudge against me."

"No," the soldier rasped. The blisters were multiplying. His hands were starting to singe.

"What you're going through, it must be excruciating. Let me end it before it gets any worse."

"No," the soldier repeated.

"Your funeral," said Redlaw, and he turned again and carried on walking back towards the factory, and behind him the soldier began to howl and then to scream.

Tina was in the doorway, camcorder in hand. Her face was ashen and her body was shaking—but she was filming.

"Are you sure you want to be doing that?" Redlaw asked as he passed her.

"No," she replied. "Are you sure you want to leave that man out there?"

"Don't."

"Don't what?"

"Feel sorry for him. He wouldn't hesitate to do as bad or worse to me, or to you."

"You're a cold son of a bitch, Redlaw," Tina said.

"Did you not know that about me already?"

"I do now."

And still the soldier screamed, as smoke rose off him and patches of black charring spread like clouds over his exposed skin.

And still, for all her qualms and squeamishness, Tina kept filming.

And Redlaw strode on, further into the shadows of the factory.

CHAPTER
TWENTY-ONE

AMONG THE ITEMS removed from the soldier while he'd lain unconscious was a phone. Redlaw turned it on. Outside, the screams were ebbing, quietening, breaking down into sporadic whimpers and sobs.

That method of interrogation had yielded some small dividend. The phone presented another possible channel of enquiry.

Redlaw scrolled through the contacts list. It wasn't extensive, just a handful of names, a bank, a telecoms service provider, a pizza delivery company. He checked the call history. The most recent incoming call had been at 2.07AM and had lasted a couple of minutes. The caller was registered only by his or her number.

A conversation of reasonable length, at that hour of the morning, had to be significant.

Redlaw thumbed the button to dial the number back.

Ten rings, and at last a thick, sleepy voice answered.

"Colonel. Is it done? Tell me it's done."

"Who am I talking to?" Redlaw said.

The voice sharpened. "Who the hell is this? That's not Jacobsen. Why are you using Jacobsen's...?" Then indignation faded to something cooler. "John Redlaw. It's you, isn't it? And Jacobsen..."

"Your friend Jacobsen is out catching some sun."

The man on the other end of the line laughed hollowly. "Oh, very good. You got the drop on him, then."

"He made it easy, coming on his own. That was very arrogant, sending just one of your men after me. Insulting, too."

"I was making the best of a bad situation. The colonel wanted you all for himself. I couldn't dissuade him, so I let him go ahead and hoped it'd bear fruit."

"Which it didn't," said Redlaw.

"Obviously."

"So I'll ask again. Who are you? I don't recognise the voice. The accent is... Boston, yes? But beyond that, I don't know anything about you, while you, for your part, appear to be waging some sort of personal vendetta against me. Seems a little lopsided, that state of affairs."

"You really have no idea who you're talking with?"

"I hope that's a rhetorical question, because that's exactly what I just said."

The man laughed again, genuinely amused this time. "Well then, you're at a serious disadvantage, aren't you? Seeing as how I know plenty about *you*."

"Perhaps I am at a disadvantage," said Redlaw. "Then again, perhaps not. I'm sure I'm right in thinking you're the one who's calling the shots round here. These vampire-assassinating soldiers are on your payroll. I'm also sure, based on the conversation we've had thus far, that you don't work on anyone's behalf but your own. You're not affiliated to any arm of the US administration or security services. You're an independent, private individual. And wealthy. Ultra-wealthy, in fact."

"You can tell all that just from my voice?"

"Voice, mannerisms, vocabulary, haughty air... And your last response confirmed it. You didn't deny anything, meaning I nailed you."

"How smart you are," said the other, a touch bitterly.

"Wasn't difficult. I've met your type before. The breed is the same the world over. Billionaire bullyboys who go round kicking the little people out of the way or buying them up like commodities. You're easy to spot."

"Ooh, you wound me, Redlaw," the man deadpanned. "I'm hurt. Really I am. 'Billionaire bullyboy.' You've hit my guilt button. In fact, I feel so bad about myself now, I'm going to give away all my material possessions and go work with underprivileged kids for the rest of my days."

Redlaw rode over the sarcasm with a weary sigh. "I had a run-in with someone like you not so long ago. He came off worse. Maybe you've heard of him. You're all members of the same special club, aren't you? You all move in the same rarefied circles. The name was Lambourne. Nathaniel Lambourne. Ring any bells?"

"Nice, Redlaw," said the other. "Well played. Waiting to see how I react when you mention him."

"A colleague of yours, then. No. More than that. A friend."

"We were close, you could say."

"Ah. Now things are starting to make sense. Why you hate me so much. Why you're gunning for me. So let me think. I'm not so conceited as to assume that these attacks on vampires have been a lure all along, designed specifically to get me across the Atlantic so that you could have me killed. That would be an unreliable and inefficient method of taking revenge. Why go to so much trouble when you could simply pay to have me bumped off in my homeland by a professional hitman? However, since I do happen to be over here and involved with the vampires you're busily trying to exterminate, it's a happy coincidence for you, isn't it? Two birds with one stone. Serendipity."

"'Luck of the loaded' is how I prefer to look at it. I've found that the more prosperous and influential you are, the more fate seems to go your way. It's like some sort of immutable law of nature."

"So come on, tell me your name," Redlaw chided. "It's not as if I can't find out for myself. Given what I know about you now—status, place of birth, connection to Lambourne—I could trawl the internet and establish your identity within quarter of an hour. Save me the time and effort. Do me a favour."

"The only favour I'm going to do you, Redlaw, is killing you," came the reply. "I've got more soldiers. I can keep sending them at you until you're well and truly dead."

"Then do. Try. Maybe you'll succeed. But shouldn't I at least know who it is I've mortally offended? Don't you want me to hear it from your own lips? Wouldn't that be much more satisfying than leaving me to dig it up from some website?"

Thin-skinned. Narcissistic. Autocratic. Pride easily pricked. In a short space of time Redlaw had built up a fairly detailed impression of his interlocutor. If he'd gauged this right...

"J. Howard Farthingale the Third," the man said.

Bingo. There we are.

"And know this, John Redlaw," J. Howard Farthingale III went on. "You have less than twenty-four hours to live. I swear it. If one of my people can find you, so can others. Make your peace with God, because you're going to be meeting Him very soon."

"When God and I do meet," Redlaw replied equably, "we're going to have words, believe you me. And if it's today, then so much the worse for Him, because I have several major bones to pick with Him. But I'm not counting on it, and if I were you I wouldn't count on it either. I'm surprisingly hard to kill. The Lord, for reasons of His own, made me that way."

"We'll see about that, Mr Redlaw," said Farthingale. "We'll just see."

The line went dead.

Redlaw's first instinct was to destroy the phone, so that its GPS signal couldn't be used to triangulate his whereabouts. There seemed little point, however, since Farthingale's soldiers already seemed to have no difficulty locating vampires. Besides, it might be useful to have a hotline to the enemy. He closed the phone and stuffed it in his pocket, then set his mind to pondering his next move.

CHAPTER
TWENTY-TWO

WE'LL SEE ABOUT that, Mr Redlaw. We'll just see.

Even as he broke the connection, Farthingale couldn't tell if it was a strong parting shot or a weak one. He was rattled. Off his game. Who the hell did Redlaw think he was? Jumped-up little British turd. A no-account nonentity from a has-been nation. The nerve of him, to talk like that to J. Howard Farthingale III, an American titan, a master of the universe. The sheer fucking temerity.

Farthingale sat up, mulberry silk pyjamas whispering against 1,000-thread-count Egyptian cotton bed-linen. He hit a button on the nightstand to open the drapes. Snow was plummeting from a smudged-charcoal sky. Deep drifts had built up overnight against the sides of Far Tintagel. The house's low-lying single-storey sections were almost entirely buried. Several of the pines were engulfed up to their topmost branches. The reach between the island and the mainland was a seamless tract of white.

Farthingale had been planning on travelling to New York today in order to supervise Team Red Eye's operations first hand. His private helicopter, a Bell 222, was stationed at Boston's City Heliport and could ferry him to the Midtown Skyport on Manhattan in under ninety minutes. But no sane pilot would fly in conditions like these.

He was housebound. Snowbound.

Frustrating though that might be, at least he wasn't completely cut off. His office was the hub from which he conducted most of his business. Like a spider at the centre of its web, Farthingale didn't have to move to know what was going on at any time in any corner of his empire. Strands of communication radiated out from his desk, his computer, his phone, and he was sensitively attuned to the data that came tingling along them. As long as he remained vigilant and in touch, nothing happened that he could not control or act upon.

His phone bleeped. Redlaw again?

No.

The call originated from *that* number, perhaps the most important of all the numbers logged in the phone's memory.

"Farthingale," said the President. "I'll get straight to the point. This ends now."

"Sir?"

"You heard me. Don't act all innocent. This bullshit you're pulling. Automatic weapons being discharged in residential Manhattan? In the heart of goddamn New York? No way, buster. It's over. You pull the plug on the whole shebang, right now, today. That isn't a suggestion, it's an order. Straight from the Oval Office."

"Sir, if I can just say—"

"No, you cannot 'just say,' Farthingale. Do you have any idea how angry I am? Can you hear it in my voice? You've been trying to provoke a response out of me. Well, here it is. I do not want your semi-vampiric soldiers. The Joint Chiefs of Staff do not want your semi-vampiric soldiers. The Pentagon and the DoD and Homeland Security and, I don't know, probably the State Department for Agriculture too, do not want your semi-vampiric soldiers. No one does. Or ever will. Because, you see, you've pushed me and you've prodded me and you've goaded me, and I do not like being pushed, prodded and goaded. I do not care for it. I do not react kindly to it at all. You've pissed off the wrong man, you entitled, old-money prick."

"But have you really thought about this, Mr President?" Farthingale said. "Thought it through? Never mind the potential for dealing with vampire immigration. What about the military applications of the Porphyrian Project? I'm offering you super-soldiers. Stronger, more resilient, less vulnerable to harm, with a broadened spectrum of senses... Surely that's a commander-in-chief's wet dream. Think if you had crack units of Porphyrian-enhanced operatives working undercover in hostile nations. Think of the antiterrorist coups you could pull off, the regime changes you could effect, the anti-American dictators you could topple. A whole battalion of treated troops would be unstoppable."

"No, Farthingale," the President said. "I'm not buying it. You are conducting criminal activities on US soil."

"I've told you, they're field-tests."

"Your people shot up a church last night, for God's sake."

"A deconsecrated church full of vampires."

"You're off the rails and flouting at least a hundred federal laws. I could have you arrested and sent to Guantanamo. I should. But because I'm a lenient man at heart, and because I appreciate that all you've been doing is trying to impress me, which is sort of sweet, I'm going to let you have this one last hurrah. The church, I'm referring to. I will—reluctantly—put procedures in place to hush it up. We can get the FBI to claim it was infighting between rival vampire factions, like a gang-on-gang drive-by shooting. That should fly. People'll rest a little easier in their beds knowing that vamps kill their own."

He sounded very pleased with this piece of extemporising.

"But that's it now," he went on, stern again. "My last indulgence to you. No more. You shut the project down and you shut it down tight."

"And what if there are foreign powers out there who'd be interested in my process?" said Farthingale. "Governments less scrupulous and sensitive? We live in a globalised economy. What's to stop me tendering Porphyrian out to the highest bidder?"

"I would advise strongly against such a course of action," said the President, deadly earnest. "Not unless you're really keen to swap those bespoke Armani two-pieces for an orange jumpsuit—forever."

"You'd infringe my right to trade freely on the international market?"

"Yes, as long as you're infringing my right to drink my morning coffee without suffering acid reflux. I've made my feelings clear, Farthingale. I can't put it any more plainly than this. Porphyrian is over. Go off and make a whole load more millions some other way. Do you understand?"

"Yes, Mr President."

"Oh, and Farthingale?"

"Yes?"

"Lose this number. You ever call me on it again, you'll be on a plane to Cuba so fast your feet won't even touch the ground."

Farthingale stared at the phone's screen, which read *Call Ended*. His knuckles whitened. He hurled the phone across the room. It collided with the walnut vanity unit, rebounded and fell to the floor. Somehow, miraculously, it remained intact. He went over to pick it up and try smashing it again.

Before he could, the door opened and in walked Clara. She was wearing her Felix Fanger pyjamas, which Farthingale had commissioned to be made specially for her, since the Transylvanian Families clothing line did not normally cater for the adult market. The fabric had repeating patterns of Felix Fanger himself interspersed with his catchphrase.

"Morning, Howie!" Clara cried merrily. "Have you seen how much snow there is outside? We can make the most massivest snowman ever! He could be a giant, like a hundred feet tall."

A wave of blind fury overcame Farthingale. Rounding on Clara, he roared, "Get out! Get the fuck out!"

His sister recoiled as though he had slapped her. "Howie...?"

"What part of 'get out' do you not understand?"

Clara's lower lip began to tremble.

"You fucking freak!" Spittle flew from Farthingale's mouth. He swatted at her. "You monstrous obese

Mongoloid! I'm not building any snowman with you, not even a 'most massivest' one. God, you're such an imbecile you can't even speak English properly. Go on, get the fuck out of my sight. I can't bear to look at you. Makes me sick to think I'm even related to you."

Tears spilled from Clara's eyes. She retreated from the room, bent and sobbing, and fled down the corridor. After a moment's hesitation, Farthingale went after her, flooded with remorse. Clara ran fast, but he had a fair idea where she would be heading. So did Rozetta, who had overheard the altercation from her bedroom and emerged in nightgown and slippers to see what she could do to assist. Together, Farthingale and the Filipina nurse chased after Clara to the safe room.

The safe room lay at almost the exact heart of the house, more or less equidistant from the furthermost point of every wing and floor. It had ventilation, phone lines, toilet facilities, enough food and water to last three people a week, and a secret compartment containing a million dollars' worth of American Gold Eagle coins, just in case. The walls were foot-thick concrete and the door was Kevlar-impregnated with reinforced hinges and lock plate. The room could, the architect claimed, withstand hurricane, terrorist attack, and brute-force entry attempt by burglar.

Opening up the safe room was a simple matter of slapping a pressure switch mounted on the wall outside. At one time, sealing yourself inside it used to be equally straightforward. Then one day Clara, mid-tantrum, had shut herself in the safe room and refused to budge. For two hours Farthingale and Rozetta had tried to winkle her out. It had taken the promise of heaps of candy, a spending spree at FAO Schwarz, and, ultimately, a trip to Disneyworld, before she finally consented to hit the door release switch. Since then, in order to avoid a repeat incident, Farthingale had had an alphanumeric keypad installed inside the room, operable by a code sequence only he knew.

Sure enough, Clara was sequestered inside the safe room now, curled up on the floor next to a stack of bottled water.

"Clara..." Farthingale began.

"Nooooo!" Clara screeched. She covered her ears.

"Clara, listen to me. Please. I don't know what came over me. I was up late and haven't slept well, and my ITP, my condition, it makes me tetchy sometimes, you know that. Howie Goat Gruff, remember? That's who I am when I'm in a bad mood. I shouldn't have said what I said. I'm under a lot of pressure. Work, that sort of thing. You understand?"

"Do you hear what Howie's saying, honey?" said Rozetta. "He's telling you he's sorry for what he did."

"Don't care," Clara snapped. "He called me horrid names. He tried to hit me. He said I'm a monster. I'm not a monster. *He's* the monster."

"I'm sure he didn't mean it," said Rozetta. "How about I make you a nice breakfast? Freshly cooked pancakes with syrup and Lucky Charms on top. Your favourite. How about that?"

But Clara just wailed with anguish, inconsolable.

"Clara," said Farthingale sternly, taking a step across the safe room threshold. "Really, that's quite enough."

Clara lashed out at him with her foot. Farthingale clenched a fist, and might well have used it had not Rozetta intervened. Pushing him gently aside, the nurse knelt down beside Clara and enveloped her in a hug. Clara buried her face in Rozetta's nightgown and howled as though her heart was breaking.

Rozetta made a gesture to Farthingale that was both reassuring and dismissive. *I've got this. You go. Nothing you can do right now.*

Reluctantly, Farthingale withdrew.

MINUTES PASSED IN the safe room. Then Clara looked up at Rozetta with a tear-streaked face and said, "Howie doesn't love me."

Rozetta replied, "He loves you very much, Clara."

"But he was so mean to me."

"People do mean things when they're upset or angry. But not on purpose."

"Yeah, but lately he's been acting so weird. What's wrong with him? Is it his blood thing? Is it getting worse?"

"I don't know, honey. I don't think so."

But what Rozetta had noticed was that her employer was spending significantly more time at Far Tintagel these days than he ever used to. It wasn't that he had become a recluse, exactly, but he was definitely not travelling as much as he had done before his ITP diagnosis. He was visiting his offices in Boston and New York far less often, and business trips abroad were almost a thing of the past. He conducted most of his work electronically.

It was as if Mr Farthingale didn't feel safe out there in the big wide world any more, knowing that a blow to the head might lead to a fatal brain haemorrhage or an accidental gash might cause him to bleed to death. On the island there was less chance of anything like that occurring, so here, as much as possible, he stayed.

His home had become something like a prison. And that, surely, could not be good for the balance of a man's sanity.

"The main thing," she said to Clara, "is that you can find it in your heart to forgive him when he hurts your feelings. Do you think you can forgive Howie, Clara?"

Clara sniffed a gelatinous frill of mucus back up into her nose. "I don't know. I think so. Maybe."

"Good girl."

But Clara's blue-green eyes were hard. "I only said maybe."

CHAPTER
TWENTY-THREE

"WE CAN'T STAY here," Redlaw told the assembled vampires and Tina. "That much is obvious. The factory's not safe any more. We need to find somewhere else."

"But where?" asked Patti Marsden. A panicky hand clutched her *Hi! I'm PATTI* badge as though it were some kind of religious talisman. "Where are we going to go?"

"And how?" added Anu Ahmed. "We can't just walk out. Not until nightfall."

"True," said Redlaw. "And we may not even have until nightfall. Sunlight poses a threat to our attackers, but not to the same extent that it does to true Sunless like you. That man out there has only been burned where his skin is directly exposed. Covered up from head to foot, he'd be fine. So it mightn't be long at all before the rest of his comrades come after us."

"What about the subway tunnels?" said Denzel Lomax. "They're right below our feet."

"How are you proposing to get to them? Dig?"

"Uh, no. I just thought..."

"Transportation. That's what we need. Some sort of vehicle we can all fit in. Getting out of Manhattan is paramount. This city's too small, too crowded, too confined. We're too easily found here. Anyone know where we could find such a vehicle? I'm open to suggestions. Tina? Anyone?"

Shrugs. Blank looks.

"You talking about a van, a panel truck, an RV, something like that?" said Anu.

"Yes."

"Going out and boosting one?"

"Borrowing," said Redlaw.

Miguel raised a hand. "I think I might have an idea."

"Go ahead."

"Well, you see, I used to be a bus driver. School buses."

"I like the sound of this already."

"I'm guessing there's no school today. Snow day. So the entire bus fleet will be sitting doing nothing at the depot."

"And where is the depot?"

"My runs were around Hamilton Heights, way uptown, and I'd pick up my designated ride from a place just off the Henry Hudson Parkway. But there's one nearer than that, in the Meatpacking District, around the Gansevoort and Washington intersection, near that park they made on the old elevated rail track, the High Line."

"How far?"

"Not very. A mile, as the crow flies. Reckon an hour on foot, allowing for the snow."

"And what's the security like there?"

"If it's anything like uptown, then minimal," said Miguel. "Wire fence. Supervisor in a hut. Maybe not even that, today. If drivers aren't going to turn up, neither's he going to turn up."

"And where would I find the keys to one of the buses?"

"Inside the hut. It's not what you'd call a sophisticated operation. Department of Education doesn't go in for infrared alarm systems and such. Hasn't got the budget, and anyway a school bus isn't high on anyone's list when it comes to grand theft auto."

"And actually driving one? Is it hard? Anything I should know?"

"Nothing to it. They don't exactly turn on a dime, and the gear ratios are for shit, but apart from that it's straightforward enough. Temperatures like these, you'll probably want to let her idle for a few minutes before moving off. If the engine isn't warm she'll stall on you every couple of hundred yards."

"Thanks, Miguel," said Redlaw. "Can you draw me a map? Quickest route to this Meatpacking District?"

"I've got a better idea," said Tina. "I'll take you there myself."

"Okay."

"But on one condition."

"What?"

"I'm starving. Haven't eaten since I can't remember when. My blood sugar's in the basement. So we stop off on the way for a meal."

"Agreed," said Redlaw. "I could do with a bite myself."

"And, er, speaking of bites..." said Miguel.

"We're hungry too," said Diane Bertorelli.

"Crazy hungry," said Mary-Jo Schaeffer.

"There are pigeons," Redlaw said. "Catch yourselves some."

"There's also the guy." Miguel jerked a thumb. "Out there. Not long dead. We could..."

Redlaw realised they were asking for his consent. And his connivance.

"All right," he said, and headed outside.

The soldier lay twisted within his bonds. His head was a hairless ovoid, hard and black, petrified almost, like a chunk of coal, ears gone, nose a misshapen lump. His hands were brittle and spindly, bone protruding through a thin envelope of charred skin.

Redlaw grabbed him by his stockinged feet, wheeled him round and started lugging him back into the factory.

Halfway there, he detected a low moan.

The soldier's rigid lips had parted. One set of eyelids cracked open to reveal a sliver of white sclera.

Redlaw paused only briefly, then dragged him the rest of the way indoors.

"He's still alive," he said to the vampires. "Somehow. Just. So you make sure you drain him fully. This is one person I do not want coming back."

"Eight empty bellies?" said Miguel. "We're going to drain him, all right."

As Redlaw and Tina prepared to leave, Redlaw said, "We'll only be a couple of hours. Sit tight. Lie low. Be on your guard."

But the vampires paid him little heed. They had already begun loosening the soldier's bonds and tearing off his battle fatigues. Soon, pale flesh was exposed, and the vampires bared their fangs and knelt down and started gnawing holes. As blood welled up they guzzled greedily and gratefully, tongues flicking in and out of the wounds. The soldier's body trembled and shuddered, and something that could have been a groan rattled in his throat.

Tina managed to grab a few seconds of footage of the vampires at their banquet, before Redlaw stuck a hand over the camera lens.

"Aw, come on!"

"No. Give them some privacy," Redlaw said.

"But it's vampires *eating*..."

"Which is something the wider public doesn't want to see."

"You'd be surprised."

"Then it's something I don't want the wider public seeing."

"Hey, this isn't some puff piece I'm putting together, Redlaw," Tina said. "I'm not doing PR for you. I'm out to show it how it is. Vampires in the raw. Red in tooth and claw and all that. Like your Sir David Attenborough and his BBC nature docs. You wouldn't try to censor me if I was him."

"But you aren't. And these aren't animals." Redlaw took her firmly by the elbow. "Now let's go and find ourselves a bus."

CHAPTER
TWENTY-FOUR

UP ON EAST 84th, Team Red Eye's five remaining members sat in stunned, dejected silence.

"So that's the long and the short of it," said the voice on the speakerphone. It was their employer, J. Howard Farthingale III. "The Porphyrian Project is being terminated, effective as of now. I can't say I'm happy about this, and I'm guessing you people won't be either. But it's out of my hands. An authority greater than myself has spoken, and I must obey. We'll begin the process of weaning you off the PP-66 straight away. This means a programme of increasingly weaker doses. That way there's no likelihood of 'cold turkey,' and the physiological side-effects of coming off the formula, if there are any, will be minimised. The techs will give you all the support and assistance they can during the decommissioning process. Our estimate is that within a week to ten days you'll be, for want of a better word, clean, at which point you'll be free to leave. Are there any questions?"

"Yes, sir," said Lieutenant Giacoia. "I have one. Under the circumstances, what's the pay situation?"

"If you check your contracts, you'll find there's a layoff clause. Each of you receives a very generous severance package, amounting to a lump sum in the region of thirty-five thousand dollars apiece, scaled according to rank. Any other questions?"

"Yes," said Abbotts. "What about Larousse? He had an ex-wife and son down in Corpus Christi. The bitch was bleeding him dry with alimony payments but he coughed up 'cause he loved that kid. You going to give them a little extra? Being as how Kyle was KIA and all."

"Private Larousse's relicts will be adequately recompensed for their loss, yes," said Farthingale. "That, too, is in the contract. Is that it? Nothing else?"

Chief Warrant Officer Berger was hunched forwards, intently scraping under the nail of one index finger with the other. Of all the five soldiers seated around the table, she seemed the hardest hit by what Farthingale had had to say.

Scowling, she looked up. "I'd like to get something straight with you, Mr Farthingale," she said.

"Sure."

"Did I hear you right about Colonel Jacobsen? He's dead?"

"I'm afraid that's the only inference I can draw."

"And"—Berger's voice cracked ever so slightly—"he went off chasing after some vampires solo?"

"Correct. I advised him against it, mostly because—"

"Because the vamps in question have a human ally. This Englishman who got Larousse."

"Indeed. And who also got the colonel."

"Then, sir," said Berger, thin-lipped, ice cold, "might

I respectfully ask that we go hunt the bastard down and teach him who he's messing with?"

"You're entitled to ask that," said Farthingale, "and a half-hour ago I'd have said yes, by all means, with my blessing. However, thanks to the aforementioned 'authority greater than myself,' I can't actually allow anything like that any more. Porphyrian is terminated and that's that. Whatever feelings you may have—and believe me, I share them—you cannot act on them on my watch. Payback in your own time, once the PP-66 has been completely flushed out of you and you're no longer in my direct employ, is entirely your own business. If you're willing to wait until then, you'll hear no objections from me. None whatsoever. In fact, I'll be cheering you on. In the meantime, though, you have no alternative but to hold your fire."

"That's it? Your final word on the subject?"

"That's it, Warrant Officer Berger." Farthingale sounded strained. "It's out of my hands. I wish it were otherwise, but it's not. Thank you, all of you, for your service. I have to sign off now. Over and out."

BERGER WAITED FOR the green status light on the speakerphone to wink out.

"Where are you going?" she said to Abbotts, who had risen from his chair.

"Uh, the rec room? I thought we were done here."

"We aren't. Sit down."

Something in her tone made Abbotts retake his seat. Immediately.

"So we're just going to leave it at that, are we?" Berger said. "Suck it up and move on?"

"What do you suggest we do?" said Gunnery Sergeant Child. "Man made it clear. Game over."

"Jacobsen—the colonel—is dead."

"And?"

"He was our commanding officer," said Berger. "This Redlaw person left him out in the daylight to burn. A horrible, undignified death. Does that sit well with any of you?"

Giacoia pulled a face. "It's pretty cold, I got to say. Sounds like the colonel wasn't even given a fighting chance."

"I'm all in favour of a retaliatory strike," said Corporal Lim, rubbing his sore arm. "I liked Jacobsen. I respected him. He didn't deserve to die that way."

"Kyle likewise," said Abbotts. "Poor bastard drowned in sewage."

"But," Lim continued, "whatever we do, it'll have to wait until we're Porphyrian-free."

"Will it?" said Berger.

"You heard the boss."

"I heard him all right. But was I listening? Properly?"

"You're saying we should ignore him," said Child.

"I'm saying if we want to do this thing, and do it right, this is the time. We hang around, Redlaw's long gone. He's in the wind. And a week from now, we'll be just ordinary humans again."

"Speak for yourself," said Child with a smirk. "There ain't nothing ordinary about me."

"You know what I mean. Unenhanced. We'll have lost our boost, our edge. Whereas..." Berger looked at each of the other four in turn. "If we go after Redlaw today, all souped up and at the peak of our abilities, we'll have every chance of catching him and settling accounts."

"Seriously fucking his shit up," said Child.

"Precisely."

"Yeah, but wait one," said Giacoia. "Jacobsen was a good guy and all, and so was Larousse, I guess, but do we have a right to run around whacking someone just because he whacked a couple of ours? I mean, this isn't Iraq or Afghanistan. We're not talking about some rabid towelhead terrorist needs putting down."

"SEALs whacked Osama," Abbotts pointed out. "And the way I remember it, no one cried. Anyone who kills Americans, especially a foreigner, becomes a legitimate target."

"But this is different. Sure, we took some casualties. Isn't that to be expected? Nobody said this would be a risk-free deal. But the campaign's over now, and we've been ordered to stand down."

"By a civilian," said Berger, "who made no bones about the fact that he'd be glad to see Redlaw offed."

"Just so long as it can't be linked directly to him," said Lim.

"And that's another reason to say fuck him," said Berger. "Let's use what we've got, what Farthingale's given us, while we still can. We do it today and we do it right. We honour Jim Jacobsen's memory, and Private Larousse's. One last outing for Team Red Eye. Maybe with an extra dose of PP-66 in our bloodstreams, just to be absolutely sure. Who's with me? Show of hands."

Abbotts's hand went up straight away. Child's and Lim's followed. That left only Giacoia.

"Lieutenant?" said Berger. "You're CO now. You going to lead this mission?"

Giacoia stroked his goatee. He was rather proud of it; it helped compensate for his receding hairline.

"Shit," he sighed. "Yeah, seems like I am."

Berger's eyes gleamed in triumph.

She didn't care which of the five of them would be the one to end Redlaw's life. As long as it happened, and she got to watch.

But if, by chance, she found herself with Redlaw at her mercy—the man who'd killed her lover—she would take her time with him. She would make it nice and slow. There would be ripping, and rending, and tearing, and she would relish every long, drawn-out, blood-soaked minute of it.

CHAPTER
TWENTY-FIVE

PRECIOUS FEW PLACES to eat were open. Eventually Redlaw and Tina found a 24-hour McDonalds where Tina wolfed down two Big Macs in a row, while Redlaw tackled an Egg McMuffin as circumspectly as though it were an unexploded bomb.

Then they resumed their trek northward, heading into the once shunned, now chic environs of the Meatpacking District. On every street, boutiques selling houseware and handicrafts jostled alongside art galleries and trendy antique shops. Tina aspired to live in an area like this, rubbing shoulders with the rich and fashionable. With what was stored in her camcorder, that goal didn't seem nearly as remote as it used to.

Not far from where Miguel had said the school bus depot lay, they passed a stationery store. The proprietor, who lived in the apartment above, was unlocking the door and raising the security shutters as Redlaw and Tina approached. Redlaw greeted her and quickly established that she sold black cartridge paper and rolls of parcel tape. He thrust a wad of dollar bills into Tina's hand.

"What am I supposed to do with this?" Tina asked.

"Buy some of that paper and tape. As much as you can get of both. And scissors."

"What for?"

"Think about it," said Redlaw. "A big vehicle with plenty of windows. Windows that let in daylight."

"Oh?" said Tina, and then, "Ohhh. Yeah. I see."

"Sort that out. Meanwhile, I'll go and procure our transportation."

Procure? Tina thought, then realised the store's proprietor was still in earshot. "Okay. So you don't need my help for that, then?"

"It's better if it's just one of us."

"Because I'd be a liability. Stupid Tina might do something wrong."

"I didn't say that."

"But you're thinking it. I know you, Redlaw."

"No." Redlaw lowered his voice. "I'd just prefer it if I have only myself to watch out for. In case there's trouble."

"Whatever. Off with you," Tina said curtly. "Go do your manly thing. I'll shop. 'Cause that's what girls do, yeah? Shop."

Redlaw was already walking away. "Twenty minutes," he said, without looking round. "I'll pick you up. Be standing there."

"Yes, dearest!" Tina called after him, in her best imitation of an upper-crust British housewife. "You bring the Rolls round, once I've finished in Harrods."

The stationery store proprietor shot her a wry smile.

"We can't help who we fall for, can we?"

Tina rolled her eyes. "Eww. Puh-leeze."

"He's not your...?"

"He's not my anything."

"Oh, God. I'm sorry. I just assumed. The way you two were bickering."

"Like I couldn't do better than Herman Munster there."

"But that accent of his," the proprietor gushed. She was the kind of plump, hippyish woman who seemed born to wear purple. "It's to die for."

"Believe me, lady, you think the British are all cucumber sandwiches and garden parties with Her Majesty? They're not. If *he's* anything to go by, they're the maddest bunch of motherfuckers on the planet. Now, am I buying stuff off of you or not?"

"Of course. Come on in."

But once inside the shop, a thought struck Tina. Twenty minutes. That was just about enough time.

"Excuse me," she said to the proprietor, "is there a restroom I could use?"

"Sure. Through that door, in back. You want I should start fetching out that paper and tape for you in the meantime?"

"That'd be great."

TINA SAT ON the toilet seat lid, camcorder in one hand, BlackBerry in the other, the two devices linked by a USB cable. Using the Media Sync app, she imported data from the camera memory to the BlackBerry and converted the H.264-format files to mpegs. These she uploaded onto her website via email. She subtitled each clip "Raw Footage, Awaiting Edit and Commentary," then composed a brief post to introduce them:

New to Tick Talk—Vampires of Manhattan

This is some truly cool stuff, straight out of my camera. Check the date stamp. You won't believe what you're seeing, but it's 100% genuine!

She clicked the Publish button and sat back with a sharp exhalation, almost a gasp of relief, as though she'd just given birth.

She couldn't possibly have held on to the vampire footage a moment longer. It was just too big, too important, too damn shit-hot. It demanded to be shared. Never mind that she'd made a pact with Redlaw not to release a single frame into cyberspace until after he was finished with his business in New York. How much longer were he and she going to be sticking together anyway? Not long. He'd probably never find out that she'd jumped the gun. He was mono-focused on getting his troupe of vampires to safety. So what harm could it do, Tina starting out on her road to fame and fortune a little ahead of schedule?

She returned to the main part of the shop, where the proprietor was busy bagging up several dozen huge rolls of cartridge paper and a stack of parcel tape.

"There you are," she said to Tina. "That's everything I've got. You've cleaned me out. I hope it'll be enough for whatever you're planning to do."

Tina shoved some of Redlaw's money onto the counter and went outside with her purchases. She checked her watch.

Twenty-five minutes since she last saw Redlaw.

Twenty-six.

She started stamping her feet to stay warm.

He was running late. What the hell was he up to? What was keeping him?

CHAPTER
TWENTY-SIX

REDLAW COUNTED AT least fifty of the yellow school buses, slotted tightly together in the parking lot like pieces of some giant puzzle. All of them wore thick berets of snow.

The fence was easy enough to scale. Chainlink was an odd kind of barrier, in that it provided so many handholds and toeholds for the determined climber to use. Self-defeating, in a way.

Barbed wire was strung along the top, but it had been applied economically, a single strand wreathed round and round the crossbar. Redlaw was able to grasp it with his gloved hands, straddle over and drop down the other side, without snagging his clothes or pricking himself.

The snow cushioned his landing, sparing his knees. Small mercies.

He padded over to the guard's hut, an aluminium-sided static trailer, and stood on tiptoe to peep through a window. No one inside. As Miguel had predicted, the guard wasn't clocking on for duty today because nobody else was.

Dozens of sets of keys hung on a rack in the hut. Redlaw cast around for something he could force the door with, a length of rebar maybe.

That was when his gaze alighted on a kennel, nestled nearby between two rows of buses.

A large kennel. With the name Zoltan painted over the entrance.

A large, *empty* kennel.

He heard the dog coming at the last possible moment. It had sneaked round behind him. It didn't bark, but its paws crunched heavily on the snow as it stopped stalking him and broke into a run.

Redlaw whirled round to face it. The dog was a huge beast, a bull mastiff. Its jowly mouth hung wide open, its teeth were fearsome, and its bloodshot eyes bore a cruel, murderous glint.

In a flash Redlaw recalled a training module at Hendon: what to do when confronted by a dangerous dog. It was thirty years ago, when he'd been a naïve young police cadet, but the techniques he'd been taught came back to him as though it was yesterday.

Zoltan the mastiff sprang.

Redlaw's left arm came up horizontally.

Better your arm than your throat. That was what the instructor, a K9 handler, had said. *You can afford to lose a hand, but not a windpipe.*

The mastiff's jaws latched on to his forearm. The thick lining of the army-surplus parka saved him from severe injury. The pressure of the bite was intolerable, almost literally like having his arm gripped in a workbench vice, and he felt teeth break his skin, but he knew the dog was capable of much worse. He'd got off lightly so far.

A surge of adrenaline made Redlaw see everything with precision. Every move he must now make was mapped out in detail in his head, a checklist for survival. Get one step wrong and the mastiff would make him pay for it, dearly.

The mastiff dragged down on his arm, trying to bring him to its own level. Redlaw hauled up against its immense weight. The thing was far stronger than him, but if he kept it up on its hindlegs it would be off-balance and unable to utilise that strength against him.

He stuck out his right thumb, rigid, and without hesitation jabbed it into the mastiff's left eye. He felt a strange kind of clinical detachment as he wormed his thumb deep into the eye socket and twisted it to lever out the eyeball. The jelly-like orb came free with a wet sucking *pop*, trailing nerve tissue and gristle behind it.

Zoltan the mastiff let out a piteous howl, and all at once Redlaw's arm was released. The dog reared back, whimpering and shaking its head. The eyeball, still attached, flopped this way and that. Gore striped the snow.

By rights, that should have been that. The shock of having its eye enucleated was supposed to render the mastiff helpless, sending its nervous system into shutdown. The dog might even have a heart attack and die.

Either the bull mastiff didn't know that, or it was made of far sterner stuff than the average hound.

Recovering its wits, it gave a baleful growl. Its remaining good eye fixed Redlaw with a look of sheer Satanic loathing.

Then the mastiff launched itself at him again.

If all else fails, the dangerous dogs module instructor had said, *you need to choke the animal. If it's large enough, the best way is this...* And he had demonstrated the method on a dummy dog, and when all the cadets, including Redlaw, had grimaced, he had said, *Trust me, you won't think twice when it's your life on the line.*

And Redlaw didn't think twice. He met the leaping mastiff with his left arm outstretched, fingers pinched into a pyramid, and he rammed his hand straight into that slobber-strung, gaping maw.

The mastiff's impetus knocked Redlaw flat, but also impaled it further onto Redlaw's arm, past the wrist, halfway to the elbow. Redlaw balled his hand, deep inside the dog's hot throat, into a fist. The mastiff was on top of him, but his arm was locked tight inside its gullet. Claws scrabbled on his chest. The dog wrenched its head from side to side, trying desperately to dislodge the blockage. Redlaw could feel its muscles straining around his forearm.

Panic lit Zoltan the mastiff's good eye. Its efforts to free itself weakened. Its whole body began to shudder as oxygen deprivation took hold. All at once it keeled over onto its flank, Redlaw's arm still inside. Spasms ran through its body, and its legs kicked and twitched. Finally its eye lost that sinister brilliance and seemed to fog over. The dog's bowels let go, unleashing a torrent of meaty faeces onto the snow. One last mighty muscular heave, and the mastiff lay still.

Redlaw painstakingly extracted his arm from the creature. His parka sleeve was ripped, saliva-sodden, and bloodied, with bits of stuffing poking out all over. Pain began to spark around the bite wounds. His head went woozy. He lay back in the snow and caught his breath and waited for his heart rate to normalise.

"Lord," he said to the skies, "I know it's your habit to test people, to try them in the fires of providence so that they can learn what they're made of and be tempered and become stronger. But this?" He flapped at hand at the dead dog. "On top of everything else? Seriously?"

Answer came there none from the heavens, other than the relentless cold white benediction of snowfall.

THE SEARCH FOR something to jemmy the guard's hut door with proved futile, so Redlaw resorted to breaking one of the windows with the butt of his Cindermaker. He reached through, undid the latch, and slithered inside.

The bus keys were organised according to vehicle size, each with a tag listing a licence plate number. Redlaw reasoned that he didn't need one of the larger-capacity buses when he had only eight passengers, nine if you counted Tina. Also, a smaller bus ought to be easier to drive, and nippier.

Soon he was behind the wheel of a twelve-seater, with the engine juddering and growling and diesel fumes pluming at the rear. The interior smelled of vanilla air freshener and children's sweat.

The depot gate was secured with padlock and chain. Both were more durable than they looked, and it wasn't until the bus had rammed the gate for a third time that they snapped.

When Redlaw rendezvoused with Tina outside the stationery store, he thought she looked disgruntled because he was ten minutes later than promised. But in the event it was the bus itself that offended her.

"The short bus?" she exclaimed as she boarded. "You went and stole the *short bus*?"

"What of it? We don't need one of the bigger ones."

"You have no idea, do you? The short bus is for the special needs kids. The retards and the disabled and the challenged. Did you not notice the wheelchair lift at the back? Nobody in their right mind would be seen dead on the short bus."

"Well, I'm not going back to steal another," Redlaw said. "I had a hard enough time getting this one." He indicated his left arm.

"Holy cow. What a mess. What happened?"

"Let's just say the place had the kind of guard who doesn't take days off."

"Does it hurt? Looks like it does."

"I've had worse." Redlaw winced as he used his left hand to pull the lever that closed the bus doors. Then he stamped on the clutch, ground gears, and drew away from the kerb. "I see you've got all our supplies. Excellent."

"Yeah, don't worry, I made good use of the time," Tina said.

Redlaw was driving an unfamiliar vehicle on the wrong side of a very snowy road, so he was too preoccupied to notice the small, hopeful smile that creased the corners of Tina's mouth as she uttered these words.

CHAPTER
TWENTY-SEVEN

FARTHINGALE BLINKED SLOWLY.

"Run that by me again."

The very frightened Porphyrian technician on the other end of the line swallowed hard, collected himself, and said, "They're gone, sir. And two of us are down. Down as in dead. I... I was one of the lucky ones. I got out in time and I ran and hid and they missed me. But they went crazy. I mean plain fucking bat-shit berserk. It was horrible. A slaughter."

"Be very exact," Farthingale said. "Team Red Eye held you all at gunpoint..."

"Yes, sir." The technician's name was Dale Postma and he was a 26-year-old MIT graduate. "They were kind of nice about it. Polite, almost. At the start. They were all, 'Sorry, guys, but we've got to do this. Co-operate and no one'll get hurt.' They had their gear on, their weapons. We weren't about to argue, not with a bunch of trained, armed killers. We're lab geeks, for Christ's sake. We did as we were told."

"And what they were demanding from you was a fresh dose of PP-66."

"Yeah, and Dr Istamboulian, he said he didn't think that was a good idea so soon after the last dose, and one of the Red Eyes, Abbotts I think it was, he said something like, 'That's not your decision to make, doc,' and threatened to put a bullet in his head. So Istamboulian backed down, because who the hell wouldn't, and we all trooped along to the treatment chamber..."

"Yes, yes," said Farthingale impatiently. "I get it. You dosed them up, like the meek little lambs you are. Then what?"

"We gave them their forty minutes, went back in..."

"You didn't think to contact me during that time? It never once occurred to any of you that it might be worth informing me, your boss, about this unhappy turn of events?"

"We were instructed not to. She said they'd know if we had and we would pay for it. And anyway, we assumed there wouldn't be much you could do about it even if you did know."

"She? Warrant Officer Berger?"

"She was the ringleader, sir," said Postma. "You could tell. The others were all looking to her for guidance, answering to her. Even Giacoia, though he outranks her."

The bitch, thought Farthingale. So *that* was why she had kept on about Jacobsen during the conference call when he'd given the team their notice. He'd had a sneaking suspicion there was something going on between those two.

Berger had lost her sweetheart and wanted someone to pay for it.

"And once the PP-66 was in their systems," he said, "they reacted how?"

"I've never seen anything like it. They broke the restraints. Literally just snapped them. And two of them, Abbotts and Lim, threw themselves at the nearest of us, the ones at the front who'd gone in first... Dr Istamboulian... Oh, God... The noise. Flesh being torn open. Jesus, it sounded like canvas ripping. And blood hitting the floor, like from a hose. And then they started drinking it. They were insane, all of them. Their eyes completely red, glowing almost, like the eyes of demons."

"Postma, get a hold of yourself. 'Demons', indeed."

"Hey, Mr Farthingale, I've just watched two people I've known and worked with months get pulled to pieces and—and *eaten*, right before my eyes. Don't tell me to get a fucking hold of myself. You get a fucking hold of *your*self!"

"A little respect for your—"

"Know what? Screw you. Screw respect." Postma was gibbering, on the verge of hysteria, his voice ragged-edged. "This whole crazy-ass project of yours, making humans vampires for a day—I always wondered if it wasn't the worst idea ever. Now I know."

"You voiced no such concerns when you signed up for the position and took the very handsome salary I was offering."

"I got student debt up the wazoo. I need every fucking cent I can get. And the jobs market being how it is, even for biotech grads, hell, I'd have applied to work in a North Korean bacteriological weapons plant if I'd known they were recruiting. Probably be safer there than here, what's more."

"Just tell me," Farthingale said. "Red Eye have gone now? They're outdoors? All five of them?"

"Like I said. I heard them leave while I was hiding in the back of one of the supply closets. They took the elevator to ground level."

"But it's broad daylight."

"If they're all wrapped up, they should be okay."

"What I mean is, they haven't got the Hummer. They're roaming the streets in the daytime in full military get-up, carrying weapons. Aren't they worried about being spotted?"

"I don't think they're worried about anything much. I think they're beyond that. They just want out. They got some piece of business they want to finish, I don't know what."

I do, thought Farthingale.

"And God help any poor bastard who gets in their way," Postma added.

FARTHINGALE DIDN'T FEEL like smashing up the phone this time, or indeed smashing anything else. He was too numbed, too appalled. He sat at his desk, head in hands, and tried to process what he'd just learned.

A mutiny. That was the only word for it. Team Red Eye had rebelled.

He knew who they were after. He knew why. But that didn't help. They were welcome to kill Redlaw any time. Just not right now. Not like this. If the President should find out—

No, there was no *if* about it.

When the President found out that Team Red Eye was on the loose and out of control, he, Farthingale, would be in the deepest shit imaginable. Those threats about Guantanamo, they were probably exaggeration, a bit of presidential posturing. Being leader of the free world was like having the biggest dick on the planet, and what good was that if you couldn't take it out and wave it in people's faces every once in a while?

So, okay, maybe not incarceration in Gitmo, but there would be severe consequences, no question about that. Red Eye had gone rogue, and it wasn't Farthingale's fault, but it would be the final straw as far as the President was concerned. Some kind of massive public prosecution would ensue. He would hang Farthingale out to dry.

You've pissed off the wrong man, you entitled, old-money prick.

That was the trouble with these fucking liberals, Farthingale thought. They couldn't handle moral compromise. They had this la-la-land view of right and wrong. Everything was either the one or the other, nothing in between. They didn't seem to appreciate that technological advances and business ventures all carried potential blowback. No reward without risk. A liberal—and the incumbent, with his healthcare reform bill and heavy tax-and-spend regime, *was* one, in spite of what the White House press officers and spin doctors said—was always looking for the easy way, the ingratiating, consensual way, the path of least resistance.

Resistance, though, was the only true test of a theory or a doctrine. Everything worth having needed to go through a painful but necessary refining process first, and fallout, collateral damage, could not always be avoided.

The development of Porphyrian itself was a perfect case in point.

The genesis of the project had come as a consequence of Farthingale's ITP diagnosis. He had been brooding on the now suddenly very personal issue of diseases of the blood and had started to wonder if vampirism held the key. A series of tentative connections had begun clicking inside his head.

Vampires lived on blood. They thrived on it. It somehow helped them be the physically superior predators they were. Was there something in the vampire metabolism that transformed blood into a sort of super-elixir, granting them strength, endurance and longevity? And if so, could it be harnessed to enhance people as well? Fix human frailties and illnesses?

It certainly seemed like an avenue of research worth pursuing. There was money to be made there, potentially quite a lot of it. More significantly, there was the possibility of a cure for his condition.

The family motto. *Sanguis ordo est*. Blood is order.

But perhaps blood was also profit.

The first hurdle was sourcing vampire DNA. Farthingale owned several pharmaceutical companies whose R&D departments he could commandeer for whatever purpose he saw fit, but there was little the men and women in white coats could do unless they had the necessary materials to work with.

Luckily, he knew a man who could help. At that time, Nathaniel Lambourne was keeping a vampire captive on the grounds of his own home. He was using the creature, nicknamed Subject V, as a guinea pig to determine the effects of the hormone vasopressin on the undead physiology.

At Farthingale's request, Lambourne sent over samples of tissue and bone marrow extracted from Subject V. All he asked in return was a 5% stake in any marketable discoveries Farthingale's people made from these specimens. Farthingale beat him down to 3.5%. That was how things operated between himself, Lambourne and Uona. Nothing was ever for free. None of them knew the meaning of the words *favour* or *goodwill gesture*. Their three-way relationship rested on a bed of mutual mistrust and common financial interest.

Farthingale appointed Ghazar Istamboulian, an Armenian expat with PhDs in pharmacology and applied genetics, to head up the project. Dr Istamboulian was the one who dubbed the project 'Porphyrian', after the rare blood disorder porphyria, the symptoms of which had once led it to be linked with vampirism. Superstitious peasants in the Middle Ages would have looked at a porphyria sufferer, whose teeth and urine exhibited a reddish fluorescence thanks to a build-up of excess blood pigmentation, and who was experiencing a degree of photosensitivity so acute that it could cause skin blistering, and might easily have concluded that some local undead bloodsucker had recently paid this person a call. The presentation matched the folklore uncannily well. They might even have decided that the best therapy was a stake through the heart. Dr Istamboulian considered the choice of name a neat ironic flourish.

He and his colleagues tinkered with the Subject V samples and, step by step, moved closer to a positive outcome. It just wasn't the outcome Farthingale had been hoping for.

"Such is the way of these things," Dr Istamboulian wrote in one of his monthly status-report memos to Farthingale. "You search for one result, by chance you hit upon another. Charles Goodyear was looking for a more malleable and durable form of rubber and clumsily spilled a mixture of rubber, sulphur and lead onto a stove. Hey presto, vulcanisation. Henri Becquerel discovered radioactivity after he left uranium rock and a photographic plate together in a drawer for a week. It wasn't planned, just a happy accident. Alexander Fleming didn't clean up his lab bench one day, and came back to find a bactericidal fungus had grown on some of his cultures—penicillin. With Porphyrian, we're not finding anything that can make improvements specific to blood chemistry or the immune system. What we are finding is something that promises to generate an overall improvement in human physiological capacity. We have synthesised a version of the vampire DNA that temporarily overwrites the recipient's DNA. We can piggyback it onto a fast-acting retrovirus to disperse it through the body in just a matter of minutes, and install a self-destruct enzyme in the package to eradicate its effects after a set period, perhaps in the region of twenty-four hours. Piece of cake, as you Americans say."

Tests on rhesus monkeys were showing a marked uptick in reaction times, reflexes and exteroception and proprioception—awareness of surroundings and self.

"Aggression, too, unfortunately," Dr Istamboulian wrote. "Put two of them in a cage, and unless they're a close pair bond, chances are that pretty soon you'll be left with only one monkey. We have to keep fine-tuning. There must be some way to tone down the violent tendencies the formula excites. It's simply a question of snipping out the pertinent parts of the genome and dovetailing the joins."

After sixty-five near-misses, he was convinced that he had finally cracked the problem.

"If the dosages are carefully measured and controlled," he told Farthingale, "I can foresee no downside. The bloodthirstiness can be held at bay. There will be aggression, yes, but not of the counterproductive kind. It will remain within acceptable parameters. I mean acceptable in a combat context, where a degree of hyper-stimulation is desirable—and combat, after all, is the venue most suited to what we've created. In that sense, Porphyrian is the ideal tool for the job."

Which it had been, until the people presently receiving the treatment had decided to take matters into their own hands. The now late Dr Istamboulian had learned to his cost that however closely you monitored and regulated an experiment, there was always an element of unpredictability. In this instance it was human nature, emotion trumping discipline.

The upshot for Farthingale was that he was facing ruin at every conceivable level.

Get a grip on the situation, he told himself. *Reassert control.*

He tried patching into Team Red Eye's comms channel via his PC. He could speak to the soldiers. A bit of sweet-talking, the dangling of substantial bribes, and he could maybe head them off before they did anything he might regret.

He couldn't get through. *No signal currently being received*, read the onscreen message.

The helmet cameras were off, too. The bastards had completely divorced themselves from him.

Of course they had.

Farthingale felt alone, and helpless, and foolish. These were unfamiliar sensations, alien, unpleasant.

It was, he decided, time to call in the lawyers. And the accountants. And the PR flacks. Circle the wagons. Get ready for the coming shitstorm.

But he couldn't quite bring himself to do so yet. It would be tantamount to admitting defeat.

Something might still turn up. The "luck of the loaded" might still hold.

CHAPTER
TWENTY-EIGHT

THE SCHOOL BUS reversed up to the loading bay on the factory's north side.

As Redlaw and Tina stepped out, a gunshot erupted. A ricochet pinged off the raised concrete dock. Tina could have sworn the bullet whistled past her ear with millimetres to spare.

Redlaw dropped into a crouch, whipping out his Cindermaker. He backed away, pushing Tina behind him, getting them both to cover round the front of the bus.

"Sorry!" someone called out from inside the factory. "Are you okay? Tell me I didn't hit anybody."

"Who the hell is that?" Redlaw barked.

"It's me. Mary-Jo."

"And why in God's name are you shooting at us?"

"I didn't mean to," the vampire replied plaintively. "I was keeping watch, and I just thought, this rifle was laying around, and I've fired a gun before, and if those vampire killers happened to turn up before you did..."

Redlaw stood and clambered up onto the dock. Mary-Jo Schaeffer hung back in the shelter of the large entranceway, whose retractable steel door had long ago been dismantled and taken away for scrap. She was petite, and Colonel Jacobsen's Colt AR-15 looked huge in her hands.

"I've been on ranges a few times," she said. "Notched up some hours."

"Handguns?"

"Yeah."

"No experience with semiautomatic assault weapons?"

"No."

"Idiot." Redlaw snatched the rifle out of her hands. "You could have taken my head off."

"I didn't realise the trigger was so sensitive," Mary-Jo protested.

"Or, apparently, that there was a round in the breech."

"I said sorry."

"'Sorry' is no good to a corpse."

Mary-Jo looked crestfallen. Harsh words from her shtriga. They stung.

Tina felt the tiniest bit of sympathy for her. "She thought she was doing the right thing, Redlaw. No need for the verbal bitch-slap."

"Would you rather it was a physical bitch-slap?"

"Just saying."

"Well, don't," snapped Redlaw. "If you want to be useful, why not start daylight-proofing the bus? Paper over every inch of window on the inside. Leave a slot on the front windscreen so that I can see out when I'm driving. Think you can handle that?"

"I think I'm probably up to it," Tina drawled. "And what'll you be doing while I'm being handicrafts queen?"

"There's an exsanguinated corpse on the premises. I'm going to chop off its head to make sure it stays dead."

"Oh."

"Unless you'd care to swap? I'd gladly mess around with scissors and tape instead."

"No. No, I'm good."

"Thought so."

REDLAW USED JACOBSEN'S own combat knife to hack through the corpse's neck. It was a grisly task, but he was used to it. Muscle and gristle cleaved easily under a ten-inch carbon-and-chromium-steel blade. There was very little mess until near the end, when he parted two cervical vertebrae and a trickle of colourless cerebrospinal fluid leaked out.

He wiped the knife clean on Jacobsen's fatigues. Nice piece of kit. Jacobsen wouldn't be needing it any more. Redlaw attached its sheath to his belt and slotted the knife there for safekeeping.

TINA WAS THOROUGH with the bus windows. She secured each sheet of cartridge paper into place with a double thickness of tape. She trimmed the paper to fit perfectly.

Every now and then she paused from her labours to take out her BlackBerry and check her site. The hit counter on Tick Talk was starting to go up. On a normal day she could count on perhaps a half-dozen visitors, if that. It wasn't surprising; it was early in the site's life and, until now, there had not been much on it that was particularly earth-shattering.

In the hour since she'd posted up the uncut vampire

footage, however, she'd had over a hundred hits. And each time she checked, the total increased. Visitors were leaving comments, too. There were the predictable jaded cynics saying that it was faked, actors in makeup, contact lenses, prosthetic teeth, it was a performance art project or a teaser promotion for some upcoming found-footage Hollywood horror. But, for every one of these, there were three or four who knew the stuff was the real deal and vowed eagerly to tweet and blog about it to their friends.

That was all Tina wanted. All she needed. Shares, retweets, links, hashtags, burgeoning interest. An exponential chain reaction in cyberspace that would see her video clips go viral and become a phenomenon. Once global critical mass had been achieved, there was no way she could not be noticed any more. Her time of rejection, of continually being overlooked, would be at an end.

Eventually the interior of the bus was fully dark, not a chink of light coming in other than from in front of the steering wheel, where she had left an aperture the size of a standard envelope.

The hit counter broke the 1,000 mark and kept on rising, far faster than she'd dared imagine, clocking upwards in leaps and bounds.

She could feel it in her gut. It was happening. Her site was making waves, the ripples spreading far and wide. Tina "Tick" Checkley was on the brink of the big time.

CHAPTER
TWENTY-NINE

THEY MOVED IN a pack, but not as a rabble. Not like hounds or wolves. Organised. Their training was deeply ingrained and still held sway. At all times four of them maintained defensive quadrants around the fifth. The point man led. The rear man checked his six at regular intervals, walking backwards for a few paces.

They crossed Central Park. Mostly they kept to the wooded areas, using rocks and the winter-bare trees for cover. At the reservoir they startled a jogger, who ran away screaming as fast as his legs would carry him. He didn't get far. Two of them overtook and overpowered him, bringing him down and tearing him apart.

Some teenagers having a snowball fight near the Belvedere Castle spotted them. They dug out their phones and started filming. It was the last thing they ever did.

On the other side of the park, a police cruiser came to a halt. Its siren blurted. Two officers emerged, sidearms drawn. They weren't quick enough to get off a single round. Their eviscerated stomachs steamed in the chilly air.

Down the western side of the city, the soldiers loped. They were tireless. They were relentless.

Not everyone who strayed into their path died. Some people were merely crippled, or knocked unconscious, or left on the critical list.

Soldiers in Manhattan. Threading through the snow-packed streets. Leaving citizens sprawled and bloodied in their wake.

Within themselves, though, they were more than soldiers. They were pure. They were free from doubts and concerns. They operated in a world of utter simplicity, life reduced to the fundamentals.

Acquire objective. Eliminate interference.

They reached the Hummer. Tracked it with a GPS locator. The stink of Jacobsen was all over the vehicle.

They dug the Hummer out of the snow with their hands. The engine started first time. They hunkered inside.

Jacobsen's final journey was marked clearly in the air, his scent trail so vivid it almost had a colour.

The Hummer drove, and all across Manhattan sirens were wailing and snow was stained red.

CHAPTER
THIRTY

ONE BY ONE the vampires darted across the dock from the loading bay to the back of the bus. They ducked through the rear door and huddled in the darkened interior. The sun was low and occluded and they were in the shadow of the factory. As long as they moved swiftly, the danger of combustion was minimal.

When the last of them, Miguel, was safely inside the bus, Redlaw pulled the door shut and headed down the aisle to the front. Tina had bagged the seat directly behind the driver's. Jacobsen's stash of weapons lay heaped on the steps that led down to the side door.

"All aboard the special needs express," Tina said. "Next stop, music therapy class."

Redlaw shot her a look.

"What?" she said. "What's with the beetle brows?"

"Poor taste."

"No sense of humour, some people."

"I didn't quite catch that. What did you say?"

"Nothing. Just grumbling under my breath. About you."

Redlaw settled into the driver's seat. "You seem in an unusually good mood, Tina."

"I'm perky. Nothing wrong with being perky. Coach trip. Yay." She pumped her fists in the air like a cheerleader with pompoms. "Anyone know any songs? How about 'Bingo Was His Name-oh'?"

Grimacing, Redlaw fired up the engine. He crunched the gearstick noisily into first.

"Hey!" Miguel called out. "Easy on the old girl. You're going to strip a cog, you keep doing that."

"If they'd just put the stick on the correct side..." Redlaw hunched forward and peered through the slot in the cartridge paper. "Well, World War Two tank drivers managed."

He bore down on the accelerator and the bus drew away from the building.

Ahead, the factory gates lay askew, dangling off their hinges. Redlaw had bulldozed through them on the way in, much as he'd done with the depot gates. He gentled the bus into the gap. One of the gates buckled and bent under the nearside wheels.

The bus trundled out along a narrow approach road lined with industrial units.

"Everyone all right so far?" Redlaw asked over his shoulder. "Don't expect a quick ride. We're never going to be travelling much faster than this, not with the restricted view I've got."

"We're cool," said Denzel.

"Just relieved to be on the move at last," said Diane.

"Yeah," said Anu. "It's good not feeling like sitting ducks any more."

"Mr Redlaw?" little Cindy piped up. "Where are we going *to*, exactly?"

"Out of Manhattan," Redlaw replied. "I haven't thought ahead much further than that. We'll find somewhere to pause and take stock eventually. Consolidate our plans there. For now, I just want to put the immediate danger behind us. Get us out of the line of fire."

A car was coming the other way along the road. It was squat and dark grey, one of those military-style vehicles that rock stars and movie stars seemed to like. Redlaw couldn't see into its windows.

His hands tightened on the steering wheel and he squeezed a little more speed out of the accelerator.

The car definitely seemed to be on the prowl. Looking for something.

It passed by, disappearing from Redlaw's sightline. Automatically he glanced in the rearview mirror, before remembering that the mirror was useless. He could see nothing at the back but black paper. He refocused his attention on the road. The snow had more or less stopped falling by now, but it lay thick and he could feel its resistance against the bus's wheels. The tyres had snow chains on, but still the bus seemed ready to slew at any moment unless he kept a firm grip. It felt more like being at the tiller of a boat in a sea swell than driving.

The car was nothing. He couldn't afford to think about the car. He had a bad feeling about it, but he couldn't let that distract him. Concentrate on driving. Keeping on the road. Trying not to—

CRASH!!!

An immense impact at the rear of the bus. The whole vehicle resounded with it. Everyone was jolted forward in their seats. The wheel bucked in Redlaw's hands. The bus swerved. He fought to straighten up and stay on course.

The vampires were yelling in consternation.

Tina cried out, "What in the name of hot holy fuck was—"

CRASH!!!

A second shuddering bang. The bus leaped like a horse that had been slapped on its hindquarters.

"Someone's ramming us!" Patti squealed.

"No shit. You think?" Tina said.

"Who is it?" said a fretful Andy Gregg. "Is it them?"

Redlaw floored the accelerator.

"Redlaw? I said, is it them?"

"I don't know. Probably. A car just went past a moment ago, one of those Hummers, I think they're called. It must have turned back. Our blacked-out windows gave us away. Now shut up, everyone, and sit tight. I can—"

CRASH!!!

The Hummer must have really poured on speed this time, and come in at an angle as well, because the bus rocked as though a landmine had gone off under its rear axle. It was thrown round, back end slewing outwards wildly.

Redlaw hauled on the wheel, turning into the skid to counteract it. He'd done a driver-training module with the Met, years back. He knew a trick or two. But a clunky Starcraft school bus was a very different prospect from a police Vauxhall Vectra, and then there was the snow to consider. Half the rules he had learned no longer applied.

The rear offside wheel struck the kerb. The bus juddered back the other way. Redlaw instinctively wanted to apply the brakes, but that was more likely to lose him control than gain it. He eased off on the accelerator instead, allowed the steering wheel to reorient itself, then stamped hard. The bus jerked forward, finding purchase again in the snow.

The road terminated at a T-junction. Redlaw threw the bus into a sweeping left turn. He had no time to check if any traffic was coming from either direction, and his scope for doing so was severely limited anyway. He just assumed the way would be clear. Given that the blizzard had brought New York virtually to a standstill, it seemed a safe enough bet. If not... Well, it wasn't as though he had much choice.

A horn blared ahead. The viewing slot was filled with an oncoming municipal snowplough truck.

Redlaw plunged the bus into the opposite lane. He had no idea how narrowly he missed the snowplough truck; he only knew that he did. From behind he heard a faint but heavy *thunk* and inferred from this that the Hummer hadn't been so successful. It must have been following the bus so closely that the driver hadn't spotted the snowplough truck until the last moment, when the bus peeled left and revealed it.

Was it too much to hope that there had been a head-on collision and the Hummer was now out of action, front end impaled on the blade of the snowplough?

A just God, surely, would have made that happen.

But you couldn't always tell whose side He was on.

Bullets whanged and gonged into the rear of the bus.

So much for that hope.

"Down! Keep down!" Redlaw shouted.

The vampires, screaming, ducked in their seats.

"Tina! Bullet holes. Are there any?"

"How the hell should I know?"

"Look, damn you."

Tina peeped over her seat headrest. "One or two."

"Low down?"

"Yeah."

"Then our passengers should be all right. For now. Fraxinus don't have the penetrating power of ordinary bullets. The bodywork should take most of the velocity out of them. But if they start shooting at the windows..."

They did. Glass shattered. Rounds punched through the cartridge paper. Spears of milky daylight lanced in. The vampires crouched still further down.

"Brace yourselves!" Redlaw ordered.

He didn't give any more warning than that. He hammered down on the brake pedal. The bus went into a straight-line skid, as though on skis. The Hummer pounded right into the back of it, propelling it forward even faster. The two vehicles bobsledded along the street in tandem, locked together. Redlaw held the wheel in the central position with all his might.

Then he jammed on the accelerator, wrenching the bus away from the Hummer. He prayed to God that he had done some significant damage to the car by forcing it to hurtle headlong into an almost stationary object. Hummers were tough things, but maybe he had cracked the radiator or even bent the front axle...

No more shooting. For a few blissful moments Redlaw was able to believe that their troubles were over. The Hummer *had* been disabled. The bus could carry on sailing down the street, unmolested, unpursued.

Then the revving of the Hummer's engine returned, growing louder. The car appeared to be pulling alongside the bus.

And then a muffled thump on the roof.

Someone was up there. Someone had leapt from the Hummer to the bus.

Without taking his eyes off the road, Redlaw pulled out his Cindermaker, racked the slide one-handed on his thigh, aimed over his shoulder and blasted six rounds into the ceiling. He ran the shots in a row down the midline of the bus. One found its mark, as he heard a shrill girlish wail followed by a succession of rolling thuds—the sound of a body tumbling along the roof and toppling off the end.

The roar of the Hummer faded. It was drawing back, no doubt to pick up the fallen soldier.

"Tina. Patch those holes."

"What?"

Redlaw pointed behind him to where rods of daylight descended from ceiling to aisle. Flakes of snow from the roof were sifting in. "The holes. Stick tape over them."

"I'm busy." Tina had her camcorder out and was popping the lens cap.

Redlaw snatched the camera off her and shoved it down in the pedal footwell. "Not now. Later. Priorities."

"All right," Tina huffed like a teenager. She rummaged in her rucksack for what was left of the parcel tape and began tearing off small strips with her teeth.

No sooner were the holes blocked than the Hummer returned, pulling level on the left-hand side again.

Redlaw veered towards it. The two vehicles touched, flank to flank. Metal squealed. Scraped. Groaned.

The Hummer drew away, then returned the favour by shouldering sidelong into the bus. A couple of windows broke, but the cartridge paper held fast. Tina had made a good job of the daylight-proofing, Redlaw had to give her credit for that.

He hared across a four-way intersection, running a red light. The Hummer stayed abreast. The bus was doing a mean 30mph, far too fast for snow as deep as this. Redlaw felt only half in control. The rest was up to providence.

Another of those muffled thumps overhead. A second soldier was attempting to succeed where his comrade had failed.

This one didn't mess about. He opened fire immediately, riddling the roof with bullets. Everyone in the bus started yelling and screaming, save Redlaw. Fraxinus rounds raked the interior. There was a howl as one of them struck home.

The shooting stopped.

Clip empty. Redlaw waggled the steering wheel as much as he dared, in order to keep the soldier off-balance and prolong the time it took him to reload.

"Who's hit?" he called out.

"Me," said an anguished Miguel. "My goddamn leg. *Hijo di puta!*"

"A graze?"

"No. It's gone right in. Deep. Hurts like a bitch."

There was nothing that could be done for him, then. A graze from a Fraxinus was survivable, if you hacked around the wound with a knife straight away and gouged out all of the flesh that had come into contact with the bullet. But since this bullet was lodged in Miguel's leg, its ash-wood would already be poisoning him, contaminating his system. The rot would spread outwards like high-speed, red-hot gangrene. Miguel was doomed.

He knew it. His face was wan, his already sallow complexion now gone the grey of oatmeal. His eyes were dark and lost, filled with dread.

"I need both hands free," Redlaw told him. "You're the professional busman. Take the wheel."

Miguel understood what was being asked of him. He didn't have long. Might as well put his last few minutes to good use, even though he and Redlaw were both aware that it was going to cause him further suffering. He limped up the aisle, through the crisscrossing bars of dim sunlight. Each beam singed his skin like a brand.

Redlaw sprang from the driver's seat and Miguel slid in to take his place. The bus decelerated momentarily but Miguel soon had it up and rolling again.

"Won't be for long," Redlaw said. "Just so that I can deal with the bloke on top. Can you hang on?"

Miguel peered into the slot as though it were a portal into the heart of a nuclear bomb blast. The skin around his eyes had already begun to redden.

"Wish I had some shades," he said. "Yeah, I can hold on. Just be quick."

"Keep her steady as you can." Redlaw patted Miguel on the shoulder, then dived for the AR-15. Holding the rifle vertical, he strode down the aisle, firing upwards at random. He didn't expect to get as lucky this time as he had the last, but he wanted the soldier on the hop, unsure.

"Stay right down," he ordered the vampires. "Yet more light coming in." He flung open the rear door, slung the rifle over his back by its strap and swung himself out. Using the backs of the rear seats as footholds, he clambered up onto the roof.

In front of him, ankle-deep in trampled, pockmarked snow, was one of the largest human beings he had ever laid eyes on. The soldier was at least six-five and massively muscled, with the proportions of a bodybuilder. His sleeves and trouser legs strained to contain his immense knotty limbs. Whether he was white, black, Asian, whatever, there was no way of telling. Not an inch of his body was exposed. Battle fatigues, helmet, goggles, face mask and gloves covered all.

He was braced with a semiautomatic rifle pointing downward, ready to send more bullets into the bus. Then he straightened. He turned. His augmented sensorium had alerted him to a presence behind him.

Redlaw threw himself flat, bringing the AR-15 to bear at the same time. He tried to line up a shot, but the soldier leapt, landed right in front of him, and booted the rifle out of his hands.

Rather than go to retrieve that gun, Redlaw grabbed the soldier's gun by the barrel. He twisted it to the side as hard as he could, hauling himself upright at the same time.

The two of them grappled with the rifle, but it was a one-sided struggle and the outcome was never really in doubt. The soldier easily gained the advantage. He yanked the rifle round hard, sending Redlaw slithering backwards across the roof.

The piled-up snow saved Redlaw, slowing his progress, giving him the chance to catch himself before he toppled off the side. He dug in with his hands and feet and launched himself back at the soldier like a sprinter from the starting blocks. Jacobsen's combat knife slid from its sheath.

The soldier stepped smartly aside. Redlaw slashed with the knife as he lurched past. Cloth tore. No wound. But that was fine. A section of the soldier's trousers split open, revealing chocolate-brown skin.

The soldier chuckled.

"Missed!"

Then he cursed.

"Oww. Shit. Cocksucker. That smarts."

Sun. Burning.

Redlaw doubled back, not so much running as scrambling on all fours. The bus was jouncing and swaying. It was tricky to stay upright.

The knife made a rent in the soldier's sleeve.

"Oh, no. You did not."

Before Redlaw could regroup for a third attack, the soldier reached out, astonishingly fast, and seized him by the neck.

"That's quite enough of *that*, little man. My turn to bring the pain."

He hoisted Redlaw up with one hand, throttling him. With his other hand he grasped Redlaw's wrist, holding the knife at bay.

"Gonna squeeze the life out of you. Gonna pop that pointy head right off of its stem."

Redlaw clutched the soldier's goggles and pulled them down.

Instantly he was dropped. The soldier fumblingly clawed the goggles back into place. This gave Redlaw time to lunge for Jacobsen's AR-15, which lay half buried nearby.

He fired the shot one-handed while lying on his side, propped up on an elbow. Not the ideal position if accuracy was your goal. His target was sizeable, and close, but still he managed only to wing the soldier, clipping his shoulder.

He didn't get the chance to fire a second shot. The soldier hurled himself at him with a feral growl. He dived into Redlaw head-first and together they slithered on their bellies along the roof towards the rear of the bus. The AR-15 slid off the roof. Redlaw felt himself swinging outwards into empty air. He fell. The soldier fell with him.

Redlaw latched on to the top of the wide-open rear door with a flailing hand. The soldier did the same. For several moments the two of them hung off the door side by side, clinging on for all they were worth, legs dangling.

Then the soldier got his act together and started kicking Redlaw. He delivered two, three, four good heel-shots to Redlaw's midriff and thigh. Redlaw could feel his fragile purchase on the door slipping. The Hummer was zooming up behind. If he lost his grip he would fall beneath the car's wheels, or bounce brokenly off its bull bar.

The knife was still in his other hand. Somehow he hadn't dropped it.

He reached across and sliced down through the soldier's knuckles. Severed fingers flew in all directions. The man screeched and tumbled away from the bus, his immense bulk landing on the Hummer's bonnet with an thunderous *whump*.

The Hummer braked sharply. With the soldier sprawled on its bonnet, it fishtailed on the snow, coming to a halt sideways across the road.

The bus lumbered onward. Redlaw, with tremendous effort, eased his legs through the doorway, then swung the rest of him inside. He hauled the door shut and lay in the aisle, panting and wheezing. His side, where he'd been kicked, throbbed. His neck felt mangled. His windpipe seemed to have been reduced to the diameter of a drinking straw.

"Redlaw!" exclaimed Tina. "God. Are you okay?"

"Never better," Redlaw croaked.

She helped him to his feet. "Looks like you did it. You saw them off. They won't be coming after us again in a hurry."

James Lovegrove

"Don't you believe it." Redlaw hobbled to the front of the bus. "Miguel. I'm back. You're relieved."

They performed another rapid changeover. Redlaw stiffly took the controls while Miguel collapsed into the nearest seat.

"About time," he gasped. "I've pretty much gone blind."

It was no exaggeration. The skin around his eyes was seared black, and his eyeballs themselves were stippled with blisters, the irises opaque as though afflicted with severe cataracts.

"You did a great job," Redlaw reassured him. "Can't fault it."

"We haven't stopped them, though."

"Afraid not. Paused them, given them something to think about, but no, they're hardly out of action."

"Damn. I guess it was too much to hope."

We've also lost Jacobsen's gun, Redlaw thought.

They had gained a reprieve. And some ground.

The chase, however, was far from over.

CHAPTER
THIRTY-ONE

BERGER AND GIACOIA helped Child into the back seat.

"Goddamn sonofabitch motherfucking *motherfucker*!" Child was clasping his fingerless hand to his chest with his forearm.

Also on the back seat was Abbotts. He had both hands cupped over his groin, holding a wad of blood-soaked surgical dressing in place. A shot of morphine from the first-aid kit had blunted his pain. One side of his face was a lattice of criss-crossing wound closure strips.

"What're *you* bitching about?" he snarled at Child.

"Asshole took my fingers off."

"Yeah? So what? He blew off one of my nuts. My fucking nut!"

"Not as if you need it. Ugly-ass cracker motherfucker like you, never get laid anyway."

"Yeah, well, you ain't got no right hand to speak of any more," Abbotts shot back. "Can't even jerk off now, bruh."

"Don't you 'bruh' me."

"What, you'd prefer 'dawg'? 'My nigga'? How about 'boy'?"

"Now listen up, you inbred piece of—"

"Enough!" Berger snapped. "You two stop the baby-whining. You've both got boo-boos, we get it. Now man up, shut the fuck up, and listen. Maintain pressure on those wounds. You're going to live. But we can't afford to take you to a hospital right now and get you seen to. We do, and we lose Redlaw, maybe for good. Doctors'll have to wait. You sit tight while we see this thing through. Got that?"

Child and Abbotts nodded.

"Good. Lim, morphine Child up."

"Yes, ma'am."

Berger slid back behind the wheel of the Hummer and reversed at full tilt. The rear fender banged into a parked car, setting its alarm whooping. Berger yanked the wheel hard round and sped off after the school bus, still just in sight.

Berger watched the Hummer narrow the gap between it and the bus. If Redlaw's intention was to escape from Manhattan and do it fast, then he was on the wrong side of the island. The exit routes along the West Side were all tunnels until you reached the George Washington Bridge way up in the upper hundreds.

A bridge was a pinch-point. A tunnel even more so.

Pinch-points were where escapees got caught.

CHAPTER
THIRTY-TWO

10.15AM EASTERN STANDARD Time. Late night in Japan. Farthingale hated himself for phoning Uona now, at his home. He knew how pathetic it looked.

"*Moshi-moshi*," said a woman, sounding sleepy and unimpressed.

Uona's wife. What was her name again?

"Izumi. Howard Farthingale. Good evening. I'm sorry for—"

There was a string of Japanese from Mrs Uona, the tone shrill and irritable. He couldn't tell if it was directed at him or not. Then he heard the sound of a phone receiver changing hands.

"Howard," said Uona. "If you have forgotten the time difference between the East Coast and Tokyo, let me remind you. We're ten hours behind. Or fourteen ahead, allowing for the date line. Either way, it's gone midnight here."

"Yukinobu, please, I'm in real trouble."

"I know."

"You know?"

"Before I turned in for the night, I received information from certain sources that your Red Eye operatives have—how to put this?—disenfranchised themselves and gone independent. I'm also led to understand that your chief executive has washed his hands of you."

"He's going to throw me to the wolves."

"That would seem likely, yes."

"You knew all this, and you didn't get in touch?" Farthingale tried to keep the hurt out of his voice.

"What would have been the advantage in that?"

"You could have offered to help."

"How?"

"I don't know. Somehow. At least showed some support."

"Do you wish me to help?"

"Yes! Why the hell else do you think I'm ringing you?"

"But what can I do?" said Uona. "Your part of the world. Your people. Your pet project. I'm seven thousand miles away. It's a whole different day here. Your today is my yesterday. Do you expect me to wave a magic wand from such a distance and make everything all right again? I am not your fairy godmother. Your mess. You clean it up."

"You're not uninvolved in this," Farthingale said. "You have interests. Shares in my companies. As I do in yours. I go down, you go down too."

"Oh, Howard. Hasn't our experience with Nathaniel taught you anything? We profit from one another's gains, but also from one another's losses. A catastrophe for you would be a prize opportunity for me."

"You vulture. Would you really—"

"I'm sorry, Howard, but this conversation is over. I have a very upset Izumi in bed beside me. She does so hate having her sleep interrupted. I shall be soothing her for the next half-hour at least."

"Yukinobu..."

"Don't beg. It's undignified."

"Yukinobu, please. There must be *something* you can do. Go on, throw me a bone."

A continent and an ocean away, Uona appeared to be thinking.

"Anything at all," Farthingale went on. "Picture me prostrating myself in front of you. Humiliating myself."

"And losing all face," Uona said.

"I'm a *gaijin*. We don't have any face to start with, do we? Not as far as you're concerned."

"Reverse psychology. Doesn't always work."

"How long have we known each other?"

"Nor does appealing to commonality." Uona seemed to soften, taking pity on him. "I will give you something. How useful it will be is up to you. Check your email inbox shortly. But remember, Howard, whatever happens to you will not automatically happen to me. I am far ahead, already moving on. I repeat: your today is my yesterday. It's always been thus."

FARTHINGALE MONITORED HIS inbox obsessively, waiting for Uona's address to pop up in the new-email window.

Come on, come on.

He was seething about the way Uona had treated him—the sheer callous indifference—yet he was also desperately hopeful that his Japanese colleague would prove to be his saviour. They were peers, but Uona was older, wiser, marginally wealthier. Perhaps he had a right to look down on Farthingale.

One thing Farthingale was certain of. If Uona ever came crawling to him asking for a lifeline, he would sure as hell think twice before throwing it.

That was assuming he managed to get through this whole clusterfuck intact. Which was far from guaranteed.

A soft ping. The email finally arrived.

No covering message. No attachment. Just a link.

Farthingale clicked on it.

He was taken to a site called Tick Talk.

Home-video footage of vampires. So goddamn what?

He nearly closed the window. Was this some kind of joke? Was Uona having a laugh at his expense? Sticking the knife in and giving it a good twist?

Almost on a whim, he played one of the video clips.

And another.

And then another.

Holy shit.

Redlaw. And Colonel Jacobsen. And the rest of Team Red Eye. And not just any bunch of vampires but the very ones Red Eye were pursuing.

There was somebody with Redlaw, then, filming his exploits and posting them online for all to see.

Meaning either Redlaw was the arrogantest, biggest-balled bastard on the planet, or he was unaware that the footage had been broadcast.

All the evidence suggested the latter.

So this woman, this Tina Checkley, she behind the camera, was a kind of spy in the enemy camp. At the very least, a conduit linking Redlaw to the outside world without his knowledge.

An asset.

And assets could be bought. They invariably had a price.

Farthingale, for what felt like the first time in months, grinned.

CHAPTER
THIRTY-THREE

MIGUEL WAS FADING fast. His wounded leg was crumbling, slow-burning with a sickly smoky-barbecue stench. His fangs were bared and clenched.

Yet, between feverish groans, he was still able to argue with Tina.

"Eleventh? Don't be dumb. Eleventh isn't—isn't two-way this far south. Stay on Tenth... until Thirtieth Street. That's the best route."

"But the Eleventh entrance is quicker."

"But it's for cars only. Don't you know anything? I've been driving these streets for years. I know what I'm talking about."

"Well, I still say we should take the Holland Tunnel anyway."

"Listen, *chica*, the Lincoln has a bus lane. A *bus* lane. And this is a bus."

"What, and you think somehow that'll stop those psychos following us? 'Oops, we can't go down there, we don't have a bus.' I don't know if you've been paying attention, but they don't give a damn about the law."

"I'm just—just trying to gain us an edge," said Miguel, and he hissed as another spasm of pain wracked him.

"Tina, leave him be," said Redlaw. "If you want to be useful, go to the back and look out."

"No way. The back is where the bullets come in. I'm not planning on getting shot."

"*I'll* shoot you if you don't do as I ask."

Tina glared at him. "You know what the trouble with you is? I can never tell whether you're joking or not."

"Presume I'm not and act accordingly."

Tina stomped to the rear of the bus and cautiously put her eye to one of the bullet holes in the paper. "Yup. They're still there. Gaining on us, but slowly."

"Can you tell what avenue we're on? Is it Tenth?"

"Looks like it. I think that's Chelsea Park we just passed."

"You 'think'?"

"Everything looks different in the snow. And I'm not a fucking tour guide."

"No, a tour guide wouldn't resort to profanity all the time."

"You're calling me on that?" Tina shot back. "Even now? Bunch of trigger-happy goons gunning for us and I'm still not allowed to swear?"

"You two, get a room," gasped Miguel.

And then he screamed in pure, all-consuming agony. The decaying process had abruptly accelerated, an exponential increase achieving overload. His body hurtled towards dissolution. He became a shuddering, smouldering thing, fiery blackness spreading through him, his clothes disintegrating with the heat. Sinews tightened, turned brittle, snapped. Bone was reduced to cinder. Hair crackled to nothingness. All at once his writhing form collapsed, spilling across seat and floor as just so much incandescent dust.

"Oh, my sweet fucking Jesus," Tina breathed.

"No!" sobbed Diane. "That was ghastly. No."

Anu had his ears covered.

Patti turned her face away, dumbstruck, appalled.

The vampires had seen many of their own number annihilated during the past twenty-four hours, but Miguel's demise seemed to hit them particularly hard. It had been so protracted, so clearly excruciating. Not the instantaneous oblivion offered by an injury to the heart.

"You're supposed to be our shtriga," said Andy to Redlaw. His voice quivered with fear and indignation. "Supposed to be protecting us. Good job you're doing of it, huh? You 'protected' Miguel pretty well, didn't you?"

"Hey!" said Denzel. "You stow that shit, you Tim Burton reject. Man's doing his best. Just put his life on the line climbing on top of the bus. Show some goddamn respect."

"I'm just saying, Father Tchaikovsky would never have let Miguel get shot like that."

"Father Tchaikovsky's not here. We got to make do with what we've got. You want to go it alone? Fine, be our guest. First chance we get, we'll drop you off. See how long you last."

"Yeah, I might just do that. Cindy'll come with me. Won't you, Cindy? We can make it on our own, the two of us."

"Uh, actually, Andy," said Cindy nervously, "I think I'd be better off with Mr Redlaw. Not being mean or anything, but he's a whole lot tougher than you are, and he seems to know what he's doing."

Andy goggled. "Cindy, I'm your sire. I made you. You're beholden to me."

"I'm not completely sure what 'beholden' is," the girl vampire replied, "but I'd much more like to be it to Mr Redlaw than to you. Sorry, Andy."

Andy's doughy features set into a glum pout. "This would never have happened to Lestat," he murmured.

Redlaw said, "I've just seen a sign overhead on that railway bridge. 'Expressway To Lincoln Tunnel,' right." He made the turn. "Tina? What's the status on our pursuers?"

"The status," Tina said, peering out again, "is that they're still behind, but kind of keeping their distance now."

"Of course they are. They can afford to. We've just tipped our hand, and they think we've trapped ourselves. Which we may have. This tunnel. Just so we're clear. There aren't any barriers or tollbooths?"

"Not going west. You pay to enter Manhattan but not to leave. Because nobody'd pay to go to Jersey."

"So we're not going to be forced to slow down or ram through anything," said Redlaw. "Good. But the Hummer wouldn't be hanging back if the soldiers didn't believe they can use the tunnel to their advantage."

"Can they?"

"Possibly. But so can we."

THE HUMMER DOGGED the school bus along Dyer Avenue and down the walled-in approach ramp to the tunnel. The bus entered the rightmost of the three tunnel tubes, and the Hummer did the same.

Suddenly both vehicles were on snow-free roadway.

The Hummer picked up speed. So did the bus. The bus's engine produced a shade over 200 horsepower, while the Hummer's was capable of twice that. The bus was also twice the weight of the Hummer. The car quickly whittled down the distance between them. In no time it was sitting right on the bus's tail. The noise of engines was amplified by the tunnel. The Hummer nosed still closer to the bus. Its bonnet was dented and one headlight was missing, broken during its glancing altercation with the snowplough truck. The bus was battered too, and acned with bullet impacts.

Lieutenant Giacoia leaned out of the passenger-side window. He had a pistol, a SIG Sauer P226 Blackwater Special. Steadying his gun hand on his left forearm, he took careful aim at the bus's rear offside tyre.

Then the bus's back door swung open and something large came flying out.

INSIDE THE BUS, the vampires were able to move freely again. They were no longer pinned in contorted crouching positions by the rods of daylight.

As soon as the tunnel roof closed over the bus, blotting out all natural light, Redlaw ordered the vampires to pull up a bank of paired seats. Denzel, Anu, Patti and Mary-Jo all bent to the task. With their combined strength they were able to wrench the seat frame free from its bolted mountings.

The bank of seats was what came barrelling out of the back of the bus towards the Hummer. It flipped end over end and slammed into the windscreen. One metal leg embedded itself in the glass, creating a perfect spider web of cracks. The bank of seats stuck fast, almost completely obscuring the driver's view.

Berger was forced to jam on the brakes. The Hummer came to a greasy, sidewinding halt. Berger and Giacoia piled out. Giacoia sprinted after the bus, loosing off several rounds from the SIG, but he was too far away and the bus was going too fast for accuracy. He took out one indicator light, but that was all.

Berger, meanwhile, wrestled with the bank of seats and at last managed to yank it free. She tossed it aside in disgust.

"LT! Get back in!"

Giacoia leapt into the Hummer as it rolled past, and Berger gunned the car for all it was worth, swearing heartily under her breath. The delay had cost them a good thirty seconds. The bus was already out of sight and probably closing in on the other end of the tunnel.

The Hummer reached the exit, coasting up into daylight and deep snow again. To the left was the toll plaza through which traffic was funnelled down into the tunnel from the New Jersey side. Beyond lay the Weehawken Helix, the pretzel of flyover and underpass that brought Route 495 through a 180° turn and merged it with JFK Boulevard. Of the school bus, there was no sign.

But among all the pairs of parallel ruts in the snow there was one that was particularly broad and deep. Berger followed this trail confidently until, at the next intersection, the ruts diverged into two separate pairs. The bus had been ghosting over the tyre marks of some other vehicle with a similar axle length. Damn.

The question was, had Redlaw turned off the freeway or carried straight on? Berger assumed the Brit would play it safe and stay on the main roads.

A mile further on, the Hummer caught up with... a

FedEx truck that was pluckily battling the elements to make its deliveries.

Berger cursed, threw the car into an about-turn, and headed back down the freeway. She wove in and out of the sporadic oncoming traffic. Headlights flashed and horns beat out an angry Morse. The Hummer hairpinned onto the off-ramp that the school bus must have taken.

"Goddamn *suburbs*," Giacoia said. "They could be anywhere."

"Tell me something I don't know," Berger growled.

Berger drove around the area, wind whistling through the hole in the windscreen. She crisscrossed Union City and Hoboken, trying vainly to pick up the vampires' scent again. She headed west along the South Marginal Highway, north along the New Jersey Turnpike, east along I-95. Nothing.

The bus was gone, lost in the wilds of New Jersey.

She pounded the steering wheel several times, bending it ever so slightly out of true.

"I don't believe it! The fuckers have gotten away!"

CHAPTER
THIRTY-FOUR

THE SUNOCO GAS station was blissfully warm inside. Tina spent a full minute in the shop just revelling in the heat. The bus, with its bullet holes and missing windows, had become a freezer on wheels.

Then she remembered she didn't have a lot of time. It wouldn't take Redlaw long to fill up the tank. She asked the attendant if she could use the restroom. The pimply teenage kid barely glanced up at her as he handed over the key on its large rectangular plastic tag. He had a bottle of Coke Zero open in front of him and looked tired and wired. He'd probably been pulling a double or even triple shift, stuck here with nobody able to come to relieve him. Tina could empathise.

In a toilet cubicle, she checked her site. The hit counter had reached five figures. Unbelievable. And the waspish and abusive comments were now few and far between. The vast majority of visitors were posting single-word positive critiques—"Awesome!"

"Amazing!" "Fangtastic!"—some with emoticons such as "8D," "@_@" and "((v=v))" tacked on.

At the washbasins she studied herself in the tarnished mirror. Grubby, ratty-haired, eyes red-rimmed from lack of sleep. She did what she could to smarten herself up. She hand-scrubbed some of the sewage stains out of her clothing with warm, soapy water. She splashed cold water on her face.

Pursued. Shot at. Nearly killed.

This was frontline journalism. Never mind the Middle East or Sub-Saharan Africa or Afghanistan. She was in the thick of a war and it was happening right here, on people's doorsteps.

She envisaged herself giving an interview, perhaps on Piers Morgan's show on CNN. Telling that slimy Limey how she obtained her extraordinary footage, what she went through to break her story about paramilitary vampire killers, the terror, the danger, the adrenalised highs and—

Her BlackBerry was buzzing. The incoming call was from an unrecognised number.

"Yes?"

"Do I have the pleasure of speaking with Tina Checkley?"

"Uh, yeah."

"The Tina Checkley who has a website called Tick Talk?"

"That's me."

Her heart started to beat faster.

"Ms Checkley—may I call you Tina?"

"I guess. Who is this?"

"An admirer, you could say. Someone hugely impressed by your work. Someone in a position to make a highly lucrative bid for your footage and your future services."

Fuck Jesus shit fuck holy frigging Christ...

Tina kept her voice even and businesslike, as cool as could be, the voice of a woman who took phone calls like this every day. "Yeah, really? You run a TV station or something?"

"I don't run one," said the man. "I *own* one. Three, as a matter of fact. Including a major network with a top-rating news outlet."

"This better not be a prank call."

"Not in the least."

"Because if you're punking me, mister..."

"Tina, I am entirely on the level." His voice was refined and beguiling. Nothing in it gave Tina any cause to suspect that he was a bullshit artist or a time-wasting crazy. His accent was Boston, but high-end Boston; not the slovenly drawl of someone from Charlestown, say, or Roxbury. "I've seen that you've been consorting with vampires, putting yourself at great personal risk to bring us some truly remarkable reportage."

"Listen, I love having smoke blown up my ass as much as the next person," Tina said, "but I'm on the clock here. Let's cut straight to it. What are you offering?"

"What am I offering? Only everything you've ever dreamt of."

"And who are you?"

"My name? J. Howard Farthingale the Third. Perhaps you've heard of me..."

TINA RETURNED TO the shop, where Redlaw was paying for gassing up the bus. She noted that he had wrapped some of the parcel tape around his left sleeve to cover up the rips in the fabric.

"Tina? Are you all right?"

"Sure," she said. "Why?"

"You're looking a little... dazed."

"No. Well, yeah. Hardly surprising, though. We've been on the go since who-knows-when and it's all been pretty, you know, stressful. Must be catching up with me."

She grabbed some candy bars and a couple of bags of Doritos off the shelf and tossed them on the counter. The attendant added them to the bill and took Redlaw's money.

"Need refuelling myself," Tina said, unwrapping a king-size PayDay as they walked back to the bus. "You want some?"

Redlaw shook his head.

"So where to now, boss? What's the deal?"

"I'm open to suggestions."

"'Cause we can keep driving around aimlessly from now until doomsday if you like. But if you ask me, we ought to be thinking about some kind of endgame. Taking the fight to these people rather than letting them make all the running."

"Where has this sprung from?" Redlaw said. "The sudden attack of gung-ho?"

"I'm tired of being pushed around, is all. And of seeing the vamps get victimised. Also, the way you're defending them, I've got to say it's pretty inspiring."

He looked askance at her. "Who are you and what have you done with Tina Checkley?"

"No, seriously. It's cool. Your dedication to them. They haven't done anything wrong except be who they are. Okay, we'll overlook the part where they were going to drink you and me dry. Blame the Russian priest for that. Bad leadership. Jim Jones in a cassock. But here are American soldiers who want to just wipe them off the map. It's genocide, pretty much. Ethnic cleansing. It's a disgrace, and we shouldn't stand for it."

"I'm not," said Redlaw. "But—"

The phone in his pocket trilled.

"Call for Colonel Jacobsen," he said, pulling it out. "Or more likely me. Yes?"

He listened to the voice on the other end. For a time he said nothing other than "Hmm" and "Yes" and "I see." Then he said, "I'll think about it. Give me a few minutes and I'll call you back." He shut the phone.

"Who was that?"

"Farthingale."

Tina frowned. "Who is...?"

"The man—and I use the term loosely—who's behind all this. Rogue billionaire sociopath. There's a surprising number of those about."

"You know him?"

"Not personally. We've talked before. Just the once. Last time he was making threats. Now..."

"What does he want?"

"A truce."

"Really?"

"Apparently. He says his soldiers have gone AWOL. He's not running the show any more. He's in over his head and he'd like to parley."

"Where?"

"His place. It's a couple of hundred miles from here. He wants us to go there and, in his words, 'try to sort out this mess before it gets any worse.'"

"And what do you think to that?"

"I think, Tina," said Redlaw, "that I'd be a fool if I didn't suspect a trap. But I also think I should go."

"Yeah, walk into a trap, that's not at all foolish," said Tina. "What good will going do?"

"Because," said Redlaw simply, "if I meet this Farthingale face to face, then I can kill him."

CHAPTER
THIRTY-FIVE

REDLAW DROVE.

He drove north-east through New England, a region that seemed to him like a cartographical remix of his own country—the names were the same, but the placements differed. He had a map, purchased at the Sunoco station, open on his lap. Portsmouth could be found due east of Manchester. Norwich lay south of Worcester. Rutland loitered way up north while Gloucester perched on a coastal promontory. It was England, but not as he knew it.

Tina had taped over the fresh holes in the bus's bodywork, so the vampires were free to occupy the seats as normal. They were asleep now. It was the middle of the day, their natural rest time.

As for Tina herself, she dozed too, and the peace and quiet, to Redlaw, was bliss. He had his thoughts to himself and wasn't having to deal with her almost incessant chatter.

It couldn't last, alas. Shortly after they had bypassed Providence and were heading for the state line between Rhode Island and Massachusetts, Tina woke up. She came forward and peered over Redlaw's shoulder into the viewing slot. It was bright out, the sky unbroken blue, sunshine glaring off snow. They passed a road sign: Boston 70 miles.

"Not far to go, huh?"

"We've broken the back of the journey," said Redlaw. "We'll give Boston a wide berth, then we're more or less there."

"At which point, what? You make like John Wayne and go do what a man's gotta do?"

"Pretty much. Farthingale left the arrangements loose enough that I've room to play it by ear." In his follow-up phone conversation with the plutocrat, they had ironed out the very vague terms of their meeting. "I intend to go to his island, handle whatever resistance he has lying in wait for me—if there is any—then bring him to justice."

"What if he's on the level, though? What if he wants to say sorry and throw himself on your mercy, just like it seems he does? You're a Christian. What is it the Bible says about sinners who repent?"

"'Joy shall be in heaven over one sinner that repenteth, more than over ninety and nine just persons which need no repentance.'"

"Exactly. If it's redemption he's after, don't you sort of have to give it to him?"

"I think things have gone a little too far for that," said Redlaw. "Anyway, it's God who does the redeeming."

"And you're the man who sends folks to the Pearly Gates so's He can do that."

"Don't make it sound so arbitrary. I don't go around killing people willy-nilly."

"Only whoever deserves it, yeah?"

"Whoever endangers that which I believe is right."

"But what gives you the right to say what's right?" said Tina.

"It's obvious. Basic morality."

"So that's how it is with you. Cut and dried. Black and white. No grey areas. Kind of childish, don't you think?"

"Tina, if someone tries to harm me, I don't let them. That's not childish. It's purely practical. I'm not going to back off from a foe or show leniency, not when my life's at stake—or the lives that are under my protection. That's not what Jesus meant when he talked about turning the other cheek."

"But according to you, Farthingale's saying he's lost control of the situation. Sounds to me like he wants you onside. He's scared now—of what he's done, and of you."

"That's if he isn't lying and setting me up."

"But if he isn't, shouldn't you give him the benefit of the doubt? A chance to make amends, anyways?"

Redlaw took his eyes off the road long enough to fix her with a curious stare. "Why are you defending him all of a sudden?"

"I'm not."

"Not so long ago you were talking about taking the fight to the enemy. Farthingale *is* the enemy."

"His soldiers are. He's... probably not. Not any more. He's Victor Frankenstein and his monster's on the rampage and he doesn't know what to do about it, which is why he's turned to you. Out of desperation."

Redlaw *hmm*ed sceptically.

"It's possible," Tina said. "You have to at least take it into consideration."

"Tina," Redlaw said after a long pause, "is there something you need to tell me?"

"No. Such as?"

"Anything you know that I don't. Anything at all."

"I don't think so. Why do you ask?"

"You didn't strike me as this conciliatory when I first met you. You're the woman who, as I recall, zapped me with a stun gun just for putting a hand on you. You're the aspiring journalist who'll stop at nothing, put up with anything, to get her story."

"I've been through a lot since then," she said. "Not surprising my outlook might have changed."

"Are you sure?"

"Sure I'm sure."

"Because if there's something I should know, now's the time to confess."

"You are so suspicious, you know that?"

"I was a policeman once. I have a policeman's instincts. When people are hiding things from me..."

"...your cop sense tingles, I get it. It's just a shame."

"What is?"

"That you don't trust me. After all we've been through together these past few days. After all the help I've given you."

Redlaw glanced at the map, then back at the road—the broad six-lane sweep of I-95. "We've another two or three hours of driving time," he said. "It'll be dark by the time we reach our destination. You do some thinking, Tina. Make up your mind. Honesty will get you much further than deceit. Take a long, hard look at yourself and let me know what you find."

Tina rolled her eyes, gave a disgusted grunt, and slouched back to her seat.

CHAPTER
THIRTY-SIX

THE TOWN WAS a pretty colonial-era sea port nestling at the tip of one horn of a large bay. In summer the streets would be thronged with tourists and seasonal residents, milling and meandering. The quaint clapboard and shingle-sided houses with their birthday-cake paintwork would gleam in the sun. The bay itself would be a glittering expanse dotted with countless yachts gliding to and fro, mainsails and jib sheets billowing, a pleasure seeker's vision of paradise.

But it was after dark now, and the dead of winter, and the town seemed lifeless and lost. Everything was closed and empty, as though the entire place had been mothballed and stowed away at the back of some wardrobe until spring. Nothing moved other than snowdrifts, their seaward surfaces sifted by an onshore wind, their crests giving off thin horizontal plumes of snow like the peaks of high-altitude mountains.

Streetlamps hummed, stoplights pulsed at intersections, and a lighthouse flared distantly in the darkness, but brighter and more constant than all of them was the near-full moon, whose glow sharply delineated everything in tones of opal and jet.

The school bus trundled down towards the harbour and came to a halt at the quayside, rocking back on its suspension like an exhausted marathon runner crouching on his haunches after the race. Steam purled off its bonnet. Hot metal ticked.

Redlaw stepped out, followed by Tina. He surveyed the prospect of moored boats before him, hundreds of them frozen at anchor, utterly motionless. The clatter of the halyards slapping against the masts in the wind created an eerie tinkling cacophony.

Out to sea a small island could be seen, silhouetted against the stars. Lights twinkled there.

"How far, do you reckon?" Tina asked.

"Couple of miles."

"And is it safe? To cross, I mean."

"Farthingale told me the strait—the 'reach', he called it—is frozen solid. The ice is several feet thick. It should be fine to walk on."

"And if it isn't?"

"No other way to get there," Redlaw said with a shrug. He leaned back inside the bus. "All of you," he said to the vampires. "Listen to me. Whatever the outcome tonight, whatever happens to me, remember who you are. Remember *what* you are. You are powerful creatures. Apex predators. You still think of yourselves as people, and you are, but you're also more than that now, so much more. When it's necessary, you have to show that. You have to do what's best for you and take what's yours. Be extraordinary. That's all I can ask from you. Understood?"

Nervous nods, but he could see his words had had an

effect. The vampires were holding themselves that little bit straighter in their seats. Their eyes showed a little more resolve.

"Any questions about what I'm proposing to do? Any second thoughts?"

Shaken heads.

"Good. Wish me luck."

They did.

"And you, Tina," he said, back outside again. "Second thoughts?"

"Nope."

"I could insist on your not coming."

"And I could insist on you not being such an obstinate, chauvinistic douchebag. I've got a job to do, a part to play." She patted her rucksack, where among other things her camcorder was stashed. "You need me."

"Like the proverbial hole in the head," said Redlaw.

THEY MADE THEIR way over a tumble of large rocks, down to the beach. Snow covered everything so thickly it was impossible to tell where the sand ended and the frozen sea began. It was only the change in the quality of their footfalls that told Redlaw and Tina they were no longer on dry land. A solid crunch became something creakier and less certain, with a kind of deadened resonance to it.

They trod warily. The ice was not smooth, rather a treacherous landscape of lumps and dips and shallow crevices. There was plenty of tripping and stumbling. Every step had to be considered and evaluated beforehand.

As they left the shore behind, they became aware of low groans and rumbles coming from beneath them. Sometimes there was even a sharp gunshot-like *crack* that brought them up short. The ice was ill at ease, fractious, flexing under internal pressures. The noises were a reminder that it was a work in progress, constantly making and unmaking itself. And below it, the sea, chafing and rubbing. It was hard for Redlaw and Tina not to think about the sea, hard not to imagine the black gelid water waiting down there—waiting for some flaw in the ice to break under their feet, waiting for one or both of them to come plunging ineluctably in.

Roughly halfway across the reach, Redlaw paused to take stock. The mainland seemed far away while the island, paradoxically, looked no closer.

"Point of no return?" Tina enquired.

"We passed that days ago," came the reply.

Onward they went over the booming, crackling floe. Redlaw could not recall undertaking a journey on foot as arduous as this one. Ice and snow conspired to create a terrain that seemed to defy being walked on. Nowhere was the going even, or firm, or trustworthy. He twisted his ankle every few minutes. Tina, for her part, cursed with virtually every step. It was a good thing they weren't trying to be stealthy.

Eventually, after one of the longest hours of Redlaw's life, the island began to look as if it could after all be reached. The moonlight picked out the trees that furred its shoulders, the luxury cruiser tethered at the shoreline, and the house which occupied the curve between its two low hills. The house was a sprawling modern affair made up of interleaving layers, and light spilled from most of its many windows, invitingly warm and yellow.

Redlaw aimed for the jetty where the boat sat. There was a ladder descending into the sea, its rungs rimed with icicles. He scaled it, Tina close behind. It was a relief to feel wooden planks beneath his feet—nice and flat and reliable.

"So we just waltz up to the front door and knock?" Tina said.

"Don't see why not. We're expected."

"I was thinking there'd some kind of reception committee."

"Be careful what you wish for."

Redlaw drew his Cindermaker and advanced to the end of the jetty. Tina unhitched her rucksack, opened it, delved in, and fetched out something. Then she jogged to catch up with Redlaw.

Redlaw had his back to her. He was scoping out the lie of the land. The trees on either side were full of shadows. Full of people too? Enemies lurking?

"I'm not looking forward to this," he murmured to Tina.

"Me either," Tina said, and moved in close behind him and placed her stun gun against the nape of his neck and hit the trigger.

Redlaw went down with a hapless, guttural cry. As he writhed in the snow, Tina bent and calmly dosed him with a second short sharp shock of voltage.

"I'm so sorry," she said. "So Christ-fucking sorry."

Redlaw's hands were claws. His entire body twitched like a dying bird's. One final huge immense shudder passed through him, and he lay still.

Tina took a step back, panting hard. "He's down," she called out, loud as she could. "Out for the count. Come and get him."

For a moment, nothing happened.

Then figures emerged from the treeline. One, two... Five in all. They converged on Tina and Redlaw from both sides. All of them bore guns and were aiming them either at Tina or at the prone Redlaw.

"All yours," Tina said, indicating the unconscious body. "One British vampire-rights sympathiser, signed, sealed, delivered."

One of the five armed figures stepped forward and nudged Redlaw with a toecap. This tentative test was followed by a wholehearted kick to the ribs.

Redlaw didn't stir.

"Oh, happy day," said the giver of the kick. "We've got him, men. At last."

Warrant Officer Jeanette Berger—for it was she—looked around at her teammates. Their grins of glee were easily as broad as hers.

"Let's take him up to the house," said Berger, plucking the Cindermaker from Redlaw's nerveless fingers, "and put on a show for the boss."

CHAPTER
THIRTY-SEVEN

FARTHINGALE FELT FULLY in charge of things, a master of the universe once more. There had been some dark moments this past day or so, periods of grievous self-doubt. But it had all come good in the end. You couldn't keep someone as determined and resourceful as J. Howard Farthingale III down for long. In hindsight, all that had happened was that there had been a hiccup or two in his plans, a touch of—what was the phrase?—mission creep. Nothing he couldn't contend with.

His call to Tina Checkley was the moment when he had started to get everything back on track, the turning point. The calls to Redlaw that had followed had put the next piece of the jigsaw in place. And then, when Farthingale had been contacted out of the blue by a disgruntled yet contrite Jeanette Berger, it had served to cement the impression that fate was well and truly on his side after all. The stars were aligning. Everything was turning his way. The natural order was being restored.

Earlier that day, his Bell 222 had touched down on Far Tintagel's heated helipad. All of the domestic staff, except for Rozetta, had climbed aboard the helicopter and been whisked off to the mainland. Farthingale told them he was granting them an impromptu three days of paid vacation. They accepted gladly and didn't question.

A couple of hours later the chopper returned, this time carrying the five surviving members of Team Red Eye. The pilot had picked them up from the helipad at the Robert Wood Johnson Hospital in New Brunswick, New Jersey, where two of the team had been receiving treatment for their injuries.

The initial moments of the meeting between Farthingale and the soldiers had been awkward. Each side felt aggrieved, betrayed by the other. But what united them and enabled them to let bygones be bygones was their shared hatred of Redlaw. Their animosity towards him outweighed their resentment towards each other.

"You want Redlaw?" Farthingale had told them. "I'm going to hand him to you on a platter."

"That's all we ask," Berger had said. "Then we're quits, right?"

"Right. You've made a wise move, coming back to me."

"Don't see as we had much of a choice. Not sure how you do it, but you always seem to know where the targets are. It was a last resort, phoning you, but I figured we'd get better results by pooling our resources than not."

"I for one am not holding a grudge, Warrant Officer Berger. It'll be a relief to have this whole messy business wrapped up tidily and discreetly. Then we can all get on with our lives."

He had refrained from mentioning the reports he'd seen on TV about a group of unidentified armed individuals leaving a trail of carnage behind them across New York that morning. "Slaughter on the Streets" was one local news channel's lunchtime headline, while one of the national news channels, which happened to belong to a network he owned, had gone with "Midday Manhattan Massacre."

Farthingale knew Team Red Eye were the culprits—who else could it have been?—but it had seemed prudent not to raise the subject and, potentially, hackles. The attack dogs were back on the leash; that was what counted. The fallout from their little rebellion was a matter for a later date. He would deal with that as and when he had to. Redlaw was now the overriding priority, the horizon line of his ambition.

Now, as Team Red Eye approached the house, Farthingale stepped out onto the terrace. Two of the soldiers were dragging a limp, insensible figure behind them by the arms—Redlaw. His feet ploughed wayward furrows in the snow.

The girl—Tina Checkley—came too, Berger marching her upslope at gunpoint. Tina was objecting loudly to this.

"Hey, I'm on your side, you know. You don't have to stick that thing in the back of my head. I gave him to you, in case you didn't notice. Remember? Knocked him out cold for you."

"Shut up and walk," said Berger. "You were with him, so you're guilty by association until someone tells me otherwise."

"*I'm* telling you otherwise, Berger," Farthingale announced from the terrace. "Let Ms Checkley go.

She's no more Redlaw's ally than I am. She's proved it, amply."

Berger did not lower the gun—Redlaw's Cindermaker. "Yeah, but isn't it a bit suspicious that she came here with him? Why'd he let her? It must have occurred to him that there was a chance of an ambush. Why put her potentially in danger?"

"He didn't want me tagging along," Tina said. "I had to talk him into it. And believe me, it was a hard sell. He's as stubborn as a mule. In the end what swung it was, I told him I could act as a kind of human shield. You know, a non-combatant, an innocent bystander. If there was trouble, having someone like me around might make someone like you think twice about opening fire."

"Shows how little you know," said Giacoia.

"Yeah, well, Redlaw bought it anyway. Plus, I think he thought having a witness around might be a good idea."

"Why so keen to come, though?" said Berger. "You got a death wish or something?"

"This is a story, my story," said Tina flatly, "and I want to see it through to the end."

"Spoken like a true journalist," Farthingale said, and a couple of the soldiers, hearing this, nodded sagely. The girl was a journalist, yes. That went some way to explaining her actions. They'd met journalists while serving. Crazy people. Certifiable. Soldiers went to war zones because they were ordered to. Journalists went because they got a perverse kick out of it.

"But also," Tina said, "I'm here on account of him." She gestured at Farthingale. "Your boss is my boss, now, too. He's offering me work."

"Come now, Tina," said Farthingale genially, "don't undersell me, or yourself. In return for all you've done today, I'm offering you a position with a national news network. Any position you like—back-room, editorial, behind camera, in front of camera. You only have to decide where on the ladder you wish to start, how high up the pecking order. I'm confident that, wherever you set out from, a glittering career awaits you. I hardly know you, but from what I've seen, I can tell you'll go far. It's my pleasure to be the one who gives you your big break."

"See?" Tina said to Berger. "There's my real motive right there. I knew if I forced Redlaw to take me with him, there might be a chance for me to really prove myself to Mr Farthingale. And when Redlaw turned his back on me down there by the jetty, I saw my moment and I grabbed it. Me and my trusty Taser. So..." She placed a hand on the barrel of the Cindermaker and gently but firmly pushed down. "Kindly get that damn thing out of my face, bee-yatch. Stop treating me like I'm a prisoner of war. I just did what none of you guys, with all your weapons and training and amped-up vamp powers, could. I took down John Redlaw. I think that earns me a little damn respect, don't you?"

Berger scowled, but she had to concede that this pinch-faced, feisty girl had a point. She gave Tina a grudging nod, and Tina answered it with a beaming smile that said simultaneously *thank you* and *fuck you*.

"You do realise what's going to happen to Redlaw?" Berger said. "What you're partly responsible for? It's not going to be pretty."

"The man's a wackjob," Tina replied blithely. "He scares me, and that's no lie."

"But you've been with him a while, am I right?"

"He's not my friend, if that's what you're driving at. He's just the story—part of it. We're not attached in any way. If you ask me—setting journalistic impartiality aside—Redlaw deserves what's coming to him. I mean, siding with vampires over humans..." Her face showed how offensive she thought *that* was.

"And that's the least of it," said Child, holding up a heavily bandaged hand. "Dude needs a serious reassessment of his values."

"Damn fucking straight," agreed Abbotts. He pointed to his face, then his crotch. "Bad enough he messed up my good looks, but to ruin another man's junk..."

He delivered a swift, contemptuous kick to the body in the snow.

"Gonna return the compliment, Redlaw," he spat. "And I won't just take the one like you did. I'll take 'em both, and I'll shove 'em down your throat. Make you choke on them."

"You'll get your turn, private," said Berger. "We all will. First things first. Let's get those clothes off him. He won't be nearly so dangerous when he's freezing half to death."

Lim and Giacoia stripped Redlaw down to his underpants. This revealed a body that carried more than its fair share of scarring. All over were the traces of wounds received in the line of duty, ranging from sets of deep parallel slashes to an ugly-looking gouge on one shoulder that had cost him a large chunk of flesh. It was a map of violence, etched out in macabre contour lines and puckered valleys of pain, and it had been added to very recently in the form of angry red bite marks on his left forearm.

Child let out a low whistle. "Shee-it. Vampires done all that to him, and now he's their best bud?"

"Amongst Britain's SHADE officers," said Farthingale, "Redlaw had a reputation for being unusually dedicated to his job."

"Well, there's dedication and then there's just plain stupid," said Giacoia. "A GI with half those injuries, he'd have been invalided out, taken off active duty and given a nice cosy desk job."

"Pretty fit-looking for a guy his age," Lim observed.

"Yeah. Fancy crucifix, too," said Child. "You could throttle a bull with that chain."

"Can we stop admiring and start tying up?" Berger snapped. "We don't want him coming round on us before he's properly secured."

"Sure thing." Giacoia pulled Redlaw's arms behind his back and lashed a plastic zip tie around his wrists. He tested the zip tie with a few hard tugs. It didn't budge. There wasn't a millimetre of slack. No way was Redlaw breaking free.

"Now wake him up," said Berger.

One-handed, Child hoisted Redlaw into a kneeling position. Giacoia slapped his face several times, increasingly hard.

Redlaw groaned. His eyelids fluttered. Snapped open.

"Good evening," Berger said to him, almost chirpy. "Welcome back to the world. How're you doing?"

"Just super," Redlaw replied hoarsely.

"Well, we'll have to do something about that, won't we?" Berger looked at Giacoia. "LT. You get first dibs."

"Hey, no fair!" said Abbotts. "The loot's not been injured by him. How come he gets a go before any of the rest of us?"

"Ranking officer," said Berger.

"But in that case, I'll be last. There won't be anything left by then."

"Look at it another way. You get the privilege of delivering the *coup de grâce*."

"Oh, yeah." Abbotts was mollified. "That's true. Just make sure he's still alive when my turn comes, everybody."

Giacoia lined himself up in front of Redlaw, fists clenched.

Farthingale looked on from the terrace, hands braced on the balustrade. He knew then how it must have felt to be a Roman emperor at the Circus Maximus, watching the Games that he had laid on, suffused with pride and a sense of his own greatness. Below was a man—a Christian, no less—who had been thrown to the proverbial lions. His life was forfeit, and it was all Farthingale's doing. Farthingale had brought him to this predicament. Farthingale was now going to preside over his slow, torturous death.

All the money in the world couldn't have made J. Howard Farthingale III feel any more sublimely powerful than he did at that moment.

CHAPTER
THIRTY-EIGHT

GIACOIA PLANTED HIS feet and landed three solid, chunky roundhouses on Redlaw's cheek. The lieutenant had done a bit of amateur boxing as a kid, and his technique was still good—pivoting off his back foot, his arm a rigid L-shape, most of the force of the blows coming from the twisting of his upper body. Redlaw's head snapped sideways with each blow.

Giacoia stepped back.

"Hit him again, loot," Abbotts urged. "Harder. Like you mean it."

Giacoia came at Redlaw again and drove a fearsome uppercut into the underside of his jaw.

Redlaw recoiled. He shook his head like a tiger clearing water from its whiskers.

"Your colleague's right," he said. "Your heart's not in it, lieutenant. You're not comfortable with this at all. I can see it in your eyes. You think it's wrong."

"Shut up." Giacoia punched him again. "Shut your

mouth." And again. "That's for Jacobsen." Again. "And that's for Larousse."

Redlaw spat blood. "Revenge is such a petty motive. So shallow."

"Sergeant Child, hold the rat-bastard still."

Child put an arm round Redlaw's neck, and Giacoia thumped him repeatedly in the abdomen.

Child let go, and Redlaw was left bent double, wheezing and gasping.

With an effort, he raised his head once more.

"After I'm dead, all you'll feel is empty and guilty," he said. He was starting to shiver with the cold, his lips turning blue. "And it won't go away. It'll never go away. You'll feel like that for the rest of your life. All of you will."

"What does it take to make you stop talking?" Giacoia said.

"More than you've got. I don't mind being martyred. I've done what I believe is right and I can go to my grave secure in that knowledge. I wonder how many of you could say the same."

With a cross between a grunt and a scream, Giacoia slammed his fists into Redlaw a dozen times more. When the onslaught was over, blood was trickling from a cut to Redlaw's forehead. One side of his mouth had begun to swell up. One eye was puffing shut.

"Uh, if I could just say something..."

All eyes turned to Tina. She had a hand tentatively raised, like an anxious pupil in class.

"Hate to butt in when you all are having so much fun," she went on, "but there's something you ought to know."

"Can it wait?" said Berger.

"Kind of not really. You see, Redlaw didn't come here alone."

"Yes. You were with him."

"No, apart from me. Others. That's why he's so calm."

"Others?" said Farthingale. "What others?"

"Who do you think? His vampire pals. The ones he shtrigas for. They crossed over the ice, too. Secretly. Behind us."

"What!? What for?"

"Backup. Redlaw's worked out this whole plan with them. He told them to follow behind us at a safe distance. In case something like this"—she pointed to the kneeling, beaten-up Redlaw—"happened. It's his insurance policy."

"Judas," Redlaw growled.

Tina shot him an apologetic but defiant look. "I've started down that road. Might as well go the whole way."

"Let me get this straight," said Berger. "Vampires are en route to rescue him?"

"Yup."

"And you only just thought to mention this fact?"

"Yeah. So? I forgot."

"Hell of an important piece of information to *forget*."

"Look, lady, a lot's been going on," Tina said hotly, "including you holding a gun to my head when you didn't have to. In all the confusion, it slipped my mind. I'm telling you now, aren't I? You still have a fair warning."

"So how many of them are there?" said Lim.

"Not many. A handful."

"What's a handful?"

"Six or seven, thereabouts."

"And are they dangerous?"

"Of course they're dangerous. They're vampires. Probably not as dangerous as you, but still..."

"Okay," said Berger with resolve. "New intel, change of plan. Giacoia, Lim, go down and run a sweep of the island perimeter. Look for these vampires. Flush them out. Terminate on sight. Got that?"

Giacoia could have resented having orders barked at him by a junior officer, but in the event he seemed relieved to be assigned a new task. Anything so as not to have to keep hitting a trussed-up, helpless human being.

As he and Lim loped off down the hillside, Berger turned to Farthingale. "Sir? Maybe you should think about going indoors, bunkering down. At least until the vampire threat is negated."

"No," Farthingale replied. "I have faith in you and your men. I feel perfectly safe. Shall we get on with teaching Redlaw the error of his ways?"

"As you wish," said Berger. "Guess I'm next." She flipped the Cindermaker round, holding it by the barrel. "A pistol-whipping with your own sidearm," she said to Redlaw. "That's going to hurt in more ways than one."

CHAPTER
THIRTY-NINE

DOWN AT THE shore, Giacoia and Lim scanned in every direction. Nothing but ice from here to the mainland.

Behind them, up at the house, they could hear the repeated hearty *smack* of gunmetal striking flesh. Each blow was accompanied by a hollow, involuntary cry from Redlaw.

"She's giving the guy a pounding," Lim remarked.

"No wonder," said Giacoia. "He killed her man."

"So Berger and Jacobsen, they were an item, huh? I never knew."

"Me, I suspected. Woman like that, all cute and fierce, she has to be boinking *somebody*. The colonel seemed as good a candidate as any. Also, sometimes I caught them giving each other these looks, you know? Like they were passing notes in class. Now, focus. I reckon we should split up. You go that way, clockwise round the edge of the island. I'll go counterclockwise, and we'll rendezvous on the other side. If you see something moving and it's not me, shoot."

"Roger that—Wait." Lim took a few steps along the jetty. "You hear that, loot?"

"No."

"Movement. Not sure where it's coming from. Somewhere out there."

Giacoia listened. "It's just the ice cracking. Sounds like a goddamn bowl of Rice Krispies."

"No, I'm sure there's something else." Lim climbed down the jetty ladder, onto the ice. He unshouldered his rifle.

"Be careful."

Lim moved out further on the ice, head cocked. Presently, Giacoia joined him. He thought that he had perhaps heard something too, buried in amongst all the glacial sounds. A kind of scratching. Claws scraping.

The two soldiers trod warily, alert, making regular visual confirmation of each other's position.

"Anything?" said Giacoia.

"No. Seems to have stopped. Maybe I—Whoa, there it is again. Still can't pinpoint it, dammit. It's like it's close enough that I should be seeing what's making it, but..." Lim's voice trailed off.

"But what?" Giacoia briefly glanced away, checking his six o'clock.

"Oh God. It's coming from—"

There was a *crack*, a shattering sound. Giacoia whirled. Lim. Where had Lim gone?

"Lim? Corporal Lim? Where the fuck are you?"

Nothing. No reply.

"Justin?" Giacoia said. "If you can hear me, answer."

It was eerie. Lim had just... vanished. There one moment out on this open ice field; the next moment, not there.

And now Giacoia discerned the scraping again. It was loud and clear this time, emanating from very nearby. The noise a vampire's talons might make when their owner was dragging them across ice.

But if there was a vamp here, where in hell was it? He'd surely be able to see the creature.

Then it dawned on Giacoia.

He looked down at his feet.

That same instant, the ice beneath him erupted. Arms shot upwards through it. Taloned hands clamped onto his legs. Giacoia was hauled down into freezing back water.

It happened so fast, he wasn't even able to squeeze off a round.

The hands pulled him down deep. He resisted. He fought. But he hadn't had a chance to draw in a breath before he was submerged. There was no air in his lungs, and already panic was taking hold, dread of drowning.

The cold was shocking, too. Numbing.

Above, a dim gibbous disc of light marked the hole in the ice he had been dragged down through. It was growing smaller and fainter.

Vampires didn't need to breathe. Giacoia did.

His lungs were crying out for oxygen.

His muscles felt weak. His struggles were getting feebler by the second.

Now the hole was so tiny, it looked like a distant star.

Giacoia opened his mouth. Inhaled reflexively.

Icy darkness roared in.

CHAPTER
FORTY

"WHAT'S GOING ON?" Clara asked for the umpteenth time.

She was growing restless and curious, and Rozetta knew this was just what Mr Farthingale didn't want.

"Let's put on a DVD," Rozetta said. "How about this one? You haven't watched this one in a long time. It's a Pixar. You love Pixar."

"No. Bored of TV." Clara had been having a kids' show marathon since four that afternoon, channel-hopping at whim between Disney, Nickelodeon and Cartoon Network. Farthingale had given Rozetta strict instructions. Clara could do what she wanted, eat whatever she asked for, stay up however late she felt like, as long as she didn't move from the den. She was to remain in the den until further notice. By no means was she to roam through the house, and she was definitely not allowed anywhere near its landward sections, which included her bedroom.

Rozetta hadn't asked why. She didn't want to know why. None of her business, just as it was none of her business that the rest of the domestic staff had been sent away and then those soldiers had arrived. Whatever her employer was up to, it wasn't anything good, she could tell. The less involved in it she was, the less she saw and could be held accountable for, the better.

But Clara was beginning to get suspicious. Rozetta was being so nice to her, letting her eat all the ice cream and candy she could manage, and it was way past bedtime and nobody had even mentioned pyjamas and teeth-brushing yet, and Clara obviously didn't mind that at all, but it was also odd. It was a break with routine, and breaks with routine unsettled her.

Something was up. She could sense it.

"I think I'd like to stretch my legs," she said, standing up. "I've been sitting on my butt for ages."

"No," Rozetta said crisply, and then, more softly, again, "No."

"Why not?"

"How about some MTV, Clara? I think there's a special on tonight about that boy band you like."

"Howie hates me seeing MTV."

"Howie will never have to find out. It'll be our secret."

"But he says it makes me too noisy, because I sing all the songs afterwards. For, like, days. Drives him crazy."

"Then sing to yourself, in your head, not out loud," Rozetta suggested.

"Oh, okay. That's a good idea."

Clara tuned the channel selector to MTV, and pounding music filled the den.

Which was handy, because Rozetta was convinced she had just heard a cry of pain coming from outdoors.

"Sandwich, Clara?"

"Nah."

"'No, thank you.'"

"No, thank you. I'm fine. Full."

"I'm going to fix myself one, okay?"

"'Kay."

"Stay put. Don't move from this room."

"What if I need to make pee-pee?"

"Hold it 'til I get back, then I'll take you."

ROZETTA HEADED OUT to the kitchen, which lay just a short corridor away. It was at the eastern end of the house, part of a block that nestled against the slope of the hillside. On the way, she listened out. No further screams. Perhaps she had just imagined it. She hoped so. God forbid that her employer had gone completely insane.

The moment she entered the kitchen, she realised something was amiss.

A chilly draught.

Her eye went straight to the windows.

A broken pane.

She sensed she wasn't alone.

A presence behind her.

She turned.

It was a man. He was dressed in black. Old-fashioned clothing. Like he was going to a funeral a hundred years ago. He was chubby, bordering on overweight. His eyes were deep scarlet.

Rozetta's hand darted to the tiny gold crucifix that hung round her neck. She was a good Catholic. She had complete, unswerving faith.

She held the crucifix forward, a shield and a weapon.

"I know you," she said to the intruder. Terror was coursing through her, so much so that she felt lightheaded and close to fainting. Yet the Lord would protect her. The Lord would. "*Aswang*. Demon. Bloodsucker. Get away from me. I command you, in the name of Blessed Virgin, Jesus and all the saints, leave me alone."

The vampire, Andy Gregg, just smiled.

"That shit don't work on me," he said. "I've lived in a church. I'm hardened."

Rozetta screeched and made a desperate dash for the knife block on the sideboard.

Andy, for all his bulk, was faster. He beat her to it, standing in her way.

"Our shtriga told us we should remember what we are," he said. "Apex predators. He said there are times when we just have to be what we're meant to be and take what's ours."

Rozetta whimpered. "Please. No."

In the Philippines, she had been raised on stories of the *aswang*, a monster who stole babies from their cribs and drained men of their lifeblood, an evil thing with a special liking for foetuses and cadavers. She could recall the many bad dreams she had had as a little girl—nightmares about terrible, red-eyed undead beings sneaking in through her bedroom window and biting open her veins and drinking deep.

The *aswang* was real. It was fact, not folklore. The whole world knew that now. What had once been dismissed as superstition was, after all, truth.

Her entire adult life, Rozetta had prayed she would never actually meet an *aswang*—her childhood nightmare made flesh.

Those prayers had held her in good stead—until today.

Fangs bristled.

So many. So wickedly sharp.

THE DEN DOOR opened. Clara didn't even glance round.

Someone came in and sat down beside her.

Only after the pop video she'd been watching ended did Clara take a look to her left.

It wasn't Rozetta, as she had expected. It was a girl. Clara didn't know her. She had never seen her before. But she was pretty, in a pale sort of way, and she had a cute, rather raggedy teddy bear with her.

"Hi," said Clara.

"Hi," said the girl.

"Where's Rozetta?"

"I don't know. Who's Rozetta?"

"My friend. She looks after me. Who are you?"

"I'm Cindy."

"Hi, Cindy. I'm Clara. Who's your bear?"

"Jingle Ted."

"Cool name."

"Thanks. He doesn't jingle any more, though. He used to, but he broke."

"Sorry to hear that."

"It's okay. What are we watching?"

"MTV."

"Is there anything else on?"

"What do you like?"

"All kinds of stuff."

"You like *Transylvanian Families*?"

"I don't mind it."

"I love it. It's my best show."

"Let's watch that, then."

"Sure. Why not? I've got a whole bunch of episodes TiVo'ed."

Clara pulled up the TiVo menu onscreen and started clicking through.

Cindy nestled up a little closer to her. "That's a great TV. You have such a cool house."

"I know. My big brother's a billionaire. Oh, this is a good one. *Felix Fanger's Night Off.* It's the one where Felix bunks off school for the whole night, and the Deadmaster keeps on trying to catch him."

Cindy linked her arm through Clara's, and together, companionably, the two of them settled down to watch the show.

CHAPTER
FORTY-ONE

BERGER WAS PANTING hard and, in spite of the cold, perspiring freely. The butt of the Cindermaker was drippingly slick with Redlaw's blood.

"You want I should take over?" Child asked.

"Just need a breather, sergeant. I'll be back to it in a moment."

"How about me?" said Tina.

All three soldiers—Berger, Child, Abbotts—looked at her.

"What you on about?" said Child.

"Well... Can't I have a go?"

"Beating him?" said Berger.

"Yeah," said Tina. "I've been through a whole heap of shit this past couple of days on account of Redlaw— literally, when we were in that sewer. Thanks to him I've been close to getting killed, more than once. I figure I owe him for that. Let me get in a couple of licks while you're catching your wind."

Berger was unconvinced. "I don't think it's appropriate."

"You don't, huh?"

"You're a civilian."

"And you're soldiers, therefore it's all right? That doesn't stand to reason." She turned and appealed to Farthingale up on the terrace. "Mr Farthingale. What do you think? You think they should have all the fun?"

Farthingale deliberated. "My view, is Tina, you're currently a witness to these events. If you join in, you become an accessory."

"So that's a no, then."

"On the contrary. As an accessory, you're more deeply involved. You're complicit. That ensures your loyalty and your silence. Look on it as an expression of your commitment to me. After this, we're bonded, you and I. You know about me what I know about you, so neither of us can incriminate the other without incriminating themselves."

"A stalemate, kind of."

"More of a mutual insurance policy. It's perfect."

"Great." Tina held out a hand to Berger. "So give me that, please."

Berger was reluctant to hand the Cindermaker over.

"Give her the gun, warrant officer," said Farthingale.

Grudgingly she complied.

Tina hefted the Cindermaker by the barrel. She approached Redlaw, who was doubled over, his ribcage heaving. The snow around him was a mass of crimson spatters.

"I wondered how long it would take you, Tina," he said thickly, head still bent. His whole body shivered uncontrollably. Droplets of his own blood were freezing to his skin. "To finally get stuck in."

"Just waiting for an opportunity," she said, moving round him. "Jeez, you're a mess."

"I can take punishment. It's one of the things I do best."

"Maybe you even like it."

"I wouldn't go that far."

She was behind him now, between him and Child. She had the air of someone gloating, relishing the humiliation of another.

"When is enough enough?" she said.

"When it's served its purpose."

"And has it?"

"Not for me to judge. But I'd like to think so."

Tina paused, then continued her circuit of Redlaw until she was in front of him again.

"Don't hold back," he said to her, finally looking up. His face was hideously distended. One eye was almost completely closed, while the other had been damaged internally so that the white of the sclera was now red.

She struck him with the gun, nowhere near as hard as Berger had, but it sent him reeling. Redlaw collapsed onto his back. He rolled and writhed in the snow.

Child stepped forward to get him back on his knees. As he yanked Redlaw upright, he noticed two things.

Redlaw's wrists were no longer zip-tied.

Redlaw had a knife in his hands.

It was Jacobsen's combat knife. Child couldn't have known this, just as he couldn't have known that Tina had been secreting the knife up her sleeve and had dropped it into the snow when she walked behind Redlaw, or that Redlaw, flat on his back, had retrieved it and used it to cut through the zip tie.

All Child knew was that, somehow, he and his teammates had been suckered.

365

And then the knife was embedded in his inner thigh, and Redlaw twisted it and pulled it out, and all at once blood was jetting from Child's femoral artery, and he clamped a hand over the wound but the blood spurted between his fingers, unstoppable, and he sank to his knees with a horrified groan.

Next second, Redlaw was making a dash across the snow to Abbotts, and the knife whipped through the air, low to the ground, and—*snick, snick*—both of Abbotts's Achilles tendons were neatly severed and he collapsed like a broken chair.

"Tina! The gun!" Redlaw yelled, and Tina tossed the Cindermaker to him.

At the same moment, Berger went for her own sidearm. She had been startled by the abrupt reversal of fortunes, the shift in the status quo. The girl and Redlaw—in cahoots all along? The whole thing just a charade? A feint?

Her pistol came up out of its holster.

But the Cindermaker was already levelled, Redlaw up on one knee, holding the bloodied grip with both hands.

Sighted.

Steadied.

Cocked.

"Guess you're not interested in a fair fight?" she said.

Redlaw fired.

"You guessed correctly," he said.

CHAPTER
FORTY-TWO

THE THREE SOLDIERS were on the ground. One was dead—Berger, the back of her head now a ragged cavity, her brains strewn across the hillside. One was dying—Child, sitting ashen-faced and helpless in a pink slush of snow and blood. One remained alive but was crippled—Abbotts, his legs useless.

Redlaw got trembling to his feet, covering both Child and Abbotts with the Cindermaker in case they tried anything. He reeled, swayed. Tina went to his side.

"Easy there, old man," she said, lending him a shoulder to lean on. "I don't know if you're ready for walking yet."

"Farthingale?" said Redlaw, searching around. "Where's Farthingale?"

Tina checked the terrace. "Gone. Big surprise. Must have hightailed it the moment you started hurting people."

"I need to..." Redlaw tried to move, but his body didn't seem ready to obey his thoughts just yet. His head was thrumming as though the bass pipes of a cathedral organ were playing inside it.

"You're in no shape to be doing anything."

"But he's..."

"Getting away? Where's he going to go? This is an island."

"He can get off it the same way we got on." Redlaw steeled himself. The pain threatened to crush him completely. Darkness beckoned—the sweet oblivion of unconsciousness. But he refused to give in to it. He would not pass out. He would keep going until he had done what he came here to do.

"Redlaw! Shtriga!"

Vampires were running up from the shoreline—Diane, Denzel, Anu, Patti, Mary-Jo—all of them soaking wet with seawater, but their faces exultant, alight with triumph.

"We got them," said Denzel. "Two soldiers. Down through the ice. Nice as you please."

"Are you okay?" Patti asked Redlaw. "Dear Lord, your face. What did they do to you?"

"They did what I needed them to do so that you lot had time to get into position," said Redlaw. "Good work, all of you. Well done."

At that moment, Child slumped sideways with a moan. The life had almost left him.

Abbotts, meanwhile, had begun crawling away. He propelled himself through the snow with just his hands and elbows, his legs trailing limply behind.

"Some unfinished business here," Redlaw said to the vampires. "Perhaps you'd do the honours...?"

The vampires accepted the invitation gladly. Two of them fell on Child. The other three made after Abbotts, who saw them coming and accelerated his clumsy progress, arms flailing desperately, but in vain.

"No," he whined. "No, this is not right. Not fair."

"Drain them," Redlaw said. "No comebacks."

Abbotts shrieked as the vampires caught up with him and pounced. His cry was high and keening, indignation mixed in with the terror.

Child, by contrast, acquiesced to his fate manfully. So much blood had pumped out of him already that he was barely conscious. As the vampires drank the rest of it and hastened his end, he looked resigned, even relieved.

"I didn't know if we could pull this off," Tina said to Redlaw. She wanted to talk, if only to blot out the sound of the vampires feasting—the chomping, flesh-rending teeth, the slobbery lip-smacks and tongue-slurps. "So much could have gone wrong."

"We did it, that's what counts. You acted your part well."

"I was making half of it up as I went along."

"It didn't show."

"Guess I'm a champion bullshitter. And you're a champion get-the-shit-kicked-out-of-him guy."

"When it's in a worthwhile cause. I'm glad you came round to our side, Tina."

"You guilted me into it. I'm not a bad person. I do have a conscience. Buried deep, but it's there. I thought it wouldn't be a problem, selling you out to Farthingale, but it turns out it was. He offered me the world, and I can't say I wasn't tempted..."

"Everyone's tempted. Nothing to be ashamed of there. As long as you don't give in."

"Besides," said Tina, "it's a better story this way. Now I don't become the weaselly villain of the piece. I retain my integrity."

"Which is a far better thing to have than worldly wealth."

"Sure. If you say so."

"Now..." Redlaw was feeling marginally better. Or rather, marginally less awful. "He'll be in the house somewhere. Farthingale. Grab me my coat. Let's get this over with."

CHAPTER
FORTY-THREE

FARTHINGALE SPRINTED FOR the safe room.

Just a few seconds. That was all it had taken for victory to turn to defeat, for gold to turn to shit.

Redlaw and Tina had, between them, pulled off a hell of a con. He couldn't get over the audacity, the sheer *nerve* of it. If this had been some kind of devious boardroom coup, he might have seen it coming and been able to prevent it. As it was, he had been hoodwinked good and proper. Tina in particular. He'd been so certain he had her in the palm of his hand. So certain she was his thrall. How could she have resisted? Who in their right mind could turn down an offer like the one he had extended to her?

This wasn't over, though. Not by a long shot. As he covered the last few yards to the safe room entrance, Farthingale was already plotting how he might regain control of the situation. He could hunker down in the safe room for days, weeks even, and they wouldn't be able to get to him. In the meantime, he could communicate with the outside world, summon help, call in favours, get the police on the scene, the rescue services, the National Guard, anyone and everyone he needed...

The safe room door stood wide open.

There was someone already inside.

Clara.

Farthingale felt a pang of shame. He hadn't even thought about his sister until now. In the heat of the moment, his only concern had been for himself.

Still, she was there, in the safe room. She had already taken refuge. Good. So he didn't have to worry about her. They were both of them going to survive this.

Clara was sitting cross-legged on the floor in a corner. She looked dazed, unsure of herself.

Little wonder, Farthingale thought. *She must have heard the gunshot and it terrified her. She probably has no idea what's going on.*

"Well done," he said to her. He didn't bother to enquire about Rozetta. She was just a nurse. Let her take care of herself. "Good girl. You did the right thing, coming here and waiting for me." He tapped the code into the keypad and the door began to swing ponderously shut. "We're going to be fine. It's going to be just you and me, just Clara and Howie. We'll hole up here, nice and snug, and I'll call in reinforcements and everything'll be okay. Okay?"

Clara didn't answer, just kept staring into the middle distance.

There was something strange about her eyes— something awry.

Farthingale leaned in for a better look.

Clara raised her head.

Her eyes were no longer blue-green, like their father's. They were vivid scarlet.

"Red juice," she said, standing.

"Clara... Oh, no... Christ..." Farthingale went numb, seeming to shrivel inside. He took an involuntary step back.

"Red juice, Howie."

Her mouth opened wide. Her teeth were not ordinary teeth any more.

The door had shut fast. Farthingale spun round and lurched for the keypad to re-input the code in order to open it. His finger fumbled. He pounded out the digits. The door gave a loud *thunk* as the bolts unlatched.

But too late. Far too late.

"Who's a monster now, huh, Howie?"

And then, with a cackle and one last ecstatic cry of "Red juiiice!" Clara leapt on him.

CHAPTER
FORTY-FOUR

DAWN WAS COMING. There was a faint whisper of warmth in the air. Over the past couple of days, the Big Freeze had slackened its grip on the East Coast. The ice in the reach had begun to melt and break up.

Redlaw was standing on the terrace at Far Tintagel, the very spot where Farthingale had stood three nights earlier overseeing what he'd thought would be Redlaw's death. He gazed out over the island, the berg-studded sea, the mainland. It was the first time since his beating that he had felt even vaguely normal. Until now, in spite of the painkillers he had found in Farthingale's bathroom cabinet, he had been a mass of aches and soreness.

The mirror was still showing him a face that was all the colours of sunset and barely recognisable from all the abrasions and contusions. His body moved as stiffly as though he was wearing a suit of armour.

But he was alive.

A winner.

For now.

Tina came out from indoors. Like him, like the vampires, she was keeping topsy-turvy hours, a night-shift existence. Redlaw was used to this, Tina had had to get used to it. Otherwise she would have been all alone during the daytime with no one to talk to and nothing to do.

"Thinking about turning in?" she said with a yawn. "I am."

"Thinking about it," said Redlaw. "But it's always been my rule never to miss a dawn if I can. This time of day is the Creator at His most aesthetically-inspired."

Silvery blue was chasing the dark away westwards.

"You had it all," Redlaw said to Tina. "Your future all wrapped up and sealed with a bow. Do you regret rejecting that?"

"Who says my future still isn't all wrapped up?" said Tina. "Tick Talk's hits are through the roof, well into eight figures. I've got nibbles from three news networks, two state, one national. I've got someone asking to agent me. I've even got a tentative book deal, though that's *sooo* old media I'm not sure I can be bothered. No, I'm not worried about what's ahead. I know where I'm going, and I'll be getting there entirely under my own steam. What about you?"

Redlaw ducked the question. "You shouldn't have jumped the gun, posting that footage on your site when you did. That nearly sank us."

Tina sighed. "Are you going to hold a grudge about it forever? It worked out in our favour, didn't it? Just remember where you are now, not how you got there. Be Christian. Forgive."

"I suppose you did redeem yourself."

"You bet your bony British ass I did."

The first streaks of sunlight tinged the sky.

"You're leaving, then?" Redlaw said.

"Soon as I can. This is your kingdom, not mine. Yours and your fangy pals'. No reason for me to stay. Once the ice clears completely, I guess I can arrange for some sort of boat from the mainland to come fetch me."

"My kingdom," said Redlaw, amused by the notion, and wondering.

It *was*, he supposed.

Farthingale was dead, killed by his sister. Redlaw had come across the body, utterly exsanguinated, in the doorway to the house's safe room. He had applied the finishing touch with the combat knife, decapitating it, just to be sure.

The sister, Clara, was now part of his vampire tribe. She and Cindy were becoming fast friends, somewhat to the chagrin of Cindy's "sire", Andy.

Far Tintagel, if it belonged to anyone now, belonged to the vampires and their shtriga.

A kingdom.

Yes.

Maybe.

Or a fortress. A stronghold. A redoubt. Isolated. Defensible. Separated from the human world by a moat of sea.

Somewhere where other vampires could come. Find sanctuary. Be safe.

A vision began forming in Redlaw's mind. A way forward. A possibility.

"You asked me if I know where I'm going," he said.

His smile was tight but brave, grim but hopeful.

A blaze of orange light turned the snowy pine trees into Roman candles.

"As a matter of fact, I'm not going anywhere."

ACKNOWLEDGEMENTS

A debt of undying gratitude is owed to the following: Adam Brockbank, who gifted the character of John Redlaw with a surname all those years ago; Mr Satyajit Sahu, consultant haematologist at the Eastbourne District and General Hospital, for inducting me into the mysteries of ITP; Chris Field, official fisticuffs advisor; and the real Chris Abbotts of Birmingham, a true inspiration.

J.M.H.L.

JAMES LOVEGROVE'S *PANTHEON* SERIES

THE AGE OF RA

UK ISBN: 978 1 844167 46 3 • US ISBN: 978 1 844167 47 0 • £7.99/$7.99

The Ancient Egyptian gods have defeated all the other pantheons and divided the Earth into warring factions. Lt. David Westwynter, a British soldier, stumbles into Freegypt, the only place to have remained independent of the gods, and encounters the followers of a humanist freedom-fighter known as the Lightbringer. As the world heads towards an apocalyptic battle, there is far more to this leader than it seems...

THE AGE OF ZEUS

UK ISBN: 978 1 906735 68 5 • US ISBN: 978 1 906735 69 2 • £7.99/$7.99

The Olympians appeared a decade ago, living incarnations of the Ancient Greek gods, offering order and stability at the cost of placing humanity under the jackboot of divine oppression. Until former London police officer Sam Akehurst receives an invitation to join the Titans, the small band of battlesuited high-tech guerillas squaring off against the Olympians and their mythological monsters in a war they cannot all survive...

THE AGE OF ODIN

UK ISBN: 978 1 907519 40 6 • US ISBN: 978 1 907519 41 3 • £7.99/$7.99

Gideon Coxall was a good soldier but bad at everything else, until a roadside explosive device leaves him with one deaf ear and a British Army half-pension. The Valhalla Project, recruiting useless soldiers like himself, no questions asked, seems like a dream, but the last thing Gid expects is to find himself fighting alongside ancient Viking gods. It seems *Ragnarök* – the fabled final conflict of the Sagas – is looming.

 WWW.SOLARISBOOKS.COM

Follow us on Twitter! www.twitter.com/solarisbooks

EPUB ISBN: 978 1 84997 341 0 • MOBI ISBN: 978 1 84997 342 7 • £2.99/$3.99

Dion Yeboah leads an orderly, disciplined life... until the day the spider appears. What looks like an ordinary arachnid turns out to be Anansi, the trickster god of African legend, and its arrival throws Dion's existence into chaos.

Lawyer Dion's already impressive legal brain is sharpened. He becomes nimbler-witted and more ruthless, able to manipulate and deceive like never before, both in and out of court.

Then he discovers the price he has to pay for his newfound skills. He must travel to America and take part in a contest between the avatars of all the trickster gods. It's a life-or-death battle of wits, and at the end, only one person will be left standing.

AN ALL-NEW EBOOK NOVELLA

 WWW.SOLARISBOOKS.COM

Follow us on Twitter! www.twitter.com/solarisbooks

REDLAW

'difficult to put down... a thoroughly entertaining novel that I would recommend to those looking for a summer blockbuster'
Sacramento Book Review on *Age of Odin*

New York Times Best Selling Author
JAMES LOVEGROVE

UK ISBN: 978 1 907992 04 9 • US ISBN: 978 1 907992 05 6 • £7.99/$7.99

POLICING THE DAMNED

They live among us, abhorred, marginalised, despised. They are vampires, known politely as the Sunless. The job of policing their community falls to the men and women of SHADE: the Sunless Housing and Disclosure Executive. Captain John Redlaw is London's most feared and respected SHADE officer, a living legend.

But when the vampires start rioting in their ghettos, and angry humans respond with violence of their own, even Redlaw may not be able to keep the peace. Especially when political forces are aligning to introduce a radical answer to the Sunless problem, one that will resolve the situation once and for all...

 WWW.SOLARISBOOKS.COM

Follow us on Twitter! www.twitter.com/solarisbooks

UK ISBN: 978 1 78108 018 4 • US ISBN: 978 1 78108 019 1 • £7.99/$9.99

Alice isn't having the best of days – late for work, missed her bus, and now she's getting
rained on – but it's about to get worse.

The war between the angels and the Fallen is escalating and innocent civilians are
getting caught in the cross-fire. If the balance is to be restored, the angels must act
– or risk the Fallen taking control. Forever. That's where Alice comes in. Hunted by the
Fallen and guided by Mallory – a disgraced angel with a drinking problem he doesn't
want to fix – Alice will learn the truth about her own history... and why the angels want
to send her to hell.

What do the Fallen want from her? How does Mallory know so much about her past?
What is it the angels are hiding – and can she trust either side?

BEN MACALLAN

DESDAEMONA

UK ISBN: 978 1 907519 62 8 • US ISBN: 978 1 907519 63 5 • £7.99/$7.99

Jordan helps kids on the run find their way back home. He's good at that. He should be - he's a runaway himself. Sometimes he helps the kids in other, stranger, ways. He looks like a regular teenager, but he's not. He acts like he's not exactly human, but he is. He treads the line between mundane reality and the world of the supernatural. Ben McCallan's urban fantasy debut takes you on a teffifying journey.

WWW.SOLARISBOOKS.COM

Follow us on Twitter! www.twitter.com/solarisbooks